Also by Chrys Fey

Charm
Halloween Miracles

Detective Heavenborn Trilogy:
Cocky Killer
Universal Killer
Cosmic Killer

Collection:
Everywhere A Killer

Disaster Crimes Series:
The Crime Before the Storm (free eBook)
Hurricane Crimes
Seismic Crimes
Lightning Crimes (free eBook)
Tsunami Crimes
Flaming Crimes
Frozen Crimes
A Fighting Chance
The Disaster Curse

30 Seconds Duology:
30 Seconds Before
30 Seconds

Of Death Duology:
Ghost of Death
Witch of Death

Everywhere a Killer

Chrys Fey

Dedication

Cocky Killer:

To my readers aka Sparklers who helped me to name characters in this story. Many ages ago. Juneta Key & Toi Thomas for naming Bow Prancer. Elizabeth for naming Soren. Sarah Rush & Sherry Fundin for naming Axel Sherman. Kelly & Sherry Fundin for naming Ashton O'Reilly. Tiff for naming Diago Wilson. Kathy Weiland for naming Mila Kinley. Cindy Schmidt Montgomery for naming Samantha Ryan.

Universal Killer:

To Ed Chastain for being a Patreon member once upon a time and allowing me to give a character your name.

Cosmic Killer:

Pink Moon Books for publishing *We Know the Truth, Do You? An Anthology to Celebrate the Raid.* And…I suppose the "raid on Area 51" itself that was all over social media in 2019. If that hadn't happened, a bunch of authors wouldn't have wanted to put together an anthology about Area 51, and I wouldn't have written a story to be included while healing for surgery. *Cosmic Killer* comes from that story.

Content Warning

Cocky Killer:

Alcohol Usage
Blood
Crime Scenes
Corpses (investigative procedures)
Dismemberment (discussed)
Murder (off page)
Strip Club
Strong Language

Universal Killer:

Arseny
Assassin
Blood
Burn Victims
Crime Scenes
Corpses (investigative work)
Guns
Murder (off page)
Strong Language

Cosmic Killer:

Blood
Crime Scene
Corpse (investigative work)
Guns
Murder (off page)
Strong Language

There's always the chance of more triggers that are specific from reader to reader, so take care, dear reader.

Cocky Killer

The Galaxy's Tease

T he peach orb of the sun poked its head above the horizon, chasing away the night. Early morning light mixed with the granite-gray atmosphere. From a wicker chair on her porch, Avrianna watched daytime slowly descend. Purple clouds hung high in the air, clinging to the blackness. The sun rose above the tree-line in the distance and shot spears of burning brilliance in all directions. Bright oranges and yellows streaked higher and higher. The pond behind Avrianna's house created a mirror image, making the sky seem that much more infinite. When the sky was transitioning to the blue of a new-born day, Avrianna rose from her chair and shuffled back into her house; she hadn't slept much last night. Bleak dreams full of snapshots of crime scenes and past cases had prompted her out of bed after a few hours of sleep.

In her kitchen, she started her coffee machine and leaned against the counter while waiting for it to brew. She stared blankly at the white cabinets and marble countertop. A microwave, coffeemaker, and can opener were the only appliances on the sparse counters. She barely used her oven and never needed to run the dishwasher. Being single and without roommates, her few dishes were the only ones that needed cleaning. She tended to wash them by hand and reuse the same few.

The coffeemaker gurgled, prompting her from her semi-comatose state. She retrieved her coffee, added sugar and creamer, and then carried the mug into the living room to her coffee-drinking chair, a chair with deep cushions and wide, wooden armrests perfect for setting down a coffee mug.

Opting against turning on the TV, she sipped her coffee in silence and looked at her living room. The couch, a couple of chairs, and a coffee table were all plain furnishings. Not even they could make the room appear lived in. The fact was, she didn't do much living in her house. She ate late dinners, slept if she could, and drank her morning cup of coffee there. She spent the rest of her time working.

Always working.

After draining her coffee, she took a fast shower and dressed in black slacks, a black button-up shirt, and boots. In the mirror, she watched her reflection closely, wondering. Always wondering. She pushed down the questions that tended to creep up whenever she spent too much time contemplating her appearance. She closed her eyes, hiding their bright green irises.

Why?

That single word broke through her barrier, hauling more words with it. *Why are my eyes so different? What am I?*

Her chest tightened, but she quickly got a handle on her emotions. It didn't matter why. Not anymore. She was different, and it was those differences that made her a damn good detective. The fact many criminals were afraid of her was a perk she wasn't sure she'd want to give up if she had the chance to be normal.

She opened her eyes and smoothed her hair into a ponytail. The silvery sheen of her hair glistened in the fluorescent lighting. Outside, in the sunlight, her hair would gleam like sterling silver. She couldn't help it; just another side effect of being a freak.

Her cell phone chimed, and she answered it on the first ring. "This is Avrianna."

"Hey, a call came in," Chuck, her homicide partner, said on the other end. "A dead body was found in the alley next to The Galaxy's Tease."

Avrianna arched a brow. "Isn't that a strip club?"

"It is, indeed."

She groaned. "Great."

"Not a fan of strip clubs?"

She scowled. "You do know whom you're talking to, right?"

Chuck laughed. "How long will it take you to get there?"

"Fifteen."

"All right. See you there."

She ended the call, strapped her firearm to her side, and slipped her badge over her head. In the next moment she was in her car, driving through the city. With the day barely begun, no one was on the road. She breezed down the streets, enjoying the emptiness. Being a detective who saw horrible things every day, she rather liked the times when it seemed no one else existed. In those rare moments, she could pretend murderers didn't exist, that drug dealers weren't spreading their filth, and criminals in general weren't overtaking her world, a world that *used to be* innocent.

The parking lot to The Galaxy's Tease swarmed with cops and first responder vehicles. She pulled her car into the mix. As she walked toward the crime scene tape, a hush fell over the workers. They all paused in their duties to glance her way. Some were bold enough to sneer in disgust.

You'd think they'd be used to me by now. But she was that much of an anomaly that it didn't matter that she'd been there her whole life. Or that they saw her at many of the crime scenes they attended.

A man in his fifties, wearing a Polo shirt and black slacks, stood in front of the crime scene tape, talking to a cop. "Hey, Chuck."

The older gentleman turned.

"Who found the body?"

Chuck pointed to five women the police had separated. "They're a cleaning service known as Nebula Cleaners. They get paid to come in every morning and perform an exorcism."

Avrianna twisted her lips to stop a smile from

forming.

Chuck pointed. "I saw that."

"I don't know what you mean." She glanced at the five women. "All five of them discovered the body?"

"Two of them came out to throw trash in the Dumpster. The other three naturally had to check it out, too."

"Naturally," she agreed.

"They said when they arrived, there was a car in the parking lot, but since the door to the club was locked up tight, they didn't question it."

"The vic's car?"

"We believe so. The plates are being run now.

She nodded. "Shall we?"

Chuck waved his arm, indicating for her to go first. She ducked under the crime scene tape and headed toward the body lying prone on the ground halfway down the alley. Blood pooled around the body from head to knees.

Avrianna stopped with her toes an inch from the puddle of blood and crouched down to examine the body. "Mid-thirties," she said. "Brown hair, brown eyes." Her gaze settled on the victim's slit throat. She'd seen the wound many times, but it never got easier. Sticky blood coated the corpse's leather jacket. Underneath, a black shirt was soaked with it, plastering the fibers to their chest.

"Here."

She accepted the gloves Chuck held out to her. Her gaze never left the corpse as she dipped her hands into them. She peered down the length of the body. With her fingers, she pinched the jean fabric at the body's knees.

When she brought her fingers away, the blue latex was stained with red. "A lot of blood. I wouldn't be surprised if the victim has other wounds. Maybe a knife to the lower abdomen."

Chuck worked out a leather wallet from the inside pocket of the victim's jacket. He flipped it open and worked out an identification card. "Axel Sherman. Male identified. The address is for Earth." He pulled out another card. "He had a between-worlds tourist visa good for a week."

Avrianna shook her head. "A tourist can't go a week without seeing half-naked women dancing around a pole?"

"Probably thought strip clubs would be different here. Androids, floating stages."

Avrianna snorted. The US had morphed New Vida into a second America. Everything America had, they had, from fast food restaurants and bars to electronics and cars, but her world was far more corrupt. You would've thought they had learned from their mistakes and would've taken the opportunity to start fresh. Not a chance. She fully believed it was a curse that the portal between their worlds was located in the Grand Canyon. She much rather would've had the portal on Earth's side located in Switzerland, Iceland, or Denmark. She'd heard the people in those countries tended to be the happiest on Earth. Perhaps then her world wouldn't be in the shape it was in.

"He would've been going back home today."

"But somehow he caught someone's attention during his one week here." She frowned at the dead man. "Who did you piss off?"

Squealing tires drew Avrianna's attention to the end of the alley as a sports car zoomed up. The driver, in jeans and a suede button-up shirt, jumped out and stormed toward the building. Two cops cut the driver off at the pass.

"That's my fucking business!"

Avrianna snapped off her gloves. "Looks like the owner has joined the party."

With Chuck at her side, she walked over to where the officers were keeping the owner at bay. "Hey, we can take it from here."

The cops sidled way, but not without casting glares in her direction. She was used to the men in her profession despising her authority and rank. The only one who never seemed to care was Chuck.

She held up her badge for the owner to view. "I'm Detective Heavenborn."

"I know who you are," the owner grumbled.

Avrianna ignored him and continued, "And this is my partner, Detective Davis. What's your name?"

"Guy Riches."

"Do you have identification?"

Grumbling some more, a card was shoved at her.

Guy Riches, male identified, New Vida residence.

"And you own this establishment?"

Guy glared. "Yes. Why the hell else do you think I'm here?"

Checking out a crime scene you created, perhaps? She kept that thought from spilling from your mouth, though.

"Do you have cameras anywhere outside your facility?" She indicated the strip club's exterior.

"I have one camera at the doors."

She glanced at the entrance. A red velvet rope blocked the double doors where a bouncer no doubt stood guard during open hours. "That's perfect. We could see if the perp followed the vic outside. Can we see the footage from last night?"

The man's thin lips puckered. He put a hand, covered in gold rings, on his hip. His mouth opened to protest, but before he could speak, she interjected, "We could always get a warrant for the video, but that would just delay things and could potentially leave your business closed until further notice."

A vein in his neck popped out and thrummed like a guitar string. "Fine," he growled. "Come on." His shined shoes clapped on the asphalt as he tramped toward the doors. He yanked the rope off its hook. It fell and hit the pole it was attached to with a clatter. Avrianna exchanged glances with Chuck. Their raised eyebrows said it all; this man was going to be a problem. He dug out a silver key from the pocket of his shirt and wrenched it in the knob. The door swung open.

Avrianna stepped over the threshold. This was her first time entering a strip club, and she wasn't impressed. Thin maroon carpet covered the floor. Small black tables and stools were scattered across the room. On one side was a pine bar complete with a rack of booze in front of a mirrored wall. And near the back was a raised stage. Chairs lined the front of the platform, and in the middle stood a metal pole where women spun and danced seductively for the pleasure of the people drooling below them. The air smelled like cigarettes, booze, and sweat. Not in the least bit appealing.

They followed Guy through the club to a backroom complete with a cluttered desk, a rusted filing cabinet, and a flat screen TV positioned on the back wall. Guy went behind the desk, squeezing past the filing cabinet, and knocked over an empty water bottle. It fell off the desk's edge and hit Avrianna's boot. The plastic bottle bounced on the scuffed tile, making a crinkling sound with each hit. Guy didn't so much as glance at it. Avrianna's foot itched to punt it as his head.

While he fumbled with his computer, she scanned the tight space. A lava lamp sat on the desk. The substance that usually bubbled through the glass tube was a solid mass of congealed whiteness. Stubbed-out cigarette butts overflowed from an amber ashtray. A strip of condoms had been left next to the landline. One of the wrappers was open. Avrianna held down her disgust. Apparently, Guy didn't believe in no sex with his employees or customers.

Her gaze lowered to the desk's drawers. The bottom one required a key. She wondered if it was locked and if it was, what he hid in there. Alcohol? He had plenty at the bar. Porn? He could just watch his dancers perform. A weapon? Perhaps a knife with the victim's DNA on it?

"Here it is," Guy said, drawing her attention to the computer.

On the screen a dark image was frozen in place. The bouncer stood there; a tall, buff man with brown skin. His large arms were crossed over his chest. He stood in front of the velvet rope and a line of customers stood in front of him. One of the customers held out an ID for the bouncer to examine.

"Thanks. May I?" She held out her hand toward the chair, indicating she wanted access to the computer.

Guy let out a huff and got out of the chair.

She took the seat, cringing inside when his leftover body heat penetrated her pants. Chuck stepped closer and leaned down while Avrianna fast-forwarded the feed for any sign of the victim. Over time, the line evaporated as customers were either let in or turned away. Every once in a while, the bouncer stood outside alone, and then someone would come up seeking entrance. The bouncer appeared firm, unflinching, ever alert, and not the type of man to put up with someone's bullshit. And he was out there all night long.

"What is your bouncer's name?"

"Bow Prancer."

"And he stays at his post until the club is closed?"

"Yes. Why?"

She lifted a brow at the owner's sharp tone. "Because he could've heard or seen something. We'll need his contact information."

Chuck gave a small nod and straightened up. "You heard her."

While Chuck hovered over the owner, Avrianna continued to scan the footage. In the corner, the time ticked by quickly, adding minutes in the blink of an eye. The Galaxy's Tease closed at two in the morning, and the time sped toward one-thirty.

The club's door opened, and a man stepped out into the halo of artificial light. He paused to dig out a pack of cigarettes from the inside of his leather jacket, tapped one out, and used a lighter to start it. He took a couple of long drags before nodding to the bouncer and walking away. Avrianna rewound the feed and paused it on the man's face. He looked relaxed. No doubt a lap dance was the culprit of the smile tugging his lips.

"Got him," Avrianna said.

Chuck rejoined her. "Play it."

She hit the enter button, and they watched him leave. They eyed the door, but it didn't open. Ten minutes went by and no one exited the club. Impatient, Avrianna double-tapped the fast-forward button. At two, the doors opened and customers spilled out. Some stumbled, some grinned from ear to ear, others laughed. All had clearly had a good time.

"Maybe the perp was already waiting for him in the parking lot," Chuck said.

Avrianna nodded. "Maybe." She pursed her lips at the feed. Her brows lowered, and she looked around the room as if she could see the rest of the building. "Is there another way out of here? Another exit?"

"There's one in the back, but it's only for employees."

Avrianna and Chuck exchanged a look that let her know they were on the same page. "We're going to need the names and contact information for all of your employees who were working last night, including the dancers."

Guy pointed at her. A gaudy gold ring with a giant ruby glistened in the light. She wondered if it was real and if owning a strip club could really bring in the sort of money that it cost to buy a gem that big. Or did Guy Riches have other side hustles?

"I don't want you harassing my girls."

Chuck pushed the man's finger out of her direction. "Watch it."

Avrianna got to her feet, relishing the fact that she was taller than Guy and now had a good three inches on him so he had to look up at her. "Questioning them about a murder that happened outside your club is not harassment. Considering you're the owner of a strip club, I would hope that you'd know what real harassment is." Her gaze drifted toward the condoms on his desk.

He puffed out his chest. "What I do is my own business."

"Sure, it is. Until it's illegal. Then it's our business."

Guy glared, and she glared right back. She had the urge to let her powers leak out, to let him see just a spark of what she was capable of when someone pissed her off, but she held back.

"We're not leaving without the information we need," Chuck added, probably sensing her broiling aggravation.

Guy's fingers pecked at the keyboard, and the printer spit out numerous sheets of paper. He grabbed them from the tray and thrust them at Avrianna. She took them, with a smile that strained her cheeks.

He crossed his arms as soon as his hands were free. "And how long are you going to be here blocking off entrance to my club?"

"You'll have to ask the CSI team that," Chuck said. "But it could be hours. They'll have to canvas the area, take pictures, collect samples, retrace the victim's steps, and remove the body.”

“That’s unacceptable. I have a business to run.”

“And we have a murder to solve,” Avrianna spat. “Let us do our job. And then you’ll be free to do yours.”

“My club better be open tonight.”

Imagine the gall someone would have to get murdered and ruin someone else’s day and the money they could earn from horny people. The fact Guy Riches cared more about money than the murder of one of his customers sent lava high up Avrianna’s neck.

“On second thought,” she said. “All of your employees will have to come in for questioning before they come in to work today. If they don’t, we’ll come here, arrest them, and hold them for questioning.”

She turned to leave. Chuck was behind her when she opened the door and heard Guy mutter, “Feminist freak with a badge.”

She froze.

Her hands balled into fists at her sides. Her eyes burned with her anger.

Chuck’s hand pressed firmly into her back and pushed her out the door.

Seething, she headed for the exit. Her bottled-up rage tightened her chest. She marched across the maroon carpet.

“Avrianna. Maybe you should take a moment before going out there.”

“I’m fine,” she hissed.

“Mirrors at your three o’clock.”

She turned her head to see her reflection. Her body was as tense as a steel rod. But her eyes made her pause; they glowed with green light. *Damn it.* She knew better than to let a slimy creep like Guy Riches get under her skin, but she had a low tolerance for men like that. Plus, she had lethal anger and a very quick temper. You would think that would make her job difficult. On the contrary, it made her job easier. Usually, people didn't push her buttons out of fear. Usually. She still encountered the idiots and jackasses who didn't know any better, or didn't care.

Her heart raced with the blood roaring through her veins…blood that had toxins swimming in it that would normally kill a human, but those toxins had the opposite effect on her. They made her damn near invincible.

She went up to the bar and gripped the top. With her head lowered, she focused on her breathing. *I should really take up meditation.* The thought made her crack a smile. She was not the type to sit cross-legged on the floor, inhaling incense, humming, and listening to calming music. Pounding a punching bag or emptying a clip at a gun range was her type of stress relief.

Slowly the heat penetrating her eyes faded to a soft sear. Eyes closed, she inhaled and exhaled. Inhaled and exhaled. She counted to ten, and then she opened her eyes and raised her head. On the other side of the bar, her reflection scrutinized her. Her eyes were normal again. As normal as they could be anyway. But she could still feel her anger lingering beneath the surface.

She peeked over her shoulder. Chuck stood by the doors, but Guy was nowhere to be seen. She lifted the door and walked behind the bar. While moving along the counter, she scanned the labels on the bottles until she found the most expensive whiskey. She picked up a clean shot glass, twisted off the cap on the bottle, poured the golden liquid to the glass's brim, and downed it in one swallow. Unlike others, she couldn't feel the burn of the liquor going down her throat, but it tasted damn good. She flipped the glass upside down and slammed it onto the counter. Tasting Guy Riches' liquor behind his back put a pep in her step.

"Better?" Chuck asked.

"Oh yeah." Grinning, she shoved open the door and stepped out into sunlight.

Andromeda

T he interrogation rooms in the police department were all occupied with strippers, but in the daylight, none of them looked like strippers. They looked like ordinary women—with heavy fake lashes, extensions, and long acrylic nails, but normal. And they all exuded fear and nerves over why they had been summoned for questioning. On the other side of the two-way mirror, Avrianna watched Chuck question a woman named Samantha Ryan whose stripper name was Nebula.

Avrianna leaned against the table with her arms

and ankles crossed while she listened to their exchange. She didn't go in for the initial questioning; she was brought in if they needed to scare a suspect. If they needed to go a level higher than bad cop, she was the girl to call. Hell, she couldn't help it if people started squirming the moment she opened a door, now could she?

Samantha picked at her glittery manicure. Avrianna noticed a sterling silver band on her ring finger and wondered how her partner felt about her stripping in front of strangers every night.

"Do you recognize this man?" Chuck passed a full-page image of Axel Sherman, taken from his ID, across the tabled.

Samantha looked at it and shook her head. "No. When I perform, I block out everyone in the room. Before and after, I stay in the dressing rooms." She peered at her fingers. "I dance for the money to pay for college. Otherwise, I wouldn't do it."

"Did you see any employees leave through the back door at any time before closing?"

She shook her head. "No, the back door is right next to our dressing room, but we keep our door closed. That's where we hang out before and after our sets."

Chuck nodded. "Thank you, Miss Ryan. You're free to go now."

Avrianna nodded, agreeing with his call. She flipped through a folder containing information on Samantha Ryan, who was studying to be a veterinarian and had recently married her partner. In fact, that was the reason why they moved to New Vida, where all people could marry freely, regardless of gender, with no restrictions.

A moment after Samantha left, another stripper was escorted into the room. She wore skinny jeans that looked like they had been painted on. Her tiny feet were strapped to three-inch heels, and her black shirt was cut so low that you could see a sliver of her pushup bra. She flung blonde hair off her shoulder with a slender hand. Seated at the table, she peered at the two-way mirror and ran a finger along the bottom her lip. Then she smacked her lips together. Avrianna rolled her eyes; she'd never been the type to care about her looks. The most makeup she used was lip moisturizer.

Chuck stated his name and the time for the record. "What's your name?"

"Mila Kinley also known as Andromeda."

Avrianna groaned. Andromeda meant "ruler of man." Guy Riches probably thought he was clever with bestowing his most popular dancer with that name.

So far, all of the strippers' names related to space science, and as someone who had taken an interest in space science as a child—after being called an alien since infancy—she took great offense to Guy Riches using the universe to attract attention to his strip club.

Venus.

Halley.

Phoenix.

Aurora.

Luna.

Calypso.

Nova.

Vega.

They had already seen a stripper with each of those

names. It was bad enough that there was a bar named Galaxy Bar that concocted drinks like Wormhole. Apparently, business owners in New Vida thought they were being clever using the galactic phenomena that made it possible for them to even have a business on another planet, located lightyears from Earth, with a simple step through a portal and only seconds of time lost.

Drinks and women. What was next? Cars? Would one of the big auto companies on Earth create a line of vehicles called the Titania? Titania Atlas—SUV. Titania Hunter—truck. Titania Solar—solar car, obviously.

Avrianna pursed her lips. Well, she actually wouldn't mind that so much, but she drew the line at strippers.

Chuck's voice drew her attention back to the conversation on the other side of the two-way mirror. "Where do you work?"

Mila shifted in her chair. "The Galaxy's Tease."

"Were you working last night?"

"Yes."

"Do you recognize this man?"

Her nails clicked together when she picked up the image. "Yes, I do. He was at the bar all night, but when I came out to dance, he came to the stage to watch. I have the best choreography." She said the last part with pride. Obviously, she took her job seriously. Nothing like Samantha.

"Around what time do you perform?"

"One o'clock every night. I dance for fifteen minutes."

So that left fifteen minutes after her dance concluded and before he left.

"What did you do last night after your dance?" Chuck asked.

"I counted my tips, and every night, after we perform, we're allowed a free drink, so I had my shot of vodka and chatted with the girls. Then I changed, took off my makeup, and left with the rest of them after closing."

"How long after closing?"

She shrugged. "Usually twenty minutes. We like to make sure all the customers are gone. Last year, one of our girls was sexually assaulted by some dude in the parking lot. He wanted a lot more than what he could have. Ever since, when the club is empty, Bow makes sure the parking lot is empty, too, and then he stands guard at the back door while we all leave."

So, Bow was outside at the time of the murder and even walked around the premise before the dancers left, which probably meant he was the last one to leave the club. Unless Guy Riches stayed after hours.

"Did you notice when Mr. Sherman left?" Chuck pointed at the image on the table between them.

Mila glanced at it again. "Nope. He was still there, front and center when I went backstage. He tossed me a lot of money, though. I think the hundred-dollar bill came from him. He was the rowdiest of the bunch. Hooting and whistling the entire time I performed." She shrugged a small shoulder. "I guess none of the other girls caught his attention." She leaned forward. "Not surprising, though." Her voice was a whisper, as if what said now couldn't be heard by others. "I'm the best. My name is the first one on all of the posters. I've gotten a lot of publicity for my skills."

Brow arched, Avrianna picked up her tablet and tapped the screen. She ran a search for "Andromeda/Stripper" on the Internet. Several results popped up. The first was a popular men's magazine sporting Mila on the cover. Her hair had been teased out into a cloud around her head. She wore a diamond encrusted G-string. A matching bikini top, two sizes too small, dangled from her neck. The strings that tied behind her back hung from either side of her slim figure. The patches of diamond-studded fabric rose so high on her round breasts that Avrianna figured they had to airbrush out her areolas. On the cover, in bold letters, it said, "The Galaxy's Tease introduces the sexiest tease of the galaxy…Andromeda."

The next Internet result was an ad for the club featuring Andromeda. She was the only dancer pictured and her name dwarfed the other dancers' names. Obviously, Andromeda was Guy Riches' moneymaker.

All that publicity would certainly attract attention. Maybe Axel Sherman really did cross over into their world to go to a strip club after all.

Avrianna set her tablet aside and refocused on the interrogation as Chuck asked, "Did you see him get into an altercation with another customer or an employee?"

Mila shook her head. Her hoop earrings swayed from side to side. "Nope. And usually when there is a fight in the club, we hear it backstage. Last night was like any other night."

Except for the fact that someone had been murdered.

"Okay, Miss Kinley. You can go. If we have any further questions, we will contact you." He held the door to the interrogation room open for her. She breezed past him on the points of her heels, strutting as if her shoes couldn't poke out an eye.

An officer spoke into Chuck's ear when Mila was out of sight. Chuck gave a brisk nod, and then he opened the door to the room where Avrianna hid. "You're up. The bouncer is in Interrogation Room Two, and he's not talking."

A slow, predator smile dominated Avrianna's lips. She went down the hall to Interrogation Room Two. As she passed, she caught a glimpse inside the viewing room. It was packed with officers, and more were hustling down the hall to watch the showdown.

She stepped into the small room and flung the door shut behind her. Bow Prancer sat at the metal table. His body was far too bulky for the chair he occupied. He had folded his arms on the tabletop, and his biceps strained from the shirt's sleeves. The cotton looked about ready to split. He didn't move when she entered, but his gaze shifted to her and followed her as she walked to the chair across from him.

She sat and gave him a silent smile.

"So, you're the muscle?" he said in a deep, gravelly voice.

"Yeah." She shrugged innocently.

He let out a small chuckle that sounded like a rockslide. "That's cute."

Avrianna barred her teeth. "You want cute?" She held up an index finger. "I can give you cute." And her finger erupted with green flames.

Bow flinched.

Smirking, she touched the tip of her finger to the metal table. The fire licked the surface. Beneath her fingertip, the metal softened. A puddle of molten steel formed, and her finger sank into it. Steam rose. The green flames burned brighter, and her finger sank deeper into the molten metal until it was up to her knuckle.

Her gaze flicked up to Bow. "You might want to move your foot."

He jumped out of his chair, knocking it to the ground, and backed into the wall. On his steel-toe boot was a drop of liquified steel. He shook his foot as if to dispel the drop like water. When it didn't budge, he bent forward, reaching out with his hand.

"I wouldn't touch it if I were you," she said. "It'll dry."

She pulled her finger from the hole in the table. The edges of it still steamed and dripped. She pointed at the spot where he had been sitting. "Have a seat."

Eyeing her still burning finger, Bow picked up the chair and dropped into it, being sure to keep his feet away from the hole in the table.

Avrianna kept her finger lifted. "I'm just beginning to have fun, but I can have a whole lot more of it." She tilted her head. "I hear you're not talking. By not talking you're just making me think you're guilty, or Guy Riches or one of the dancers are guilty. I have ways to make people talk." With a blink, the flames surrounding her finger winked out, and she laid her hand on the table. "We have footage of Mr. Sherman leaving the club at one-thirty in the morning. He paused to light a cigarette and nodded at you before he left. Do you remember him?" She jutted her chin at the image of Axel that sat on the table between them.

"I saw him."

Well, that's a start.

"Did you see anyone approach him in the parking lot?"

"He made a left turn, out of my line of sight."

"Toward the alley?"

"Yes."

"Did you hear the sounds of a confrontation?"

"I'm not paid to listen."

"But you're paid to watch, right?" She looked him square in the eye. "You make sure the dancers leave safely. Wouldn't you have seen a car in the parking lot after all the customers cleared out of the club and taken that as a sign someone was still there? Possibly to harm one of the dancers?"

"I check to make sure no one is lingering in the parking lot. The car was empty, and no one was around."

"Except someone was around." She paused. "Mr. Sherman was bleeding to death in the alley." She cocked her head to the side as she studied him. "Did you check the alley?"

He glared. "I glanced at it."

"Can a glance really reveal whether someone is lurking in the shadows or hiding behind the Dumpster?"

The muscle in Bow's jaw throbbed. "I had a MagLite with me. I pointed the light down the alley."

"Can you get up and show me?"

Grumbling, Bow shoved out of the chair. He lifted

his right arm as if he were holding a flashlight. With his body at an angle, he waved his arm from side to side.

"And what do you shine the light on?"

"The Dumpster."

She gave a nod. "So, you wouldn't see someone lying on the ground in the middle of the alley."

His dark brown gaze connected to hers. His face was taut with anger and her unvoiced accusation that he didn't do enough to make sure the premise was deserted after closing hours.

She pointed at the chair again. Without a word, he sat. "How far away would you say the alley is from your post?"

"Ten feet, maybe."

"And at one-thirty in the morning there's hardly any activity on the streets. A man was attacked ten feet away from where you stood, his throat slit from ear to ear, and you didn't hear a thing?"

"The music in the club is loud. I have the bass pounding behind me."

She nodded again. "At two o'clock, several people left the club. Did any of them turn left, in the same direction Mr. Sherman headed when he left thirty minutes before?"

"No. They were all parked out front. When they were gone, I made my rounds."

"What do you do when you make your rounds? Walk me through it."

Bow let out a sigh. "I checked the alley. Then I went to the front parking lot. I saw the car, went up to it, and looked in. When I didn't see anyone, I figured someone had car trouble and left it there to be towed.

It's happened before. Then I continued to the back where the employees park. I unlocked the gate and checked around each car before I knocked on the back door. Guy opened it, and I stood guard while the girls and bartenders left. Guy locked up, and I watched him leave before I got into my vehicle, locked the gate, and went home."

"When Mr. Sherman went to the left at one-thirty and a car didn't drive past you to exit the parking lot a moment later, you didn't question that?"

"No. We've had customers park in neighboring parking lots to keep jealous spouses from driving by, searching for them, and finding out they were spending their time at a strip joint instead of home in bed. If you head to the left and hop through the bushes past the alley, you're in the small grocer's parking lot. That's a favorite spot for married guys to hide their cars."

"Would it be fair to say that the murderer could've come from the grocer's parking lot and had slipped through the bushes to wait out Mr. Sherman?"

"Yes."

Avrianna tapped her finger against the table. Her nail created a soft ticking sound with each contact. The action and noise had Bow glancing uneasily at her finger. She tapped her finger a few more times, letting the time and silence stretch.

Finally, she spoke. "I didn't have the pleasure of seeing the employee parking lot. You said there's a gate?"

"Yes."

"Was the gate always there?"

"No. Guy had it installed after a dancer was

attacked a year ago."

"But even with the gate there, you still check around all the cars. Why?"

Bow crossed his arms over his chest. "Because a dude scaled the gate a few months ago and was hiding behind a car, waiting for the girls to leave. I found him." He gave her a look that said he was good at his job, no matter what she thought.

She ticked her nail a few more times against the table's surface. "So, with the gate in place, the only people who have access to that area, unless they scale the gate, of course, would be the employees of The Galaxy's Tease. Is that correct?"

"That's right."

"And the door to the club that the employees use to come and go is located within that gate?"

"Where else would it be?"

"You're the last one to leave, which means you lock the gate behind you?"

He nodded.

"Who locks the gate after all the employees are there and the club opens?"

"I do."

"Are you the only one with a key to the gate?"

"No. Guy has one, and there's a spare in the back for anyone who may need to come and go during hours, but they have to put it back when they return."

Her finger lifted and dropped with a steady beat.

Tick-tick-tick.

Her gaze didn't stray from his.

Tick-tick-tick.

But he broke eye contact to watch her finger move

up and down.

Tick-tick-tick.

"So, if someone were to leave the lot from the left as Mr. Sherman had, they would likely be going through the hedges to the grocer's lot?"

He kept watching her finger. "Yeah."

Tick-tick-tick.

"Or the alley, which has access to the gate and back parking lot?"

"Yeah."

Tick-tick-tick.

"Since no one passed by your watchful eye, following Mr. Sherman…and unless someone else came through those hedges…the only other way someone could get to Mr. Sherman from where he was found, is if they came from the employee parking lot?"

"Yeah."

Tick-tick-tick.

"Like an employee."

Tick-tick-tick.

"Yeah."

Her finger stilled.

Bow blinked. Startled, his head shot up. "No, that's not what I meant!" He surged to his feet. "You fucking tricked me. You put words in my mouth!"

Avrianna got to her feet, too. When she lifted her finger, it was like a mini tiki torch. She pointed with it. "Sit." Her voice was several octaves lower. Some would call it demonic.

Bow sank onto his chair.

She walked around the table. "I'd like to thank you for your cooperation."

Bow sat stiffly, looking straight ahead.

When she was beside him, she extinguished her finger out of sight and touched it to his bulging bicep. "Tss."

Bow toppled out of his chair. He swatted at his arm. It took him several seconds to realize he was perfectly fine. From the floor, he peered up at her with wide eyes.

She held up her finger. This time, it was normal. "Cute, right?" She walked around him. At the door she paused to add, "Thanks for the fun, Mr. Prancer." And she left him there, still on the floor, oozing embarrassment.

3

Lighter

Chuck waited for her on the other side of the interrogation room.

From the viewing room, the laughter of several officers escaped out into the hall.

"I have to say," Chuck said. "You outdid yourself on that one."

"Thanks."

"Simone has something for us. How 'bout you handle that while I continue the questioning?"

Simone was the medical examiner for the department. If she had something, that meant going down to the ME office where corpses were inside drawers that spanned a wall, and Chuck hated it down there.

"Wimp." She gave him a teasing smile.

"Whatever, Lighter."

She lowered her brows. "Lighter?"

"That's what they're calling you in there." He jabbed his thumb over his shoulder at the viewing room. "They said your finger looked like a lighter."

Avrianna figured her display in front of all of those cops hadn't helped her cause in proving she was just like them. Oh well. Nothing she could do about that now. She could peel a banana from either end, and they'd still claim she'd done it like an alien.

"I'll catch up with you later." She took the elevator downstairs. The hallway that led to the morgue carried the faint stench of death under the odor of strong chemical cleaners. She pushed open one of the double-doors. On the examination table, beneath a large light and under a white sheet, lay Axel Sherman.

Dr. Simone White stood next to the table, writing notes on a clipboard. She flipped a piece of paper over and made a quick notation. She wore her favorite black scrubs, and her black hair was tied into a bun at the top of her head. Her pale skin appeared moon-kissed, and her lips were painted the brightest red Avrianna had ever seen.

"Hey, Sim, what do you got?"

Simone peered up from the clipboard. "It's what Mr. Sherman doesn't have that's the problem."

Avrianna stood on the other side of the examination table. "What do you mean?"

"Someone castrated him."

That was far from what Avrianna had expected to hear. "Really?"

"Yeah, do you want to see?" Simone reached for the white sheet covering Axel.

"No." Avrianna held up her hands. "I'm good. Thanks. I'll take your word for it."

"You want to know the weird thing?" Simone wondered.

"As if castration isn't weird enough?"

"Whoever killed him, rezipped and buttoned his pants after the fact."

Avrianna looked down at Axel's crotch. Thankfully it was fully covered, but she wasn't seeing the sheet; she was back at the crime scene when she first examined his body. His zipper had indeed been zipped and the button clasped. If they had been undone, she would've figured sexual assault had been a part of his death. She bit her bottom lip. Maybe it still was. She paced along the side of the examination table.

Castration was usually done by a specific type of person—women getting revenge on cheating spouses or women seeking vengeance against a man who had raped or sexually assaulted them. They hadn't found proof of a spouse or girlfriend, so Avrianna considered the latter option.

Had Axel gone too far with one of the strippers? Mila, herself, said he got rowdy during her performance. Had he snuck backstage for more? Grabbed her, touched her, forced himself on her? Avrianna didn't detect a victim beneath Mila's conceited demeanor, but that didn't mean she wasn't one.

"Does Mr. Sherman have any other wounds or signs of a struggle?" she asked.

"None. Whoever killed him had a clear path to his throat."

"No scratch marks? Bites?"

"Not a single one."

Avrianna frowned at his bare feet. "How tall is Axel?"

Simone lifted her clipboard. "Six-foot on the dot."

"Where are his boots?"

Simone pulled out the bag of Axel's belongings. Avrianna measured the boots' soles with gloved fingers. "This would add a couple more inches to his height." With an idea brewing, Avrianna removed her radio from her belt and brought it to her mouth. "Hey, Chuck, radio back when you're alone."

"Go."

"How tall is Mila Kinley?"

There was a pause on the other end. "Her file says five-foot-two."

"How tall are you?"

"Six-foot-two. Why?"

"Hold that thought." Avrianna eyed Simone up and down. "How tall are you, Sim?"

"Five-five."

"And Mila Kinley wears three-inch heels. That's perfect." She lifted the radio again. "Chuck, meet me and Simone downstairs."

"On my way."

A few minutes later, Chuck joined them. She got him up-to-speed on Simone's finding, or lack thereof, and then she instructed Simone to stand next to Chuck. "The two of you represent the height difference between Mila Kinley and Axel Sherman. Axel is six-foot and had on boots with two-inch soles. Mila is five-two and had on three-inch heels during her interrogation. Would a woman of your height, Simone, be able to cleanly cut a man's throat who is as tall as Chuck?"

Simone looked up at Chuck. "Only one way to find out." She gripped her pen like a knife. From behind Chuck, she reached around to lay the pen against his throat, but she could only get the pen to the middle of his throat. She lifted up on tip-toe and managed to set the pen under his chin but at an angle. If she were to attempt to cut his throat, it would be a diagonal slit. Simone dropped flat on her feet. "It's hard to stand on tip-toe if you're in heels, though," she said.

"So, it wouldn't work?"

"If a woman of my height killed Mr. Sherman, his Adam's apple most likely would've been severed. Or, it's possible she could've cut the submental triangle." She indicated the part of Chuck's throat beneath his chin. "But she would not have the height to cut him from ear to ear." She pointed to Axel on the table. "The path that blade took was clean. The murderer had height to his or her advantage."

Avrianna took the pen from Simone and brought it to Chuck's throat. She had no problem reaching the sweet spot. She ran the length of the pen across his neck in a perfect arc, matching the path the blade followed when the perp killed Axel.

Chuck stole the pen from her fingers. "That's a

little scary to know," he said while rubbing his free hand over his throat.

Avrianna shook her head. "Please. You know me better than that." She turned to Simone. "But that lets us know that someone at least as tall as Axel, or taller, is the murderer."

Simone nodded in agreement. "I would say so."

"What are you thinking?" Chuck asked Avrianna.

"I'm thinking it's a woman. Castrating a man is a very murderess thing to do for pay back. Plain and simple. A few years ago, Lexie operated on a man whose wife castrated him. The wife had found out her husband was having an affair, she pretended she didn't know, got him into bed, forced him to reveal the truth with a blade to his penis, and when she heard the truth from his lips, she finished the job. And last year, remember the college student who confronted her rapist? He didn't recognize her, so she flirted with him until he took off his pants. Then she grabbed him between the legs. At knife point, she told him who she was and what he had done to her, and in turn, what she'd do to him. She did it, too. She was celebrated by every woman who had ever been assaulted. It was a huge thing."

"I remember that," Simone said. "I was one of the ones cheering 'You go, girl!'"

Avrianna nodded. "And we could have a similar case here. From what I know, Mr. Sherman was single, but there's no telling what he could've done while on vacation."

"But why zip and button his pants if you want the world to know his transgressions?" Simone asked, bringing them back to that weird factor.

Avrianna's brows lowered while she considered that. "Maybe she didn't want the world to know. Maybe this was a private act and she wanted it kept between them, in the same way the assault had been between them."

"But someone sure had a lot of blood on their hands," Chuck added.

Avrianna recalled all the blood soaking Axel's pants. "And all the girls had on long fake nails, too. It can be hard to get residue completely out from under your nails. We'll have to collect samples from all of them, even if that means we have to pry off each and every one of their acrylic nails."

Chuck pulled out his cell phone. "I'll also contact CSI to make sure they check the employee parking lot for signs of blood and take samples from all of the sinks in the club."

"Thanks, Chuck. And thanks, Sim. I'll be in my office if you need me."

For the rest of the day, Avrianna watched the videos for the interrogations she missed. She made note of all the employees who were five-eight or taller. Only a few girls fit that description, including Nebula…Samantha Ryan, the college student.

Avrianna removed the last CD from her computer after watching the final interrogation. She dropped her pen to the yellow legal pad she had been using for notes. On it was a short list of possible suspects, and Bow Prancer was not on that list. He'd never moved from his position at the door until all the customers left, and by then, Axel Sherman had already bled out. But

Guy was on the list. He had a key to the gate, and being the boss, he could come and go without anyone noticing or caring.

Too bad there isn't a camera at the back door. She sat up. *And why isn't there?*

Bow Prancer had said someone jumped the gate once. If the gate was put up for protection, why not a camera, too?

Wanting the answer to that question, she snatched up her phone and dialed the number Guy Riches had provided.

"This is Guy."

"Mr. Riches, this is Detective Heavenborn with the Aurora Police Department. I have a follow-up question I'd like to ask you."

"What is it?"

"I found out you had a gate installed around the employee parking lot located behind the building for safety reasons, but you said the only camera you have is above the entrance. Why didn't you ever install a camera at the back door?"

"I never thought of it."

She lifted a brow. "Really? You thought to put up a gate, which to some would seem extravagant and wouldn't even cross their minds as an option, but you didn't consider more security cameras? Not even after a man had jumped the gate and hid behind a car to get closer to your dancers?"

"I already told you I didn't," he snapped.

Avrianna clenched her jaw. "Then might I suggest you get one?" Her voice came out in a growl, and she dropped the phone to its holder before he could reply.

"What a little dipshit."

"Dipshit? Really?" Chuck's amusement met her ears.

She eyed his smirk. "Yes, you heard me right. I said dipshit. Guy Riches is a little dipshit. He never thought to have a camera installed at the back door despite everything that had happened there."

"He could do illegal dealings back there."

"That wouldn't surprise me." And she wished she could catch him in the act, but she had something bigger to do first: catch a killer.

"Chief Logan wants to see you."

Avrianna blinked. "Did he say what about?"

"Nope, just that you're to report to his office."

"Okay. Thanks." She walked down the hall, past the cubicles and desks to the large office at the other end. Out of the corner of her eye she glimpsed a group of officers in plain clothes whispering to each other. When she got closer, they elbowed each other. Their whispers died, and they all watched her approach Chief Logan's office. The door was shut. Shoulders squared, head held high, she knocked.

"Come in," a deep voice called out.

She opened the door and stepped in. The smell of stale coffee choked the air. Chief Logan, a man with thinning brown hair, sat behind a desk half-buried by piles of Manila folders and stacks of stapled papers. A half a dozen pens were scattered over the desk's surface. He set down a coffee cup that had dried coffee drippings down its sides.

"Ah, Detective. Have a seat."

She quietly closed the door and perched on the

edge of the chair in front of his desk. Chief Logan leaned back in his chair and linked his fingers across his paunch. He didn't say anything, and she wasn't about to ask why she was there. After a moment, he took a deep breath and then said, "I heard you melted a hole through one of our tables."

She didn't so much as blink. "Yes, I did." She almost shrugged, but she forced her shoulder to remain still. "I'll pay for it."

For a handful of seconds, he didn't reply. Then his head moved marginally, and she realized he was bobbing his head. She almost started to bob her head along with him, as if it had a hypnotic effect.

"Okay," he said, "you can go."

"Thanks, sir." She popped to her feet and slipped out into the bull pen. With her back to the door, she turned her head to the group of nosey co-workers. Smiling, she lifted her hand and crooked her index finger up and down a couple of times in the way people do to say "hi," but what she really meant was "fuck you." They got her message clearly and scattered as if on fire. She chuckled under her breath.

Okay, so maybe it sucked being treated like a freak, but she sure got a kick out of it sometimes.

Infinity Grocer

That night, Avrianna made a stack of pancakes for her late dinner. She doused them in maple syrup and sprinkled on powdered sugar. At her kitchen table, she devoured them alone while thinking about strippers and murder. Afterward, she turned on the late-night news. There was nothing about the murder at The Galaxy's Tease. She wondered how Guy Riches managed that. Did he have contacts in the news? Did he pay them off? Surely someone getting murdered after watching his best dancer perform would be bad for business.

She went to bed, without any hopes of actually sleeping. Bleak dreams managed to pull her into a fitful state. Glittery nails scratched down blackboards. Stilt-like spikes of high heels spun around on glass. Bloody hands twisted around silver poles.

Her alarm shattered the quiet and sent her heart rocketing up into her throat. She shot into a sitting position, and her hand instinctively reached out for her gun on her nightstand. Her fingers touched the cold metal, shocking her back to her senses. She blinked a few times and felt the heat pouring from her eyes with each bat of her lashes.

The alarm continued to screech.

She snatched up her phone and jabbed at the button to get the wretched noise to stop. Then she dropped the device onto her bed and cupped her head in her hands. The images from her dream continued to dance in her mind—black, pointed nails fingered grotesque slits in men's throats, the lethal points of stilettos stabbed the empty eye sockets of skulls, and stripper poles dripped with dozens of bloody handprints.

"Get. Out." She whacked the sides of her head with each word.

Groaning, she rolled out of bed and dragged her feet into the bathroom where she stood under the hot spray, letting the pulse of it beat against her head, hoping it would drum the images out of her thoughts and down the drain to the septic.

She downed a cup of coffee without moving from the counter. Gasping for breath, she grabbed the pot and filled the cup again. This time, she brought it to her coffee-drinking chair. She pulled her knees to her chest, lowered her head, and pressed her forehead to her kneecaps. She stayed like that for several minutes, as water from her wet hair slithered down her neck and dampened the back of her shirt.

One thing she longed for was a peaceful night's sleep. Luckily, she didn't need sleep to function; a perk of being abnormal. But she could use the peace, the quiet, if for nothing else but to stay sane. Instead, her nights were haunted with disturbing dreams that continued to cling to her in her waking hours.

She drank her second cup of coffee and finished getting dressed. Her hair was still wet, so she wrestled it into a bun before leaving. At the department, she went straight to her office to go over her notes from yesterday. Fifteen minutes later, a knock sounded on her opened door. Chief Logan stood at the threshold.

"Find Chuck," he said. "A body was found at Infinity Grocery."

Avrianna let out a breath. *Great another case.*

"His throat was slit."

She looked up at the chief's words.

He shook his head. "A lot of blood."

Shit.

"I'll find him now." She hunted Chuck down in the breakroom where he was selecting a cherry-filled jellied donut from a box of pastries. "You might want to hold off on that."

He turned to her with the donut halfway to his mouth. "Why?"

"A man's body was found with his throat cut at Infinity Grocery. And please, please don't tell me that's the grocer next door to The Galaxy's Tease."

Chuck set the donut on a paper plate. "Sorry, kid."

She blew out a breath. "Damn."

Crime scene tape roped off half of the parking lot to Infinity Grocery. A single, silver car was within the boundary, and a group of investigators circled around that vehicle. Avrianna parked her car next to the tape. Chuck got out of the passenger's seat, and she joined him on his trek toward the crime scene. They rounded the silver car and came face to face with the gore. A man in a suit lay there. With his tie gone and the first several buttons of his shirt undone, she could clearly see the gash in his throat. There was so much blood that he appeared to be floating on it.

"He looks like a man who wanted to decompress after a long day in the corporate world," she said. He had removed his cuff links, un-restraining himself from the bonds of work, but he wore a wedding band. "Apparently Bow's theory about the married gents parking here is accurate." She turned toward The Galaxy's Tease. From where she stood, she could see the roof of the building and the bushes that separated the two establishments.

She waved over a crime scene investigator. "Backtrack from the crime scene toward those bushes that lead to The Galaxy's Tease. Check the dirt for footprints. Check the leaves for blood and the branches for fibers. See if there's a trail of blood heading into the back where the employee's parking lot is, check the gate and its lock for signs of blood, too."

"Yes, ma'am."

"Thank you." She turned back to the scene. Blood had sprayed from the victim's neck and slithered down the driver's side door from the window to the ground. More blood had left a pattern of splatters on the roof of the car. "He was probably unlocking his car when the perp came up behind him."

Except, the body was parallel to the car.

"The perp coaxed him down so the car would shield him." Her gaze lowered to the man's crotch. Blood soaked his pants, and Avrianna had a feeling where all of that blood had come from. "And maybe to hide while she finished her task."

Chuck looked at her. "She?"

Avrianna shrugged while slipping her hands into gloves. "She, he, they." She squatted next to the body and lifted the sides of his jacket to see if the victim's wallet was inside one of the inside pockets. The corner of a piece of paper stuck out of a square of silk lining. "I got something."

A crime scene investigator joined her and handed her a pair of plastic tongs. Avrianna used them to slip the paper free without getting bloody prints from her gloves on it, but it wasn't a piece of paper. It was a white paper napkin spotted with blood. She carefully turned it over to see The Galaxy's Tease logo. Something else accompanied the design—a phone number scrawled in ink.

"Hey, Chuck." She showed him the napkin. "Do you think we'll be lucky and the perp forgot this?"

"We could only hope." With the help of another investigator, he shifted the body slightly. "I've got his wallet." And he worked it out of the man's back pocket as Avrianna dropped the napkin into an evidence bag.

"Ashton O'Reilly," Chuck read off the ID in the

man's wallet. "Forty years old. And he's been a citizen for twenty years."

He didn't appear to have anything in common with Axel Sherman, except for The Galaxy's Tease, but that didn't necessarily mean a thing. People could be friends with anyone, even someone you wouldn't expect them to bond with. Just look at Avrianna. She had close friends from all walks of life, and she was by far the strangest one of the bunch. If you could only be friends with someone you had things in common with, Avrianna would be shit-out-of-luck in the friend's department.

On her feet, she scanned the eaves for a sign of a surveillance camera. The car was parked in the second-to-last spot on the side of the building. "How much you wanna bet this is a blind spot for whatever cameras Infinity Grocery has?"

And she was right. The grocer had several cameras inside and three outside along the front of the building, two of which were at the corners, but not one showed the bushes or the victim's car.

"You know what this means, right?" Chuck asked.

She grimaced. "No."

"Yes, you do."

"I refuse."

"Wimp."

She glared at him. "Fine, but I can't guarantee that I won't punch him."

They waited for Guy Riches to show up at The Galaxy's Tease. Today he wore a black silk shirt and pants. He waved a hand at them as he pranced toward the front door. Avrianna bit her tongue as she waited for him to unlock it. The smell of his cologne made her lightheaded.

Back in his office, she noticed a second condom wrapper had been opened and left on the desk. She took a breath between clenched teeth. Man would she love to teach him a thing or two, and a few slaps may be part of that lesson.

He called up the footage on his computer. As he stood, he waved his hand at her again. She gave him a toothy smile that she figured looked like a lioness' grin and got to work searching for the victim. At two o'clock, a gaggle of men in business suits left the club. They divided and half of them went right and the other half to the left. She slowed the footage and zoomed in, but they were so close to each other that they blocked out each other's features. If the victim was among them, she couldn't point him out. Immediately after the men in suits flooded out the doors, the flow of customers continued. There were even several women. But with so many people leaving at once, she couldn't tell if any of them followed someone with malicious intent or not.

With an annoyed sigh, she got to her feet. "Well, thanks for allowing us to view this feed, but you know what'll really help? More. Security. Cameras."

"It's not my fault these men are getting murdered."

She put a hand on her hip. "They both died after spending time at your club."

"You can't prove he was here. You couldn't even find him in the footage."

She showed him her teeth again in a way that had him taking a step back. "I didn't need to find the victim in the footage. We know he was here last night. He had one of your napkins in his jacket pocket. And there was a phone number on it." She took a step toward him, enjoying the fact that he was pressed up against the wall. "You have a murderer in your club," she said in a low voice. "If I were you, I'd watch my back. You could be the next target."

His Adam's apple bobbed.

"Have a good day, Mr. Riches."

She led the way out of the club, grinning the entire way.

Knock On Wood

Avrianna pulled up to a picturesque house with shutters painted blue, flowers planted along the walk, and a wooden swing on the front porch. She hated this part, notifying loved ones of the worst news they would ever have to hear. At the door, Chuck knocked, and she clasped her hands in front of her, trying to strike a non-threatening pose. Heck, she could have a pacifier in her mouth and still look threatening.

The door opened to a brunette woman. Her hair was done up in a low ponytail. Stragglers framed her face. A burp cloth was draped over her shoulder, and a trail of spit-up flowed down it. She held a baby bottle.

Oh shit.

Chuck took point. "Mrs. O'Reilly?"

The woman nodded. "Yes."

"I'm Detective Davis and this is Detective Heavenborn."

The woman looked at Avrianna with wide eyes. She turned back to Chuck. "What happened? Is it Ashton? He didn't come home last night."

"May we come in?"

She peered again at Avrianna. The apprehension was there. Should she let the demon child into her home? Where her own child was? "O-okay." She held the door open and flinched away when Avrianna passed by her into the hallway.

Mrs. O'Reilly led them into the living room. A blanket was spread out on the carpet for a baby's tummy time. Avrianna stepped around it and sat on a chair, trying not to touch too much of it; she'd seen people grab cans of disinfection the moment she got up to spray down chairs, as if being a freak was contagious. Chuck took the other chair beside her, and Mrs. O'Reilly lowered onto the couch across from them. She stared at them with wide, frantic eyes.

Chuck cleared his throat. "We're so very sorry to have to tell you this, but Ashton O'Reilly was killed last night."

Mrs. O'Reilly continued to stare.

"His body was found at Infinity Grocery. We believe he was at The Galaxy's Tease."

She blinked. "W-what's The Galaxy's Tease?"

"It's a strip club, ma'am."

She shook her head. "No. No, Ashton doesn't go to strip clubs."

Chuck pulled out Ashton's ID from his pocket. "He had this on him."

Her hand shook as she inspected the card.

"Is that your husband?" Avrianna asked.

The woman's eyes flashed with resentment when she looked up at Avrianna. "Yes, but it's not what you think."

Avrianna licked her lips and picked her words carefully. "Ma'am, a man was killed in The Galaxy's Tease's parking lot two nights ago, and we believe Ashton is the second victim."

Tears plunged down her cheeks. "You're wrong." She snatched up her phone and attempted three times to unlock the screen. When she finally put in her four-digit code correctly, she accessed her contacts and brought the phone to her ear.

Avrianna and Chuck exchanged glances. The longer the phone rang, the more Mrs. O'Reilly's resolve crumbled. Her shoulders shook, and she bent forward, as if her body was caving in. Heaves broke free. The call rolled to voicemail, and she poked her finger at the screen, calling back her husband who would never answer the phone again. At that very moment, his phone was in an evidence bag. She could keep calling, but it wouldn't change the truth of the matter, the truth that she was painfully coming to accept.

She covered her eyes with her free hand, but she kept the phone pressed to her ear in utter desperation. When the call went to voicemail again, she let out a wail, and the phone fell from her fingers to the floor.

They let her cry.

The sorrow she emitted made the air heavy. After several moments, she swiped the tears from her face and looked at them with bloodshot eyes. "W-why are you h-here?"

"We have a few questions for you." Chuck's voice was soft.

"What?"

"Had Ashton stayed out late frequently?"

She removed the stained burp cloth from her shoulder and used it to wipe her runny nose. "He'd work late, and sometimes he'd have drinks with co-workers."

"Would he say where they'd go to have drinks?"

"No." She sniffed loudly.

Chuck met Avrianna's gaze, tagging her in.

"How often would he stay out late?" Avrianna asked.

Mrs. O'Reilly glared through wet eyelashes. "I don't know."

"A weekly estimation," she prodded.

She balled the burp cloth into her fist. "Once or twice a week."

Avrianna took a slow breath. "I'm sorry to have to ask this, but is there a chance that he was having an affair?"

Mrs. O'Reilly jaw hardened. Her face turned several shades of red. "How dare you!" She threw the burp cloth at Avrianna. It hit her square in the chest and uncurled on her lap. "I want you out of my house. Get out! GET. OUT!"

Avrianna got up and left without a word. She shut the door while Mrs. O'Reilly continued yelling for her to get out and went all the way to her car where she closed herself in. It was as far as she could go without leaving her partner.

Breathing in and out, she gripped the steering wheel. No matter what she did, she'd always take the brunt of everyone's anger. They didn't understand her. They listened to the rumors, whether they were real or fabrication. If they didn't fear her, they hated her. Or they feared AND hated her. How could she compete with what had been ingrained in them since she was a newborn, found by sailors as if she were a piece of ship wreckage? She couldn't. So, she gave people space and left when they wanted her to leave.

Ten minutes later, the front door opened and Chuck stepped out. He climbed into the passenger's seat. "She said he didn't have any enemies and swears that he was a loyal husband."

"Loyal enough to keep a woman's phone number," Avrianna said.

"Unfortunately, you can never really know the people you love."

Avrianna started the engine. "Yeah." She backed out of the driveway and headed in the direction of the police department.

***

Down in the medical examiner's office, Avrianna approached the table holding Ashton O'Reilly's body. Simone stood beside him, clipboard in hand.

"I have a feeling I know what you're going to say,"

Avrianna said.

Simone nodded gravely. "Castrated."

Avrianna squeezed her eyelids shut and pinched the bridge of her nose. "Okay. Two men. Both castrated after going to The Galaxy's Tease. What links them other than the location and method of murder?"

She began to pace. "There's still a chance that this is a woman's act. We could be looking at a partner scheme. Axel Sherman was only on vacation here for two weeks, but if he had frequented the club, he could've met Ashton there one night and the two of them could've devised a plan to sexually assault their favorite dancer." She spun on her heel. "Both of these men could've pissed off the wrong woman in another way, though. Maybe they'd rejected her."

"Or she's playing Russian Roulette and randomly picking men to slay," Simone offered. "She could have a huge distaste for men and has finally snapped after having men ogle over her with hard-ons in their pants night after night."

Avrianna paused and regarded Simone. "You make a good point. If that's the case, what worries me is the possibility of another murder tonight."

"You better knock on wood."

Avrianna scowled at Simone as she picked up her pacing again. "You know the one thing I can't figure out? What is the killer doing with their…" She paused and moved her hands around while searching for a good noun to use. "…body parts after castrating them? No appendages have been found anywhere at the two crime scenes. Not even in nearby Dumpsters."

"Maybe the killer is keeping them for souvenirs."

Avrianna scrunched up her nose. "Ew. How would that even be possible?"

Simone scribbled something on her clipboard. "Well, if you have a jar and some formaldehyde, you could keep them for a long time."

Avrianna's phone chimed just then—a saving grace. She plucked her phone from her belt, hoping it was something that could take her away from his conversation. Lucky for her, a text from Chuck waited.

—We matched the phone number on the napkin we found on Ashton with a name. She's in Interrogation Room One now.—

"Gotta go, Sim. I'll talk to you later."

Relieved, Avrianna hurried to Interrogation Room One, but instead of finding the questioning already underway, Chuck waited outside.

"What's up?" she asked.

"We thought we'd shake things up and let you do this one."

Frowning, she took the print of Ashton's photo. "Okay." She entered the interrogation room. Sitting at the table was a young woman wearing a ripped shirt that showed off her rather busty cleavage. Her hair was bleached blonde and fell down in waves to her hips. A silver lip ring sparkled in the middle of her bottom lip, which was painted a bright, bubble-gum pink.

Avrianna cast an eye toward the two-way mirror. They all probably thought this was funny; pairing up Avrianna Heavenborn with a woman who looked like a porn star.

Bastards.

She took the chair across from the woman, who

eyed her up and down. Avrianna forced a smile and stated the date and time. "This is Detective Avrianna Heavenborn questioning…" She paused. "Can you state your full name for the record?"

"Kat Kirkpatrick."

"Miss Kirkpatrick, did you go to The Galaxy's Tease last night?"

"I sure did." She batted her thick, feathery lashes.

"What time did you arrive?"

Kat pursed her lips, making the lip ring stand out even more. "Hmm. I think I got there at midnight."

"Did you go with anyone?"

"Nope. It was just little ole me, but I was meeting someone there."

Avrianna's interest piqued. "Whom were you meeting?"

"My friend, Samantha Ryan. She's one of the dancers. She told me she had a new routine and wanted me to see it. While I waited for her performance, I had some fun." The corner of her mouth tilted up.

"Did you see this man at the club?" Avrianna pushed Ashton's photo over the table.

"As a matter of fact, I did." She purred with the memory. "He's older but sexy as hell. I mean look at those dimples and baby blues." Her tongue came out and flicked her lip ring. "I flirted with him for a good hour. He bought me drinks, and in return I bought him a shot, which I put right here." She leaned forward and pulled down the collar to her shirt, showing off the crevice between her voluptuous breasts. "His buddies got a real

kick out of that and cheered him on." She lifted a

shoulder. "I like to entertain."

Avrianna nodded. "So, you had drinks with him?"

"Oh, we did a little more than that. He said he'd never kissed a girl with a lip ring before, so we made out." She giggled. "He was afraid he'd pull out my lip ring and hurt me. It was incredibly cute."

"Did you do anything else?"

Like kill him?

"Unfortunately, no." She pouted. "I left after Samantha performed. I had class early this morning and couldn't skip again."

"Did you see Mr. O'Reilly before you left?"

"Of course, I did. I gave him my number."

"You wrote it on a napkin, didn't you?"

Kat blinked. "Yes, I did. How do you know that?"

"Because I found it in his jacket pocket. He was killed last night after leaving The Galaxy's Tease."

Kat's face paled. "Well, damn." Her shoulders slumped. "My God." She stared off into space. "I-I made out with a man who was murdered?"

"He was also married."

Kat waved her hand, dismissing Avrianna's words. "I make out with married men all the time, but I've never made out with a man with the Grim Reaper on his ass."

Avrianna squinted her eyes at the young, flirtatious woman across from her.

"What did he do when you gave him your number?"

"He kept it. Obviously."

"I mean, did he say anything, do anything. Did the two of you do anything?"

"Well, I sucked on his earlobe and whispered in his ear to call me. He blushed. It was so adorable. Then I said goodbye to Samantha and left."

"Where were you parked?"

"Out front."

"You said you left right after Samantha's performance. Where is she on the lineup?"

"She's the second-to-last act of the night, right before Andromeda."

Avrianna kept her features neutral but inside her thoughts were clicking into gear. Samantha fit the height requirement of the suspect. Performing before Mila Kinley, as known as Andromeda, the club's most popular talent, could entice the green-eyed monster to come loose. Especially if you saw a man, who not so much as looked your way during your performance, gravitate toward the stage, as if hypnotized, during the act that followed yours and toss a hundred-dollar bill.

"How close are you to Samantha?"

"We're best friends now, but first I was her girlfriend."

And especially if you see one of the men making out with your ex-girlfriend.

Avrianna gave a nod. "Thanks, Miss Kirkpatrick. That's all for now." She pushed out of her chair and started for the door.

"Wait." Kat leaned forward so the collar of her shirt sagged to reveal her breasts.

"Did you see it?"

Avrianna had no idea what she was talking about and almost thought she was referring to Ashton's body. Or worse, his missing appendage. "Did I see what?"

"The napkin with my number on it?"

Her brows furrowed. "Yes."

"Good. Give me a call sometime." She winked.

And all Avrianna could do was stare. She couldn't believe that had just happened. "You do know who I am, right?" Not even men had the balls to come on to her. In college, she had heard the rumor that the male student body thought their penises would burn off if they tried, but here she was, getting hit on by a woman with breasts that made her own boobs look like mosquito bites.

Kat sat back. Her gaze trailed up and down Avrianna's body. "Absolutely."

Avrianna's cheeks burned when she realized Kat hadn't been eyeing her out of indifference when she first walked in, she'd been checking her out.

"I'm sorry," she said. "I'm straight, and even if I wasn't, I wouldn't cross that line with a potential suspect. Thanks for your cooperation." She escaped out the door.

On her way past the viewing room, she noticed all the officers watching had their mouths hanging open.

Fun-Sucker

The next day, Avrianna expected to get a call about a third victim, but one didn't come. Either that meant that there were no other targets, or the killer hadn't been tempted last night. And that gave her an idea.

"You want to do what?" Chuck asked when she told him her brilliant idea.

"I want to put someone in, as a customer, to stake out the place. We'll fit her with a camera and a wire. She'll also have a mike in her ear to hear me."

"Her? You already have someone in mind?

"Yup."

"Please, don't tell me it's Sassy."

Avrianna looked horrified at the thought of her foster mom in a strip club. "Are you out of your mind? A strip club would be a playground for Sass. No. Someone better."

"Okay. I'll bite. Who?"

She smiled. "The only girl for the job…Simone."

Simone sat behind her desk, taping away at a keyboard while a recording of her findings during her last medical examination played back to her. Instead of a rolling computer chair, she sat on a large purple yoga ball. Her white coat floated around it, and she moved her hips, causing the ball to sway from side to side. She had perfect posture while balancing on the ball, with her back straight and her shoulders back. If Avrianna were to attempt that, she'd probably end up popping the ball. With a bullet, because she was not the yoga type.

Avrianna stood by quietly, waiting for Simone to finish. When she did, she bounced around on the yoga ball to smile up at Avrianna. "Hey, Ave, what can I do for you? I don't have a body for you today."

Avrianna glanced toward the empty examination table. That part of the room was dark. "I know, but I have a job for you to do, if you want to. I won't pressure you."

Simone put her hands on her waist and rotated her hips around in circles. "That sounds intriguing. What sort of job are we talking about here?"

"You could help me catch the killer castrating

men."

"I thought I already was."

"Oh, definitely." Avrianna didn't want Simone to think her work wasn't important or appreciated. A lot of the time, she found something on a corpse that could be led back to the killer. And her reports on the method of murder were crucial. "What you do always helps us to catch the bad guys. But what I mean is that you could go out in the field, where the action takes place."

Simone raised her eyebrows. "I do like action."

Avrianna grimaced at the sexual note in Simone's voice. Not to mention that she was still rotating her hips in circles. "Well, you'll be undercover for us in The Galaxy's Tease. We'll have a camera on you, probably in a necklace or something, and you'll also be wired to capture sound. Plus, a mike in your ear will let you hear my instructions."

"Oh, now that sounds exciting. I've always wanted to be wired."

"So, are you in?"

Simone winked. "I'm in."

Later that evening, Simone met Avrianna at her house. Simone had a pile of clothes in her arms and a bag over her shoulder full of shoes. "I brought all of my best clubbing outfits."

Avrianna blinked. There must've been ten outfits, and there was no telling how many pairs of shoes that bag carried. "Did you leave anything in your closet?"

Simone set the clothes on Avrianna's couch. "As a matter of fact, I left my church clothes behind. I didn't think it would be appropriate to mix the two."

"So, no leather and sequins for church?"

"Oh, I have a leather dress for church. It's white. It's for Easter."

Avrianna nodded slowly. "Why exactly did you bring so many outfits?"

"Because I need to match what I'm going to wear with whatever you have that has the camera in it. I mean, what if you have a gawdy necklace for me? I can't wear that with a bubble-gum pink halter top."

A sigh escaped Avrianna's lips. She hadn't anticipated being part of a fashion lesson before their undercover work. "Well, I don't have a necklace for you. We vetoed that because of your height. We'd only be capturing people's shirts, not their faces."

"Are you calling me short?"

Avrianna looked down at her. "A little bit."

Simone laughed. "Okay. Well, if no necklace, then what do you got for me?" She rubbed her hands together. "A tiara? And then I can pretend to be a bride having fun for her bachelorette party." She hopped up and down. "Oh! Then we can invite the girls, and they can be my bridesmaids."

This was not going the way Avrianna thought it would. "No tiara. No bachelorette party. No girls. Strictly work."

"You know how to suck the fun out of everything."

Avrianna shrugged. "Yup, that's me. Fun-sucker." She picked up the prop that Simone would wear from the stand beside the front door. "Here. You'll be wearing this."

Simone gasped. "You want me to wear a hat?"

"Yup. We've already established that you're on the short side. This Stetson will help with that. It's black with this silver heart on a band. That's where the camera is." She handed it to Simone.

"Well, at least it's cute." She brought it over to her stack of clothes. "I think I have something that'll work with this."

While Simone dressed, Avrianna went through the details of the case again. The problem was, they didn't have a definite lead. The perp could be one of the dancers. Or a bartender, for all they knew. And Guy Riches definitely wasn't off her radar. That left a whole lot of people on the suspects list.

What would lead someone to want to kill men who went to a strip club? Aside from the sexual assault theory. Maybe the men were bad tippers. Even the smallest slight could set someone off, especially if that person had been treated poorly for too long. Anything could make someone with a fragile mind snap.

A dancer could be offing men who mistreated her simply because of her profession. Or even because they gave their attentions to another. That thought led Avrianna to think of Andromeda. The woman was conceited. She thought she was the center of the universe. At least, the stripping universe. What would happen if a frequent customer who usually rained her in bills started to do that to another dancer, her rival on the pole? A woman like that would take matters in her own hands and remove the people who slighted her. Or remove the competition. If the perp was a dancer, they had to nail her before she went that far.

But perhaps the killer was someone else at the strip

club. She considered Bow Prancer, the bouncer. He took his job seriously. A man like that, looking out for a dozen or so dancers, could think of himself as their protector who would do anything and everything to keep them safe, especially from rowdy customers who posed a threat.

Could Guy Riches do the same to protect his girls? *His* girls? If he viewed the dancers at his strip club as more than employees, as property, he could very well off customers who tried to take what was his. Or hurt them in some way. What better of a way to make sure banned customers would stay away than to kill them?

And yet, the killer could be someone unexpected, like a bartender. A female bartender tired of competing with the entertainment, or having to put up with men's unwanted advancements just because she was a woman.

At this point, anyone could be the suspect. And their motive could be any numbers of things.

The thump of heels coming down the hall had Avrianna looking up. Simone came out in the open wearing low-riding jeans, boots, a laced corset top, and the Stetson on her head. The corset top was so sight that her pale breasts were pushed up to her collarbones, like twin moons.

Avrianna put up her hand to shield Simone's boobs from her vision. "Dang, girl."

Simone peered at her bust proudly. "My girls are always hiding under scrubs. It feels so nice to have them out. Aren't they beautiful?"

Refusing to look again, Avrianna kept her gaze up toward the ceiling. "Ugh. Sure. You ready to go?"

"I think so. How does my makeup look?"

Avrianna hadn't even noticed her makeup. She lowered her gaze to Simone's face, trying really hard not to look any lower. Simone's lips were painted vixen red, and her eyes were covered in several layers of black—liner, mascara, and smoky eyeshadow. And Avrianna was pretty sure only half of her lashes were real.

"You look like you could be performing."

"Great. That's the look I was going for."

Avrianna picked up a tiny transmitter from the coffee table. It had two wires a couple of inches long, with a round piece on one end. "This is a miniature recording device. You can…ugh…put it between your…ugh…"

"Girls?"

"Sure." She quickly handed Simone the wire and averted her gaze while Simone slipped it between her breasts and got them situated.

"Let me make sure it won't fall out." Simone moved her shoulders back and forth, shaking her breasts from side to side. "It stayed put. We're good. You can look now."

Ignoring that, Avrianna selected another item from the coffee table. "This inserts into your ear. It's a mike. When I talk into my radio, you'll be able to hear me." She gave the mike to Simone to slip into her ear. "I'll go into my room to test it out."

In her bedroom, with the door closed, she raised the radio to her mouth and decompressed the button. "Testing, testing, one, two, three. Can you hear me?"

"Holy shit," Simone shouted. "That's cool! Now whisper something sexy to me."

Avrianna put the radio to her forehead and closed her eyes. This was her friend. She loved Simone, and wouldn't be able to solve crimes without her, but dang the girl sure had a kinky mind.

Avrianna spoke into the radio, "No more playing around."

"I was kidding," Simone yelled back.

Avrianna left her bedroom. "Okay. It's almost midnight. I want you to be there for the last two hours before it closes. It only makes senses that the perp and the victims are there late until closing."

Simone nodded.

"You good?"

Simone gave a thumbs up. "My breasts and I are ready to party."

I'm A Slave 4 U

In the parking lot of The Galaxy's Tease, to the left of the doors where the first crime had taken place, Avrianna pulled out her laptop. Simone occupied the passenger's seat of her car. "I just want to make sure that the camera is working properly." She booted up her laptop and connected it to the camera. A dark image appeared on the screen. She could make out part of the dash and the view through the windshield. With her gaze locked on the laptop's screen, she reached over and waved her hand in front of the cowboy's hat. Her hand flashed across the screen.

"All set," she said and turned to Simone. "Now, remember, there could be a killer somewhere in that club, so you need to be careful."

"I know."

"I want you to try to talk to the bouncer a little. And keep an eye on the dancers, especially if they seem to favor a certain customer or have some sort of altercation with one. And try to check out the bartenders, too. Just be yourself. Not even a killer would be able to resist talking to you. Or flirt with you, for that matter."

"Is that a compliment?"

Avrianna smiled. "It is. You're extremely friendly and fun to be around."

Simone smiled back. "Thanks."

"You're going to do great. And I will be there with you, giving you advice and instructions. I'll be listening and watching everything, too. I've got your back."

"I wouldn't want anyone else to have my back." She leveled her balled fist, and Avrianna gave her a pound.

"We have an undercover male officer inside. He's just going to be nursing drinks and appearing to watch the show. Lowkey. And Chuck is on the other side of the parking lot, ready to enter if need be."

Simone nodded. "Sounds like it's as safe as could be. For a place where two people have wound up dead, that is."

"*Men* have wound up dead," Avrianna corrected. "So, you're good there."

Simone cupped her breasts. "Thank goodness."

Avrianna laughed. "Okay. Time to put your girls to work."

Simone took a deep breath before getting out of the car. Avrianna turned in her seat to watch Simone walk away. When Simone turned toward the entrance of the club, out of sight, she shifted back to her laptop. A visual of Bow Prancer, with arms cross and feet shoulder's width apart, appeared on the screen.

"Twenty-dollar admission fee," he said in a bored voice. No doubt, having to say that over and over again every night would be tiring.

Simone passed him a bill.

"You can go in."

"Oh, I'm not in a rush. You look like you could use a little company."

He shrugged.

"What's your name?"

"Bow."

"That's a strong name. Perfect for you. I'm Rose."

Good girl, Avrianna thought, proud that Simone had given her last name instead.

"Do you mind if I stay out here with you for a bit?"

Thanks to Simone having to look up at Bow, Avrianna watched as Bow lowered his gaze to Simone's breasts and licked his lips.

Scumbag.

"You can stay here with me," he said.

The image shifted a little as Avrianna assumed Simone shifted to the side to lean against the building. "Tell me, what is it like being bouncer?"

"It pays decent. I get free drinks and free lap dances whenever I want." He eyed Simone, sending her some serious lustful vibes.

"Lucky boy," Simone said, playing him up. "Have you ever had to tackle someone or deck them?"

"I avoid getting physical with the customers, but I have had to bar entrance to guys who were obviously drunk or high on something. And sometimes a customer inside gets too frisky with a dancer. When that happens, I have to restrain them and escort them out the doors."

"And none of them have hit you for that?"

"They've tried, but I'm fast."

The feed bobbed up and down as Simone nodded. "You look it." Her voice had dropped an octave, deepening to a sultry tone. "I bet you do a great job keeping all of those girls in there safe."

A smile cracked Bow's stiff face. "I do what I have to do to protect them."

"Of course. They're lucky to have you." She inched closer. "You probably have a ton of stories. What's the craziest thing that's happened here?"

Avrianna leaned forward in her seat when Bow stepped up to Simone and dipped his head. "Well, I shouldn't be talking about this, but a man was killed in our alley. And another man was killed next door."

Simone gasped. "No way. That's pretty exciting. Do you know how it happened?"

"Not really, but I was interrogated by the police."

"They thought you did it?"

Bow shrugged. "They were grasping at straws."

Avrianna scowled. What a jerk.

"So, you didn't do it?"

Bow laughed.

"Come on, you can tell me."

"Me? Nah. I'm not that kind of guy. I don't even knock the guys' lights out who bother the girls. Though, there are times when I would love to do nothing more."

The camera moved up and down again. "You're a good guy, Bow." She reached out and patted his arm. "I'm going to get a drink now and toast you. See ya later."

Bow's mouth pulled down at the sides, clearly disappointed he wasn't going to get something more from Simone. "Okay. Enjoy your time."

"Oh, I think I will."

Avrianna imagined Simone winking at him before parading into the club. During working hours, the club had a completely different atmosphere than when Avrianna had been there during the early morning hours. The lights were dim, giving the space a passionate feel with red lights shining along the walls and votive candles flickering on the few round tables positioned in the back.

On the stage, a woman wearing a bikini that looked like a bunch of skinny red belts across her butt danced to "I'm a Slave 4 U" by Britney Spears. With that outfit, she definitely looked as though she enjoyed bondage, which was likely the point. Men hooted and howled as she flung her blonde locks in seductive head whips. Her hands rubbed her body, and she parted her legs and gyrated her hips to the music.

Simone made her way to the bar, and Avrianna took that opportunity to talk to her. "You did very well with Bow. He does seem genuine." A little shift in the feed told Avrianna that Simone gave a slight nod of agreement. "At the bar, try to give me a good look at who is there."

Customers occupied the stools on either side of the bar, where two bartenders were busy getting them drinks. Simone took a spot in the middle. She swiveled on the stool, giving Avrianna a nice view of the customers' backs who were eagerly stuffing bills into the straps along the stripper's bare butt cheeks.

The camera shook, blurring the image.

Avrianna squinted, trying to make out distinctive features of the customers and what they wore in case they later had to be identified on security footage, but she couldn't see clearly.

"Sim, stop bobbing your head to the music."

Instantly, the feed stilled.

"You can tap your foot or your fingers to the music."

A humming sound started up, matching the lyrics to the song.

Avrianna smiled when she realized Simone was singing the tune under her breath. She didn't mind that. Seeing was important. Hearing would come into play if Simone spoke to someone or they spoke to her.

None of the men in front of the stage stood out. They all seemed like normal guys. A group of them were likely twenty-one and experiencing the erotic fun for the first time. Several men stood or sat alone, wearing all sorts of clothes—suits, leather, jeans and T-shirts. They were drinking beers or liquor in highball glasses and enjoying the show. The dancer on the stage didn't appear to care about them, and they certainly didn't give a damn about each other.

At one of the tables, off to the side of the stage, sat a man and a woman, who was clearly an employee. She wore a halter top in a red flannel pattern that revealed her midriff and a tiny, matching skirt. They spoke with their faces close together. Whatever they were discussing, to Avrianna's eyes, they were enjoying each other's company. And no one else in the club paid them any mind.

Another man and a woman came out of a side door. The woman held the man's hand and led him to a table. She wore a bra covered in rhinestones that shot off bits of light whenever she moved. The door probably led to a private room where lap dances could be performed. Apparently, the man with a stupid grin on his face and a dazed look in his eyes had just had an amazing lap dance. When he sat in a chair, she rubbed his shoulders before heading to the bar.

"Hey, Ricky. I need a whiskey sour for that fella. Put it on his tab."

A moment later, the woman sashayed back over and delivered the drink to the man. She took the seat across from him as he took the first swallow of his drink. Her job was to get men to spend more money. She'd be back to the bar again. Or maybe she'd even lure him to the private room for another show before he headed home.

Avrianna watched the two of them interact for a while. Nothing unusual happened between them. No one cared that Ms. Rhinestone was giving all of her attention to this man. Nor did she appear to hate the role she played or what she had to do to make some money. As for the john. Well, he was giddy.

When the song ended, Avrianna trained her attention back to the stage to see the bondage-covered stripper taking her leave. The customers were bummed to see her go, naturally, but none of them were putting up a fight, demanding her to come back, or creating a scene. If the killer was a customer, he wasn't there. Or, at least, he wasn't tempted. Yet.

Suddenly, a dark object flashed across the screen.

Simone turned and tipped her head back.

"I noticed you while I was backstage." The dark shape became a shirt, a par of shoulders, and a face.

Guy Riches, the sleaze ball.

"Oh, and what were you doing backstage with the girls?"

Guy gave her a disgustingly charming smile. "I own this place."

"Really?" Simone slathered her voice in awe. "You own this joint?"

"I do."

"It's nice. Kudos."

"Thank you." He scanned Simone with his hungry eyes. "What's your name?"

"Rose." And just how she said it would make any man blush.

"Do you dance, Rose?"

Avrianna clenched her jaw. No way was this prick trying to pick up her friend, an innocent woman out for a good time, in order to recruit her as his newest stripper.

"As a matter of fact, I used to. I danced ballet all through grade school and high school. And in college, I took salsa lessons."

"That's hot. Would you ever consider exotic dancing?"

"Hmm…maybe."

"You could start your set with a salsa number. Then you could remove your dress to reveal ballet flats and a tutu-inspired mini skirt. You could add ballet moves to a slow, seductive dance around the pole. We could even play a classic song remixed with a sexy thump."

"A stripper en pointe? Now that would be different."

"That's what I'm all about. That's what this is." He spread his arms wide to indicate the club. "I think outside the box to bring men their inner fantasies."

Avrianna groaned.

To Simone she said, "Show reluctance and ask him about the murders."

The camera lowered as Simone tipped her head down. Her hand came into view as she tapped her fingertips on the bar's top. "Well…honestly…this is my first time coming here. I came because I've been curious…about the murders."

"Oh, I wouldn't worry about that."

Simone looked up. "Why's that?"

"The protection of my employees is of upmost importance. I do whatever I can to keep them safe. And if you worked here, I wouldn't let anything happen to you."

Avrianna's brows drew together at that. How would he guarantee that? By killing anyone who offended them? Threatened them?

"Ask him how."

Simone tilted her head. "How'd you do that?"

"Easy. The dancers are guarded inside the club at all times. Especially when they're on the stage or in a private room. They're even watched over in the employee parking lot when they come and go. You'd be safe here."

"I guess it's a good thing that the victims have been male customers then, huh?"

"I wouldn't say it's a good thing. Not very good for business."

The view changed to show the club from corner to corner. "It doesn't look as though it had hurt your business any. There are a lot of people here."

"They come for the girls."

And the girls could be the reason why they're getting killed.

Avrianna chewed on her bottom lip. If Guy Riches was concerned about business and male clientele being afraid to come, he wouldn't be killing them off. He certainly wouldn't have continued after the first one. And he most definitely wouldn't commit any more murders in the future that could hurt his business.

"And they'd come for you," Guy told Simone, and he flashed her a sleazy smile.

A shiver snaked through Avrianna's body. Still, she did not like the man.

"Guy!"

The camera turned to show a dancer in a full leather body suit standing at the hallway off to the side of the stage where only employees were allowed to go. She lifted her arm and waved him over with long, red nails.

He turned to Simone. "Tell me you'll think about it."

"Yeah, I'll think about it."

"I hope to see you again, Rose." He gave her a wink before departing.

When he was out of earshot, Simone mumbled "Ick" under her breath.

"You can say that again," Avrianna said. "But don't. I don't want anyone seeing you talking to yourself."

Simone let out a soft laugh.

"And no laughing."

She snorted.

Avrianna covered her eyes with her hand. "Oh God." This wasn't going to be good if Simone broke cover now and revealed her earpiece.

"Was he trying to recruit you to join his cult?"

The voice came from off screen.

The camera moved around to show a young woman behind the bar. She had a rag in her hand that she used to wipe down the bar. She wore black pants and a low-cut black tank top. Her lips were painted a magnetic purple that matched her nails and the streaks in her blonde hair.

"Cult?"

The bartender laughed. "Cult is the wrong word. *Payroll.*" She put her hands on the bar. "What can I get you?"

"A glass of pinot noir, please. And how'd you know that he was trying to get me to be one of his dancers?"

The bartender selected a bottle and a wine glass.

She filled the glass half-way with red wine while she spoke. "A few times a week he's always hitting on a hot woman with a unique look, trying to get her to be one of his dancers." She set the glass on a napkin in front of Simone.

Simone put her fingers around the stem glass. "Unique look?"

The bartender nodded. "Yeah, like a girl with a hoop in her nose. Or—" She lifted a hand in front of Simone. "A dark haired, pale-skinned beauty with Angelina Jolie lips and bright eyes."

"Now if you were the one trying to get me to join the payroll, I'd be filling out an application right now. You know how to give a girl a compliment." Simone took a sip of wine before adding, "But…I'm not sure if I'd feel comfortable working here. With what's happened lately."

"Oh, you mean the…" The bartender's smile faded, and the color of her cheeks diminished. "Yeah. That's understandable."

"Do you feel safe here?"

The bartender put her elbow on the bar and leaned toward her. "Yeah. Bow, the bouncer, makes sure that everyone gets to their cars safely when we close. And if customers get rowdy, wanting more to drink past the limit, security comes over and handles them for me." She pointed off screen.

Simone turned to show two men standing off to the side, keeping an eagle's eye on everything that was going on. Avrianna wasn't aware of the club's security being interviewed about the murders and made a mental note to have that done ASAP. Where were they at the time two men had lost their lives? Did they see something that had happened in the club that could be the killer's motive?

A pair of customers came over to the bar, bumping into Simone to ask the bartender for drinks. Simone got up and took her wine farther down the bar where it was empty. She sat there, quietly drinking her pinot noir and enjoying the music. After a while, the other bartender came over and asked her if she wanted a refill.

"Yes, please. Pinot noir."

"Don't drink too much," Avrianna said. "You have a job to do."

"I can hold my drink," Simone said aloud.

The bartender smiled as he set the freshly filled glass of wine in front of her, apparently thinking she had spoken to him. "Are you enjoying your time here?"

"I sure am," she said and took a long drink. "Do you like working here?"

"Sure." He shrugged.

"Have you ever seen a fight break out?"

"It happens from time to time. Security takes care of it fast, though."

From Avrianna's perspective, the bartenders weren't much help. They didn't know much of what happened beyond the barstools.

Simone looked toward the stage as another dancer did her number. Avrianna lifted the radio to say, "Ask the bartender if Nebula is there."

The image changed.

"Hey, is Nebula going to perform tonight?"

"No, she's off."

Avrianna pressed down the button to the radio.

"Andromeda?"

"What about Andromeda?"

"She'll be the final performer."

The murders happen after closing, after Andromeda's performance.

Coincidence? Maybe not.

Simone finished her wine.

"Hey, Sim," Avrianna said into the radio, "sit at a table in the corner so I can have a view of the entire room."

From Simone's seat in the corner, Avrianna watched the happenings of the club. Nothing noteworthy occurred. The customers consumed alcohol and cheered and got boners. The dancers sashayed and stripped and collected money. Security didn't move, didn't talk to anyone. Guy didn't return.

When a song came on over the speakers and a dancer wasn't on the stage, Simone suddenly said, "I've got an idea."

The camera rose as Simone stood, and the footage spun in circles.

Avrianna stared at the wobbly, chaotic feed, attempting to make sense of what she saw. Somewhere in all that, she realized that Simone was drawing the attention of the male customers. All of them. Avrianna snatched up her radio. "Take off your hat and set it on the table so I can see."

Once the hat was in place, Avrianna was able to make out the faces of the men and their excitement at seeing a drunk woman dancing her ass off. Simone was giving them what they wanted, and they were eating it up, visually.

They shouted cat calls, hooted, and whistled. And in the corner, by the stage, Andromeda stood there with her arms crossed, watching as her audience drooled over a random woman dancing to a pop song. She didn't look happy to have competition or to have the attention of the men in the club robbed from her approaching performance.

Avrianna smirked. "Andromeda's watching you, and she doesn't look happy."

When the song ended, Simone took her seat and fanned herself dramatically.

A moment later, Guy announced Andromeda.

Instantly, the men in the place turned toward the stage, forgetting about Simone, which was fine by Avrianna, because she was watching the performance, too. More specifically, her eyes were on Andromeda, looking for any sign of the stripper targeting one of the men with the plan to punish him for not being completely devoted to her. Andromeda did her thing, but she didn't single out any of the men. Instead, she played it up to them all, likely knowing she'd get more tips if they all felt loved.

When the show ended and men began to filter out, Simone returned to Avrianna's car. The two of them stayed put as the vehicles left one by one. The undercover agent was instructed to be the last to leave, and he had just gotten into his vehicle. Sighing, Avrianna lifted her radio to her lips. "All the customers from the front have left. What's your status, Chuck?"

"Clear," Chuck said. "Employees haven't left yet, but there's no customers back here. I don't think the killer is going to strike today."

Avrianna nodded. "Agreed. Well done, everyone. Especially Simone." She smiled at her. "We knocked some suspects off the list, I think. Nothing happened tonight, but this isn't over yet. We're not going to give up."

8

A Real Cocky Killer

As a matter of fact, three more days went by and nothing happened. All of the dancers went through a second round of questioning and all of the samples taken from their fingernails had come back clean. Avrianna couldn't pin the murders on any of them, not even Andromeda, and that meant the murderer was still out there, roaming free.

She lay in bed on the fourth night, gazing up at the ceiling. Sleep didn't want to lure her into its dark realm. *I should just stop trying to sleep.* She debated on whether or not she should continue her staring contest with the popcorn ceiling or get up and workout. Her phone going off ended her debate. Without blinking, she picked up her phone and answered it.

"Detective Heavenborn."

"Bad news," Chief Logan said.

She sat up.

"A man's body was found at Space Station Gas. Looks to be related."

"Cameras?" she said the one word while jumping out of bed.

"Several of them. We've already viewed the footage. A dark sedan stops next to the vic's car. The front passenger door opens. Whoever it is, he or she ducked around the vic's car and was blocked by the gas pump."

"Gas pumps aren't that tall," she pointed out as she ripped a pair of pants and a T-shirt off hangers in her closet.

Chief Logan said two words in reply. "Ski mask."

"Damn it." She tapped the speakerphone icon, set her phone on her dresser, and tugged her shirt off her head. "License plate?"

"The car backed out. No view of the plates."

"Color?"

"Black and white feed. It could be any dark shade."

She gritted her teeth as she shoved her feet into a pair of black pants and pulled them to her hips. "Make and model?"

"We're working on it."

"Anything on him that says he was at The Galaxy's Tease?"

"His debit card was on the ground next to his body.

I put in a favor and got the bank to pull his pending purchases. He used it to pay for his bar tab."

Avrianna grabbed her keys. "Is the body still there?"

"No, it's on its way to Simone now."

"Okay, I'm on my way to the ME office."

"I'll call Chuck and have him meet you there."

"Thanks, sir." She hung up and checked the time—two-forty. They were getting closer and closer to the moment the suspect killed. While rushing through her house, she called Simone, who answered on the second ring. "Are you at the department?"

"I just arrived and so did the body." Simone's words were labored from rushing.

"I'll see you soon."

"Okay. Bye."

The connection ended.

Avrianna drove quickly through the city. Traffic was sparse and to her advantage.

She arrived at the department ten minutes later and went straight downstairs. In the hallway outside the medical examiner's office, she fired off a text to let Simone know she would wait outside the door until she was finished, as Simone needed privacy and zero distractions while completing her report.

A text came in a moment later from Chuck. He had called Guy Riches and was dragging him back to the club to view whatever security footage they had.

While she waited, she paced. When pacing got tiresome, she leaned against the wall outside the doors, with her arms and ankles crossed, and tapped her fingers against her arm in a rapid beat.

Simone pushed open one of the swinging doors twenty-five minutes later, making Avrianna jump. She straightened off the wall and lowered her arms. "Well?"

"You already know what I'm going to say."

Avrianna followed Simone into the office. A faint odor, unlike what you'd usually smell, touched her nostrils. "What's that smell?"

"The poor guy got gasoline all over himself. When he went down, he was still holding the nozzle and yanked it from the fuel filler."

"So, the perp could've gotten gas on themselves?"

"That's a strong possibility."

Simone held out her hand. "Avrianna, meet Diago Wilson. Severed esophagus and castrated. Diago, this is the woman who will find the sicko who did this to you."

Avrianna gave a weak smile. Diago Wilson had golden skin. His black hair was shaved close to his head. Diago and the other two victims were vastly different from each other. She no longer considered that they had anything in common, which meant she had to discover what was making the murderer pick them, and she had to do it fast.

Simone shook her head. "We've got a real cocky killer on our hands."

Avrianna eyer her. "Really?"

Simone's face was all innocent. Her dark lashes batted. "What? Too much?"

Avrianna held up her hand with her thumb and index finger a couple of inches apart. "Just a bit."

"Oh, I'm sure they weren't that small."

Avrianna froze with her hand in the air and her

fingers still measuring out two inches. The meaning behind Simone's words had her turning away. "I'm leaving now."

She was at the doors when Simone called after her, "Oh, come on. It was funny!"

In the hall, Avrianna allowed a small giggle to escape her lips. She had to admit, it had been funny. The situation was bizarre, and Simone had no problem pointing out just how bizarre.

Chuck was in his office when Avrianna dropped in. "Any helpful footage?"

"Not really." He turned around his laptop. On the screen were two security footages. One showed a gas station's parking lot, and Diago was on the other. "The same car from the gas station was seen following the vic's car out of The Galaxy's Tease. Both cars came from the left of the parking lot. Guy Riches says a couple of his employees have dark colored sedans and it could be any one of theirs."

Avrianna sat in the extra chair. "We have to stop this person. Even if that means it's Samantha Ryan. Someone's going around castrating men, and it needs to end now."

Chuck winced when she said "castrating."

She pressed her lips together. Working this case had to be hard for him and the other male investigators. And she was twisted enough to have fun with that.

"They're losing their manhoods, their joysticks, their disco sticks. Someone's taking their family jewels so they can never plant another jewel. This killer is giving an all-new meaning to meat sword. Men left and right are being neutered."

"All right!" Chuck put up his hand. His face was contorted with horror. "I get the picture. Thanks."

Avrianna couldn't stop her laughter. "Sorry, Chuck. But for the record, I won't let the killer take your family jewels." She patted his shoulder.

"I feel so much better."

"But seriously…we know the killer uses The Galaxy's Tease as their hunting grounds. There's no denying that. This killer could be there every single night, and we know this person parks to the left, near the alley and the gate to the employee parking lot that only employees and Guy Riches have access to. It's obvious that footage isn't going to help us, and the killer will never wave at a camera. On top of that, there's no DNA evidence. We could get warrants to search all the cars that match the one in the videos, which would be how many?"

"Four."

She nodded. "Or we can do something extreme and catch the killer red-handed, preferably before their hands are red with blood."

Chuck crossed his arms. "How extreme?"

"We put a plant in The Galaxy's Tease as a stripper."

"And who would that be? Simone again?"

She looked him straight in the eye. "Me."

Bad Romance

Miracle of miracles, Guy Riches agreed to let Avrianna go undercover in his club with a few officers, one of which would be Chuck. To make sure she wouldn't be recognized and could play the part of a stripper, she ventured to Evony's beauty salon. The sound of blow dryers and the smell of fake nails greeted Avrianna when she stepped into the salon. Evony stood behind a chair cutting a woman's hair.

"Someone will be right with you," Evony said before glancing over at the door to see who she was talking to. When she did, a grin split her face. "Oh damn! It's my girl!" She dropped the scissors and comb onto her workstation. "Hey, Mary, take over for me." And just like that, she ditched her customer. She flung her arms around Avrianna, who, despite not being a hugger, embraced her in return.

Evony stepped back to get a good look at Avrianna and tsked. "Don't hide that hair in a bun, girl. Let it flow free."

"It was wet this morning," Avrianna said in way of an explanation.

Evony took her arm and turned her toward the closest workstation. "Let me introduce you to a blow dryer. It's this crazy invention that dries hair." She gasped and laid brown fingers over her lips. "Wicked, I know."

Avrianna smiled. "I know how much you're dying to teach me all the ins and outs of beauty tools and products, but I'm here for another reason. I need a disguise."

"Really?" Her dark eyes lit up with excitement and possibilities. "What will I be turning you into this time? A junkie? A gun dealer?" She grinned. "A dude?"

"A stripper," Avrianna whispered.

Evony jumped up and down. "This will be so much fun." She spun toward the rest of the salon and shouted, "Avrianna Heavenborn's going to be a stripper!"

The customers under the hair dryer chairs and in the styling chairs beneath black aprons cheered. Even the person reclining back while getting shampooed put their hands in the air. And the stylists shook their various tools in the air.

"Ev, this is for work," Avrianna hissed. "I don't want everyone to know."

Evony waved her hand. "Whom are they going to tell?" She swished her hand to the side, as if sweeping away Avrianna's concern. "Now come on back to my laboratory."

Her "laboratory" was the large back room of the salon where she designed clothes, concocted her own makeup, and had a large supple of wigs. "Do you have any ideas for your costume?" Evony asked once they were alone.

Avrianna walked along a counter lined with plastic heads that showcased a variety of wigs from curly to bobs. She reached out, catching a chunk of silky black hair with her fingers. "Gothic stripper. Black hair, black lips, black leather everything."

Evony clapped her hands. "Oh, this is going to be so much fun."

And Avrianna braced for the torture.

By the end of it, she had on a black wig that stretched down her back. Her fingernails and lips were black and glossy. Evony had given her smoky cat eyes and blush for color. "Gothic, not dead," she said as she swiped the brush along Avrianna's cheeks. Black leather boots tied up to Avrianna's knees. Fishnet leggings dug into the skin on her thighs, and she had squeezed into a pair of tiny black leather shorts and a matching halter top that did it's best to make it look like she had cleavage.

"Hmm." Evony twisted her lips while scrutinizing her work. Then she held up a finger. "I know what we need—" She opened a drawer and came back with flesh-toned silicon inserts for bras.

Avrianna took a step back. "No."

"Oh, come on! You need a little more junk in the…front."

"Not. Happening." On this Avrianna wouldn't budge.

"Fine." Evony tossed the cutlets over her shoulders. They plopped onto the floor. "But you do need a bit of color." She pulled out a contact container and unscrewed the caps. Inside, red contact lenses swam in clear solution.

"Red contacts?"

"It'll give you that vampire stripper vibe with a touch of evil, which men love."

Avrianna didn't move to accept the contacts.

"I could go all out and give you fangs."

Avrianna grabbed the contacts. "How do you even know these will work on me? My green eyes always shine through."

"I've been experimenting."

Tipping her head back, Avrianna placed each contact on her eyes. Evony held up a mirror for her to see the results, and she was surprised. She couldn't see a trace of green. What was strange, though, was that the red glowed.

"Are they supposed to glow?"

"No. That's all you, honey, but it works. Now don't move." She put up her hands. "There's one more thing we need to complete your look."

After her last two ideas, dread filled Avrianna. What could she possibly have in mind now? A snake? A dog collar? A whip?

Evony went to a clothing rack of what Avrianna could only describe as theater clothes and rummaged through the articles, pushing one hanger aside after another until she found what she was hunting for. "Ah-ha!" She removed a hanger and brought it over to Avrianna. "You'll have this on, and then when you get on the stage, bam! You whip it open and show off those awesome abs and skyscraper legs." She held out a patent leather trench coat with a sash.

"Now this I like." Avrianna slipped it on and tied the sash. It reached down to the tops of her knee-high boots, making her feel a little less naked. "But I don't have any plans to take it off."

"Party pooper." Evony lifted the collar for a more dangerous, sexy look. "All right. My work here is complete." She dusted off her hands. "Government worker by day, sexy gothic stripper by night." She smiled. "No one will be able to recognize you."

"That's the idea."

At midnight, Avrianna met Chuck behind The Galaxy's Tease. She got out of her car and made sure her coat was covering all of her with a quick tug of the sash. Her heels clicked on the asphalt. Chuck turned to her while tipping back a water bottle to his mouth. When he saw her, he coughed violently and wiped the back of his hand over his mouth to clean away the water dribbling down his chin.

She squinted at him—risking her heavy, thick lashes sticking together—and held up a warning finger. "Not a single word." She rapped on the backdoor.

While waiting for it to be answered, she eyed the other cars in the employee parking lot. Two of them were the approximate shape and size of the vehicle captured on the security footage at Space Station Gas.

The door opened to Guy Riches. He wore velvet pants and a silver button-up shirt that sparkled in the streetlight.

She waved her gloved fingers. "Trick or treat."

His jaw dropped. "This is genius." He reached out to touch her hair.

She smacked it away. "No touching." She pointed to the cars behind her. "Whose cars are those? The gun-metal gray one and the purple one."

"Gun-metal gray belongs to Andromeda and purple is Nebula's."

His words struck her. No matter how much Avrianna hated the thought of Samantha, also known as Nebula, being a killer, that didn't make her innocent in the eyes of the law, and Avrianna was supposed to have those eyes at all times.

"Speaking of which," Guy said. "Have you thought of a performer's name?"

"Pandora."

Guy nodded. "Appropriate."

"I thought so, too."

He opened the door wider, allowing Avrianna and Chuck to enter, but he put up a hand. "Did you notice?" He pointed a manicured nail up at the corner of the building. A brand-new camera looked down at them. "I had it installed this afternoon."

"That's a good start." And she couldn't help but feel a little proud of him for finally doing what was necessary to help her investigation and protect his customers.

Thumping music surrounded her when she entered through the back door. The bass felt alive in her veins, in her blood. He showed them around. The first thing he pointed out was the nail in the wall by the back door where two silver keys dangled from a small loop. She was about to rattle off how unsafe that was but held her tongue. To the right of Guy's office and down the hall was the girl's dressing room. The voices and laughter of a dozen women seeped out into the hall.

Guy knocked on the door. "Cover up, ladies." And before giving them a chance to actually cover up, he opened the door. "Ladies, this is Pandora. She'll be performing after Andromeda. Make her feel welcome." He turned to Avrianna. "Good luck." With that, he shut the door, leaving Avrianna alone with a roomful of strippers.

She thought they'd want to rip apart their competition with claw-like nails and string her up with their G-strings. Instead, they hopped to her, all smiles.

"Welcome!"

One after the other they hugged her. Each embrace brought a new perfume. Arms slick with baby oil and sparkling with glitter wrapped around her. She was thankful for her coat as a barrier to keep their oil and glitter from smearing off on her.

The last one to hug her was Samantha. She wore a shimmery, rainbow dress with glow-in-the dark heels. "Hi. I was the last newbie, so I know what you're feeling, but we're all pretty supportive of each other."

Supportive enough to kill for each other?

"Thanks," Avrianna said.

"Make room, girls!"

A gap formed in the crowd.

Andromeda, in a tiny red teddy complete with a garter belt, came forward. She even had on a red lace mask, her trademark accessory. "Pandora, huh? Nailed it!" Her blood-red lips revealed too-white teeth. "May I?" She indicated at the sash on Avrianna's coat.

"Um. Sure."

Giddy, as if she was unwrapping a present, Andromeda whisked away the sash. "Oh, damn." She snapped her fingers. "You picked the perfect outfit. Men may not like to admit it, but they get off on the whole twisted girl thing. You're going to be making many of their fantasies tonight, girl."

Avrianna forced a smile. "Thanks."

"But it's weird that Guy is putting you on after me. Usually I close the night."

Was that jealousy?

"Guy said since you draw them all in, we'll really be able to see how they'll react."

Andromeda nodded slowly. "I get it. I lure them in with my sexy mystery, and then you'll end the night on a creepy, dark note."

Nothing said creepy and dark more than murder.

"And to top it off, you have a killer bod. How'd you get those abs?"

Avrianna almost said, "By taking down killers."

She shrugged. "Pilates."

"Gotcha." Andromeda removed an ankle-length red coat from a rack and slipped it on. "You look like you need to loosen up. Let's get a shot." She hooked her arm through Avrianna's and led her to the door. Avrianna quickly knotted the sash as Andromeda pulled her down the hall.

"Is it okay to go to the bar with all the customers there?"

"Absolutely. I do it all the time. I like to flirt with the gentlemen at the bar. It gets them that much more invested in my act. They think I'm only dancing for them." She laughed. "I'm wicked, I know, but I didn't get this good by being an angel."

Definitely not an angel.

"Although there is a girl here who dresses like an angel and gets a good response. Just as much as men like the dark ones, they like the virginal ones, too." They made their way through the crowd to various cat calls, sexual innuendos, and whistles. Each one made Avrianna's skin crawl. And she was attracting a lot of attention. Even before Guy Riches could make the announcement, they all now knew there would be a new dancer tonight.

"Damn. I'll be your voodoo doll, baby."

"You could spank me all you want."

"Sacrifice me!"

She kept her features calm. Chin lifted, she portrayed an air of royalty. These men were beneath her; she was Pandora, after all. But inside, she seethed. You had to have an impenetrable wall to be a stripper to feel empowered by expressing your sensuality. Avrianna *was* impenetrable; not even a bullet could break her flesh, but she wasn't built to be in the spotlight for entertainment. Especially not this kind of entertainment.

At the bar, Andromeda pushed her way between two men. "Two Kick in the Crotches, Ricky."

Avrianna's brows lifted. *She did not just order that.*

Behind the counter, the bartender, a man in a long-sleeved black shirt, mixed the drinks, expertly tipping over bottles and pouring the right amount of liquor. He set two shot glasses on the bar top. The alcohol was purple with a hint of blue at the very bottom of the glass.

"Thanks, Ricky." Andromeda picked up the shots and handed one to Avrianna. "We should toast to you having a killer-good first night." She tapped her glass to Avrianna's and tipped her head back to down the shot.

One could only hope.

Avrianna threw her shot back. She set her glass down beside Andromeda's. Both shot glasses had their lip prints on the rim—one black, one red.

Andromeda leaned over the counter to call for Ricky. "Do you have any cherries?" She winked at Avrianna. "I always play with a cherry when I talk to the guys at the bar," she revealed in a conspiratorial whisper.

Ricky came back with a crystal dish of red, tart cherries. Andromeda selected one, pulling it by the stem with her red fingernails. The upper-half of her body was draped over the counter as she reached. Avrianna's gaze rose from Andromeda's back and landed on a man across the way. He sat alone at a high-top table with a pint of beer in his grip. His long, brown hair was tied back into a bun by a piece of leather. He wore faded, ripped jeans; a weathered, leather jacket;

and scuffed biker boots. A beard covered half his face, and his gaze was latched onto Andromeda. He lifted his beer and gulped down a couple of swallows without shifting his attention from her. And that attention did not ooze warmth. Rage simmered beneath his mask.

"There's a man behind you shooting daggers at you with his eyes," Avrianna said under her breath so only Andromeda could hear.

"Really?" Andromeda twisted around to get a good look. "Oh, him?" She laughed. "That's Soren, my fiancé." She gave him a finger wave.

He saluted her with his beer.

"Fiancé? You're not wearing a ring."

"Of course, I'm not." She looked aghast at the idea. "I have to appear available."

"And your fiancé doesn't mind that?"

By the way he glared, it appeared he minded it greatly.

"That's why he's here every night." She folded her hands over her heart. "He wants to look out for me. His protectiveness is a major turn on."

Protectiveness? Avrianna would call that *possessiveness*.

"He's here every night?"

"Yeah. Well, he was out of town for five days, but now my man is back."

Maybe that's why we didn't have luck when we put Simone in the other day. And why nothing had happened in...five days.

She glanced at him. "Would you call him a *cocky* man?"

Andromeda's brows drew together. "What do you

mean?"

"Is he…arrogant?"

Her laughter was like champagne bubbles. "Definitely. But arrogance can be sexy, especially when you've got a bad boy."

A new song came on over the speakers, and a dancer strutted out on stage. She had on a skimpy black dress that her butt hung out of and was slit up to her navel. A fake badge was pinned to her chest, cuffs dangled off her hip, and a black captain's hat sat atop her blonde head.

Avrianna ground her teeth. Why were the careers of cops and other first responders, even nurses and doctors, degraded with stripper costumes and sexy Halloween costumes? She wished she could ban them.

"That reminds me." Andromeda's voice drew her attention away from the stage and the dancer who was grinding against the metal pole. "What song did you choose?"

Avrianna glanced at Soren, who was sucking on a cigarette and eyeing Andromeda through the smoke. "Bad Romance."

10

Guys Are Weird

Backstage, Avrianna stood to the right with a clear view of the club and the customers. Guy Riches introduced Nebula, and the lights were dimmed. On stage, Nebula's shiny, rainbow romper glowed, and her shoes made bright streaks in the air as she spun around the pole and did cartwheels. Her dance was mystical, like a dream. She moved with grace and sensuality. The stage became her own planet, her own universe, making everyone who watched feel as though they were racing through a worm hole to a new star source. At the end, she bowed and left the stage in a gentle flash of magical color. The lights came back on, and with Nebula gone, it made you think she had been an illusion. But backstage, Avrianna watched her snatch up a towel and press it to her face and chest. Another dancer, in a devil costume, handed her a bottle of water. She took a swig from it. Then she exited the stage.

Avrianna discreetly pressed a finger to her ear to hear Chuck's voice from her earpiece. "Nebula and the other dancers are in the dressing room," he said.

Guy Riches announced Andromeda and a huge uproar broke out in the club. Men got up from their places at the bar, all vying for a seat at the stage. Soren stayed at his table, but now his attention was on the stage for the first time all night.

"Watch a pro at work," Andromeda said as she sashayed past Avrianna.

A seductive song with a thumping beat came on, and she started to move. She contorted her body, gyrated her hips, and rolled her torso like a belly dancer. Every pose she struck, every motion she made was to entice men to imagine her in bed. And they all reacted energetically.

One of the men sitting front and center tossed a handful of bills. "Yeah, baby, I like it like that." He bantered with the other men around him. When Andromeda made a backbend, he threw back his head and howled like a wolf.

Soren glared at the back of the man's head. His beer had been drained, and his cigarette butt sat at the bottom of the pint. He sat forward with his hands in fists.

Andromeda spread her legs wide, and the man

called out, "I'd eat that!"

Soren's face turned a deep shade of red. The veins in his neck bulged.

Avrianna dipped her head toward the mike hidden in her halter top and whispered, "Does anyone have eyes on the man sitting alone to the left of the stage? Leather jacket, bun?"

"I'm in the hall by the dressing room," Chuck's voice came from her earpiece.

"Anyone?" Avrianna hissed.

"I don't have a clear view from the bar," an undercover agent said.

"I'm outside in the employee parking lot," came another.

"I'm by Mr. Riches' office."

Avrianna ground her teeth. "We need someone on him now."

The song ended. Andromeda blew a kiss to her audience and then breezed backstage. The man by the stage tossed back the rest of his drink and clapped the men on either side of him on the back. He got to his feet and moved away while his friends stayed put, but someone did get up—Soren.

Avrianna's heart shot into her throat. "It's Andromeda's boyfriend. Get him."

Soren caught up to the man. He put his arm around him, as if they were pals, and said something that had the other man throwing back his head in laughter. They walked toward the exit.

"Where is he? I lost him." One of the undercover agents stood at Soren's abandoned table, looking left and right.

From her place on the stage, she watched the two men get closer to the exit. "They're leaving through the front."

"I'm in the back."

"I don't see him."

"Avrianna, stop him!" That came from Chuck, and with his blessing, she took off down the stage stairs. She whipped around the corner and shoved people out of her way as she raced after the men ahead of her.

On the stage, Guy Riches announced, "Don't leave yet. I have a surprise for you tonight, our newest talent, Pandora!"

Applause erupted, but Avrianna was long gone.

Several paces ahead, the two men went through the front door. She plowed through the customers in her way, with her gaze pinned on the opening. They passed Bow and kept on walking down the concrete path toward the parking lot. Then the door swung closed, blocking her view.

Damn it.

Desperation had her heart racing. Her heels pounded the floor. She didn't so much as slow a fraction when she got to the door and threw her body into it, causing the door to bang against the wall behind it. Bow jumped around, with his fists raised.

"Which way did they go?" she demanded as she blew past him.

"Left!"

Her heels skidded on the asphalt as she hurried around the building into the parking lot. Several steps ahead of her, Soren still had his arm around the gentleman's shoulders. Their voices drifted toward her.

Anyone would see them as two friends who'd just had a good time. No doubt they appeared that way to Bow. But Avrianna knew better.

Several feet away from them, Avrianna zeroed in on Soren's hand. It disappeared into his pocket and came back out grasping a small piece of plastic. A blade shot out of it.

Avrianna's mouth went dry. She couldn't let him kill someone else, not with her just feet behind them, so close to stopping it.

Soren held the switchblade at his side, ready to use it. The man he planned to kill stopped beside a red convertible. And Soren lifted his hand.

Avrianna stopped and held out her hands. She cupped her clenched right fist with her left hand. "Freeze! Soren, drop the knife."

Soren froze, as if stunned to finally have been caught.

His intended victim whirled around. "What the hell?"

"Sir, back away for your own safety."

He stumbled backward to the car's bumper.

"Soren, drop the knife. Now!"

"Do what she says."

Avrianna glanced to her left.

Bow stood beside her. He nodded.

The switchblade fell from Soren's hand and clattered onto the asphalt.

"Put your hands on the back of your head." She inched closer to him, step by step. "Slowly. Do it now."

He raised his arms into the air on either side of his head, and then he laced his fingers above his ponytail.

Avrianna dropped her hands and the imaginary gun she held and launched herself at Soren. She wrenched his arms behind his back. Without proper cuffs, she resorted to the next best thing and yanked the leather sash from around her waist. She secured it around Soren's wrists and completed it with a figure eight knot.

"Soren, you're under arrest for the murders of Axel Sherman, Ashton O'Reilly, and Diago Wilson. And the attempted murder of—" She looked up at the man shivering by the taillights of his car. "What's your name, sir?"

"Jack Madison."

Keeping her knee pressed firmly to the middle of his back, Avrianna repeated the man's name and finished reading Soren his rights. She hauled him to his feet, giving him a clear view of who had arrested him. Without the sash to tie her coat, he could see her entire outfit and every inch of her exposed skin.

"A stripper? I was arrested by a stripper?" He let out a laugh.

"If I were you, I wouldn't make fun of her," Bow said.

She smirked. Apparently, her threat had done him some good.

Chuck ran toward them, followed by the undercover agents and half a dozen strippers.

"Can someone escort Soren to a police cruiser?" Avrianna asked.

"I got him," an agent said. He grasped Soren's arm and led him away.

"Stop!" Andromeda ran forward, still in her costume and mask.

Chuck intercepted her. "Ma'am, he's being arrested."

"No, he hasn't done anything wrong." She caught sight of Avrianna. "Pan-Pandora, what's going on?"

"My name's not Pandora." She removed her wig to reveal her silvery-blonde hair. "It's Avrianna."

Andromeda gaped. "Y-you. You?" Anger morphed her features into sharp lines. "You, bitch! How dare you! What did he do, huh?" She screamed in Avrianna's face. "What did he do?!"

"He murdered three men," she said in a calm voice.

"What?" Andromeda shook her head. "No, he wouldn't do that."

"He was about to kill this man." She pointed at Jack.

Andromeda's mouth fell open, but no words came out.

"Ma'am?" An agent came over to Avrianna with an evidence bag. "He had this on him." Inside the bag was a black ski mask. "And it still smells like gasoline."

Andromeda peered from the mask to Avrianna and back again. "Gas?"

"The last man he killed was at Space Station Gas."

Andromeda blinked. "Gas." She stood there a moment, staring off at nothing. Her eyes widened, and then she spun around. "That's why my car smelled like gasoline?!"

Across the parking lot, an officer had Soren up against a cruiser. He turned his head over his right shoulder to shout, "I did it for you, babe!"

"Oh my God." She covered her mouth with one hand and put the other hand on her stomach.

"I did it for you," Soren shouted again. "Those men deserved it! You're mine, and they needed to know that."

Andromeda dropped her hand. Her eyes blazed, and she charged toward her fiancé. "This is my job!" Avrianna jumped forward and caught her arms to hold her back. "You did this for you! Not me." She put a hand on her forehead. "Oh my God. I almost married a murderer."

"They thought with their dicks," Soren roared. "They thought about *you* with their dicks. I did what I had to do."

"We met at the strip club, you idiot! You were just like them."

"They never loved you. *I* love you!"

Andromeda shook her head. She turned away and put her forehead on Avrianna's shoulder, an act that momentarily shocked Avrianna. She reluctantly put her arms around Andromeda and patted her back.

Soren continued to holler his undying affection.

"Get him out of here," Avrianna ordered.

With a hand on the back of Soren's head, the officer restraining him pushed him into the back of the car and slammed the door when Soren twisted around to yell more words of psychotic devotion.

Andromeda's friends swept her up in their tide of feather, sequins, and love. Nebula was the first one to wrap her up in a hug. A smile tweaked the corners of Avrianna's lips. She had been wrong about the two of them, and she was glad for that.

Guy Riches approached Avrianna. "You know, I've got a club full of men who'd still like to see

Pandora dance."

Avrianna pulled the sides of her coat together and crossed her arms. "Not happening."

She changed into comfortable clothes—jeans and a T-shirt—and scrubbed all traces of her stripper makeup off her face. Now she felt like herself, in the place more of a home than her actual home—her office at the police department. She finished filling out her report, slapped the folder shut, and dropped her pen to her desk. Closing a case would never get old. She lived for it.

Chuck sauntered into her office. "I've got some news." He sat across from her. "I'm coming straight from Soren's interrogation. He told us everything."

Avrianna leaned back. "That was nice of him."

"Indeed. He said he initially wanted to silence the men and their come-ons directed at his woman, but once he cut Axel's throat, he didn't feel that was enough. He thought all of them wanted to fuck her. His words. So, he castrated them to make sure they never could."

"As if killing them first wouldn't be effective enough," Avrianna muttered.

"He claimed it was symbolic, that they wouldn't even be able to fuck in the afterlife. His words."

Avrianna put up her hand. "I get it, but there's one thing I don't get." And she regretted her next question. "What exactly did he do with their…appendages?"

Chuck squirmed. "Well, there's a seafood store in the neighborhood. Their Dumpster is full of fish and fish guts. He threw their parts in there."

Avrianna scrunched up her nose, unable to stop the visualization from popping into her head. Or the odor. "Ew."

"You can say that again." Chuck stood and pulled a flier from his back pocket. He settled back into the chair as he held it out to her. "I saw these posted around town."

Curious, Avrianna read the announcement: *Now introducing Pandora at The Galaxy's Tease*!

She blinked. The advertisement even had a picture. "Guy has lost his mind if he thinks I owe him a dance."

"Look closer at the picture," Chuck said.

She did. After a moment, she noticed a sparkling silver ring in the middle of the woman's bottom lip. "Kat Kirkpatrick?" The woman she had interrogated and who had hit on her, much to her astonishment and to the amazement of all the officers who had been watching. "She looks just like me as Pandora. That's kinda creepy."

"I talked to Guy, and he admitted that Kat and him had been having a tryst in his office. She was after a job. When he realized how excited the guys were to see you…or rather, Pandora, perform last night, he called her up. Now they are both happy."

So that explained the opened condom wrappers on Guy's desk.

"The two are a pair."

Chuck nodded and got to his feet. "Anyway, the guys want to get sushi in honor or Axel, Ashton, and Diago. Want to come?"

Avrianna cringed. "No thanks."

Guys are weird.

Universal Killer

The Veil

T he call came after midnight, for murderers never rest. Not even in other worlds.

Avrianna snatched up her cell phone on the second ring. "Detective Heavenborn."

"Someone was killed at the Veil," Chief Logan said.

Avrianna sat up in bed. "I'm on my way."

With a jab of her finger, she ended the call.

In her small closet, she tugged a pair of black slacks off a hanger. She yanked them on and then buttoned up a black, collared shirt with cuffs. After giving her teeth a fast scrub, she tied her silvery-blonde hair into a bun. On the way out the door, she grabbed her firearm, badge, and cuffs. Then she drove through the sleeping neighborhood and made her way to the heart of the city.

The closer she got, the more the Veil became visible. The crystal arch rose high into the sky so that the peak was hidden by clouds. Inside the arch, an opal sheen moved like a waving flag. During the day, a line of cars to the right could be seen waiting to drive through it to Earth, and next to that, a flow of vehicles appeared as if from thin air, entering her world—New Vida.

After dusk, authorities restricted access to the Veil on both sides. Now, law enforcement vehicles clogged the roads. Avrianna parked her car among them.

The officers securing the crime scene, and the guards who kept the Veil fortified at night, parted for her as if she had the plague. No, she wasn't a carrier for a catastrophic disease. Nor could she cause death with a touch of the hand, or by breathing in their direction, or even with a look. That didn't stop others from steering clear of her, however; for what they did know about her—knew to be fact—was enough to warrant the distance.

Nearing the Veil, a humming sound met her ears. The air crackled with static electricity. No one knew how the Veil came to be, just that it had always been, like a sacred force.

Avrianna's gaze swept across the ground, searching for the dead body. Except, there wasn't one. Well, not all of one, anyway. A pair of black leather shoes and a set of ankles poked through the Veil. Whoever had been killed there, the rest of their body wasn't even in her world.

A middle-aged man with dark hair that reached the collar of his white Polo shirt stood a few feet away, staring at the feet and jotting notes in a pad. She joined him. "Hey, Chuck." She put her hands on her hips and eyed the leather shoes. "So, is this the Wicked Witch of the East's spouse?"

Chuck looked at her with wide, blue eyes. "Did you make a joke?"

Her lips quirked at the corners. "I'm not a robot. I can make jokes."

"I've never known it to happen."

She rolled her eyes.

"Do you want to go through or shall I?" Chuck indicated the Veil.

"I'll go."

Chuck's brows lowered. "Are you sure?"

"Of course." She waved off his concern. "They love me over there."

"Right. I'm sure they're getting out their party hats now." He pointed to the uniformed men standing to the side. "I'll question the guards here. Save me some cake."

She shot him a grin before moving closer to the Veil. A camera positioned outside the guard's station pointed down at her. She took out her ID, flipped it open, and held it up to the camera. Then, with her other hand in the air, palm facing outward as if in surrender, she stepped through the Veil. The shimmering curtain of transcendental light tickled her skin. A gentle warmth caressed her. With one step, she transitioned from one world to the next as New Vida gave way to

Earth. The city she left behind transformed into orange rock formations, shadowed in darkness. Her feet went from asphalt to dirt. Now, she stood in the Grand Canyon.

And ten U.S. soldiers pointed automatic weapons.

With her hands still raised, she said, "I'm Detective Heavenborn of the Aurora Police Department, New Vida. I—"

"They know who you are, Detective," a voice called out.

The soldiers parted for a blond man in a suit. They shifted so the man wasn't in their line of fire, but they kept her in their sights.

"Who you are is exactly why they're pointing their weapons. We know what you can do."

She smirked. *You* think *you know what I can do.*

"I am here as a representative of New Vida to investigate this murder." Her smile widened. "I come in peace." When none of them moved, she tilted her head. "I'm going to lower my hands now." Slowly, she brought her hands to her side to slip her ID into her pocket.

The soldiers surged forward.

Avrianna froze. "Easy, boys. I'm just putting away my ID. My piece is on my other hip." She eyed the detective, hoping for some level of cooperation.

"It's all right," he told them.

The soldiers inched back, but not far enough.

She finished tucking away her ID and lowered her arms to her sides. "And whom am I speaking to?"

"Agent Asher. FBI."

Avrianna arched a brow. This was her first

encounter with an FBI agent, and by the way this one was going, she hoped it'd be her last. "How would you like to proceed?"

"About what?"

She blinked. Surely an FBI agent couldn't be that dense. "About the body." She pointed at the ground by their feet. "That body."

They peered down at it. The victim wore tan slacks and a white button-up shirt that was half untucked from his waistband. His dark hair stuck up in multiple directions, as if he had raked his hands through his hair in frustration. A bullet hole in the middle of his forehead leaked a stream of blood.

Squaring his shoulders beneath his ironed and starched jacket, Agent Asher eyed Avrianna. "The US wants no part of this."

That didn't surprise Avrianna. Murder at the Veil, on the American side, would lead to complications. They couldn't let this get out, couldn't let the states or other countries know it was unsafe at the Veil. They relied on the import/export business between worlds. And let's not forget their nasty habit of sneaking their criminals through the Veil…right under New Vida's nose. They were the reason why New Vida needed law enforcement and adapted their system with an ugly history to try to fight back against the onslaught of criminal activity.

They hadn't just colonized. They had corrupted.

Avrianna glared at Agent Asher. "Most of the body is on your side. The body's identifying features are on your side."

"But his feet are on yours."

Avrianna studied the body and the Veil that cut him off at the ankles. "That's true enough, which is why New Vida would like the United States' cooperation in this investigation."

"You don't seem to understand, Detective. This man was shot on your side. If he hadn't been so close to the Veil, he wouldn't have fallen into ours. He was shot in the head, likely died instantly. Therefore, the murder took place in your world. This is your mess. Not ours."

Inside, Avrianna smiled. She rather liked the job being hers. The less she had to deal with them, the better. "Fine, but our crime scene investigators will need to come over to take photos, canvas the area, collect samples, and remove the body."

"I can grant that."

Avrianna glanced at the security post equipped with computers to scan IDs and passports, as well as to monitor the travelers leaving New Vida. The US had demanded to have their cameras on New Vida soil as a "security measure," but they had rejected New Vida's request for the same, claiming it put the US at risk by having foreign entities viewing their operations.

Yeah, their illegal operations.

But perhaps, in this case, they'd offer an olive branch. Or maybe a twig.

"Will you grant approval to allow us to view the footage from these cameras before and after the murder happened?"

Agent Asher's brows stitched together, making gray strands stick out. "What for?"

They wouldn't like this. Not one bit, but she said it anyway. "To see if the cameras caught the murderer."

Self-righteousness flitted across the agent's face. He—just like the rest of the US officials—thought New Vida and all the people in it were beneath him.

Because of that look, she couldn't bite her tongue anymore. "And to make sure the suspect hadn't fled through the Veil to escape justice."

"What are you getting at?" Agent Asher snapped.

"What we both know is true, that countless US criminals *somehow* sneak past this armed post into my world, with their records wiped clean because the US purposefully keeps them from us."

A soldier marched forward, aiming his weapon at her chest. "Are you claiming we let criminals through?"

Avrianna glared. "You know very well what you do without me having to say it." She restrained the urge to unleash her powers, to reveal her wrath at their unlawful practices. If she did that, though, they'd open fire and whatever fragile alliance the two worlds had would be shattered. She couldn't let that happen, and certainly didn't want to be the one to cause that disastrous fallout.

"If you want the surveillance footage, you'll have to ask the Director of the FBI yourself. Until then, your CSI team can come and do their job. Take it or leave it."

Well, a splinter of an olive branch was something. Still, she couldn't stop herself from grinding her teeth. "I'll take it," she growled. "But if I find out the killer came through here and was let go, there will be severe consequences."

"Is that a threat?" the same solider barked.

Her gaze flicked to him. "Yes, it is. And when the

CSI team gets here, not a single gun will be pointed at them. Is that understood?" She glared from him to Agent Asher, who nodded. That one motion had the soldiers lowering their weapons again.

"Appreciate it."

She passed back through the Veil. Crime scene investigators stood back in a cluster, holding their kits and supplies and staring at her. She gave them a nod. "We've been given access to the crime scene, and it's all ours. I doubt they'll let us back in to search for new evidence, so be thorough."

Chuck came up to her. "No cake?"

She managed a smile. "Nope. They didn't even have ice cream."

"Damn." He tilted his head, and all humor vanished from his face as his features became hard. "Will they let us see their footage?"

Avrianna arched a brow. "What do you think?"

Chuck's jaw clenched. "Did they give you trouble?" She continued to stare at him, and he cursed under his breath. "Of course, they did."

She shrugged. "Nothing I didn't expect." She glanced back at the CSI investigators as they prepared to pass through the Veil. "We should go. I want to make sure they don't get any grief."

Once more, she flagged down the security camera recording her every move and entered US territory ahead of Chuck and the CSI team. The soldiers had taken up residence a safe distance from the crime scene. Their weapons were still in their hands, but they weren't holding them at attention. Agent Asher, however, stood beside the body.

"My people are coming," she said. "If you could kindly step aside."

Asher eyed her, and she didn't so much as blink. If she were getting that sort of treatment from someone in her world, she'd let her eyes flare brightly with her power to show them she didn't put up with that sort of bullshit, but she couldn't do that here. Even so, her glare had Agent Asher flinching. He backed away and retreated to the side with the soldiers in time for Chuck to come, escorting the CSI team.

The investigators did their job to the letter, and under heavy scrutiny from the soldiers and Agent Asher. They discovered that the bullet had passed through the back of the victim's head and had traveled through the Veil, meaning it was somewhere out there, possibly embedded in a rock formation or buried under a sheet of orange dirt. A crew of investigators with metal detectors walked one foot in front of the other, scanning the terrain. The metal detectors went off frequently to notify them of some bit of metal—a lost coin or a bolt that rattled off a car while it was coming or going through the area.

While they did that, Avrianna and Chuck examined the body. With protective booties over her shoes and gloves on her hands, she knelt on the ground.

Chuck hunkered down on the other side of the vic.

"To fall backward through the Veil, and with the GSW here"—she pointed at the bullet hole in the middle of the man's forehead—"he hadn't been facing the Veil. The suspect had to have been right in front of him."

Chuck shook his head. "I questioned our guards.

No one else was there. He came running toward the Veil, shouting 'she's going to kill me' and asked to go through, but with access to the Veil restricted after dark, the guards denied him entry. They said he became desperate, begging them. He kept looking over his shoulder. Then, when he turned around, his head went back, there was a spray of blood, and he was dead."

Avrianna's neck snapped up. "A sniper?"

"Could be."

She studied the corpse from bullet hole to ankles. His features were contorted into a look of sheer terror. Whoever killed him, he had been genuinely terrified of her, and she had been a really good shot.

Avrianna slipped his wallet out of his pocket, flipped it open, and worked out the identification card from its slot. "Benjamin Holmes," she read. Her brows lowered at the familiarity of that name.

Chuck noticed. "Do you know him?"

"I'm not sure. I think I've heard of him, but I can't place him." She handed the ID to Chuck to run once they stepped back into their world.

"We found something," an investigator called out.

Avrianna and Chuck went to them. The investigator held out an evidence bag. Inside it lay a hunk of metal, but it was no ordinary bullet. This bullet was two inches long and in the shape of a spiral. Avrianna's brows lowered. Through the plastic, she held the bullet between her thumb and forefinger.

"What kind of gun did that come from?" Chuck asked.

She shook her head. "I have no clue, but maybe we can find out." She handed the bag back to the investiator.

Back at the body, she frowned at the victim. "Who were you so afraid of and why did she want you dead enough to kill you with that?"

Of course, he had no words to tell her. Anything he had to share with her she would have to uncover in the evidence and whatever he left for her at his home and workplace. And she planned to find out who the murderess was and why she killed him. Giving up and letting killers go wasn't in her job description.

"I've got your back," she whispered.

With a wave, she brought the coroner over. "The body can be bagged and removed. Have it brought straight to Simone Rose's ME office at the Aurora PD."

Avrianna stayed behind to supervise the transition. When the workers wheeled the body back through the Veil, Avrianna took up the rear of the line of CSI workers. A voice stopped her a foot from leaving.

"Detective Heavenborn."

She looked toward Agent Asher.

"The blood."

She peered at the pool of blood beside her. Yes, it was still there. Yes, cleanup had left it. Yes, she had told them to.

She smirked. "Consider it our parting gift. Enjoy."

Still smirking, she passed through the Veil to see New Vida slowly becoming conscious with soft grays and lavender streaks in the sky.

Hands on her hips, she studied the surrounding rooftops. A skyscraper—Sterling Tower—with tinted windows stood erect directly across from the Veil. Tipping her head back, she eyed the roof with a perfect vantage point for a sniper to execute a kill shot in the dead of night unseen. But how did the sniper get up there? As far as she knew, no break-in had been reported. Unless, of course, the perp had access to the building by means of a key or an accomplice on the inside, such as the night guard or a janitor. And since the sniper would've needed to be on the property, security cameras would've caught her.

"Hey, Chuck, I'm going to check out the perimeter of Sterling Tower for signs of the perp. Can you see if you can get a hold of someone in charge to let us up to the rooftop and to view security footage?"

"No problem. I'll do that while waiting for results to come in on our vic." He flashed the victim's ID card that he held between his fingers.

"Thanks." She headed across the road and cut through the parking lot to the skyscraper. The entire time, she kept her gaze on the pavement, sweeping it from side to side, to make sure she didn't miss a scrap of evidence. At the front doors, she spotted two security cameras posted in the corners, pointing in opposite directions. Circling around the building, she found two more cameras in the back, but none would show the vantage points to the sides of the building.

Curious, she went to the left side of the building and stared up at a solid wall of glass. There were no windows or terraces with sliding glass doors. No fire escapes. No pipes, drains, or gutters. Nothing that could get someone in or out undetected.

Her gaze trailed down the shiny, gray glass. At eye-level, she spotted a white shoe print. She blinked. Surely that was a trick of the pre-dawn light and the clouds overhead. She took a step closer. But, no, there it was—a dusty-white shoe print, flat on the glass. The right foot. And another print for the left foot was stamped slightly higher. From there, the trail continued up the glass, gradually fading until the prints became invisible.

Lifting her arm, she placed her elbow close to the heel of the imprint to estimate the shoe size. Her own shoe size was twelve inches, and since the length from elbow to wrist matched the size of your feet, she was able to guess the shoe was about six inches. Tiny feet.

She unclipped the radio from her belt, pressed down the button, and spoke into it, "Chuck, I think our perp is Bat Girl."

"Two jokes in one morning? That's a record."

"I'm not joking this time. There are shoe prints, roughly size six, heading up the side of the glass building."

A pause lengthened on the other end of the radio. "I have no words."

Peering up at the roof, she also didn't have any words. The only way someone could scale a wall was if they had a piton or a cam, but with this smooth surface, crack climbing couldn't be achieved, not as it could be if the building were made of brick or had a sizable crack in the structure. Suction cup marks weren't even visible. She frowned. Or were suction cups only used in movies?

"We need CSI over here ASAP. Alternate light sources could make the print visible in photos, and they may be able to lift a couple with electrostatic dust-prints."

"On it."

The investigators collected photographic evidence, prints, and measurements.

They were finishing up when the CEO of Sterling Tower, a man named Richard Sterling, arrived. Even in the dim lighting, his fake tan glowed an unnatural color. Wisps of black hair clung to a large, smooth, shiny head. He wore a gunmetal-gray suit and a black tie. The bottoms of his Italian shoes clicked and scraped against the asphalt. By the way his eyes narrowed on her made it clear he felt horribly inconvenienced.

Yes, murder was an inconvenience for everyone, especially the dead.

"Hello, Mr. Sterling. I'm—"

"I know who you are." He stopped a full two meters from her.

She wondered if she should stop introducing herself altogether. "Thank you for coming out this early. Will you allow us access to the rooftop to further our investigation of the murder that happened across the street?"

"What in the world could Sterling Tower have to do with your investigation?"

"Well…" She pointed at the progress taking place with the shoe prints.

Richard's beady eyes widened. "Remove that now!" He shoved an investigator to the side and reached out his hand to swipe the print away with a hanky he had whipped out from the inside of his jacket.

Avrianna sprang forth and caught his arm before he could ruin their only link to the killer. "You can't do that, sir. That's evidence."

He turned stiffly toward her. "Take your hand off me."

She released him instantly.

He angled his shoulders more so that he stood directly before her, and he pointed a manicured finger in her face as he said, "You have no right to touch me. Me, the CEO of the most prominent business in this damn world. You are a lowly citizen, a blight on this universe. Never touch me again. Do you hear me? If you do, I'll sue you."

Avrianna clenched her hands into fists. "This lowly citizen and blight on this universe has a badge that says I can and will stop you from doing something that'll jeopardize this investigation. The next time I see you about to destroy our evidence, I will tackle your ass to the ground and handcuff you." Then she did what she had been restraining herself from doing since stepping foot onto US soil and unleashed her powers. Heat emitted from her eyes. Bright green light reflected on Richard's face. "And the next time you point your finger in my face, you'll be sorry. Do *you* hear *me*?"

His nostrils flared as he huffed and puffed. He was the kind of man who would never relent to the opposite sex, and probably thought of himself as being above men with higher positions and titles than he himself possessed—a real chauvinistic pig. So, Avrianna didn't expect him to back down or apologize or say, "I understand."

Taking his silence as a good sign, she waved an officer over. "Please escort Mr. Sterling to the front door so he can unlock it and let us up to the roof." She cocked her head to the side, challenging Richard to try to get in the way of her investigation again. Lucky for him, he didn't say a word and followed the officer. The moment he unlocked the door, she breezed through it, without so much as a glance toward Richard.

She rode the elevator to the top floor then took the final stretch of stairs to the roof. On the other side of the door, she found a helicopter pad. Her boots thudded on the concrete as she made her way across the rooftop, cutting across the helipad, to the left side of the building. Lining up where the investigators were hard at work below, she came to the barrier directly above them. She leaned closer to see cuts etched into the stone from sharp blades—the killer's climbing device.

The door behind her opened, and two investigators crossed over to her. She pointed at the mark. "I think the perp used a grappling gun. It looks as though it caught hold here."

"We can get a mold off these impressions," one investigator told her as the other investigator snapped photos.

"Thanks." Avrianna got to her feet while pondering what kind of woman would scale a building to kill someone with a spiral bullet. Not the kind of woman anyone wanted to come face to face with, that was sure. And you certainly didn't want to get caught in her crosshairs as poor Mr. Holmes had done.

"Avrianna?" Chuck's deep voice came from her radio.

She brought it to her mouth. "Go for Avrianna."

"The result came back on Benjamin Holmes. He was a lawyer and had his own small firm. Holmes & Holmes."

Avrianna's tread along the helipad halted. Her foster mom worked there.

Sassy

Avrianna and Chuck went to Holmes & Holmes. Sassy's red, fancy car sat in a parking space marked "Reserved." Seeing that car sitting there both relieved Avrianna and gave her a fresh dose of anxiety. At least Sassy got to work okay, but what would Avrianna find inside the office? Would Sassy be slumped over in her assistant's chair, with a spiral bullet buried deep in her forehead?

Swallowing, she walked up to the frosted glass door. The words "Benjamin Holmes, Attorney" were printed in black letters on the glass. She knocked briskly. Something large and pink moved on the other side and approached the door. A moment later, the lock whisked to the side with a *thunk*, and a bell made a soft tinkling noise when the door opened.

"Avrianna, sweetie, how are you?" A blur of pink blinded Avrianna as Sassy embraced her with a maternal hug. Avrianna's face sank into a mass of red, wavy hair that smelled strongly of hairspray.

Sassy wasn't your usual mother figure. She had a daughter of her own, Veena, who Avrianna considered a sister, but Sassy didn't believe in mom jeans or giving up her unique style, which often involved feather boas and leather skirts. Her pink A-line dress, with a sweetheart neckline that showcased her voluptuous curves, was adorned with a shiny silver belt. The heart-shaped buckle was encrusted with tiny, sparkling diamonds, all fake, of course. On her feet, she wore silver shoes. White fuzz lined the strap by her toes, which were painted the same bubblegum-pink as her dress.

"Hey, Sass. Can we come in?"

Sassy batted her lashes in Chuck's direction. "Why, of course. I always have time for you and your good-looking partner in crime."

Holding back a laugh, Avrianna slipped into the office. A few wood and leather-cushioned chairs were positioned around the room for clients waiting to see an attorney. Across from a flat screen TV hanging on the wall, magazines sat atop a mahogany coffee table, and in the corner was a table with a coffee maker, a dish stuffed with packets of sugar and creamer, a tower of plastic cups, and a handful of red cocktail straws sticking out of a coffee cup with a smiley face on the side. Aside from a couple of paintings of Vidian sceneries—like Mystic Lake, a lake of lavender water and blue stones—the only source of color in the whole place, aside from Sassy, was Sassy's desk. Positioned outside the door that led to Benajmin Holmes's office, Sassy's desk burst with color and personality, from the pink-haired troll baby standing next to the computer screen, to the line of nail polishes and lipsticks behind the cordless keyboard. And Avrianna knew if she rounded the desk, she'd see a photo of a shirtless man as the computer's background. On the coat rack just inside the door hung a white feather boa. Avrianna looked at it with a smile. Yes, her foster mom was unlike any other.

"It's not every day that I get a visit from my two favorite detectives." Sassy sashayed to the coffee station. "Would either of you like coffee?"

"No, thanks, Sass. We have something to tell you. Why don't you sit?"

Beneath her layers of makeup, her face paled. "It's not Veena, is it?"

"No, no, Veena is okay. It's actually about your boss." Avrianna ushered Sassy over to one of the leather chairs and waited for her to sit down. "Sass, Mr. Holmes was killed this morning at the Veil."

Sassy blinked her thickly-mascaraed lashes. "You're mistaken. He'll be here at six. I always get here twenty minutes early to start the coffee."

Avrianna shook her head. "He's not coming in. I was called to a crime scene this morning. He was shot at the Veil. Someone killed him."

"It was her, wasn't it?"

Avrianna and Chuck exchanged glances.

"Her, who?" Chuck asked.

"His obsession."

Without another word, Sassy got up, went to her desk, and removed a single key from the top drawer where she stashed chocolate kisses and red licorice. On the tip of her finger, she dangled the tiny keyring. "Have a look." She tilted her head toward the office door. "Look inside the armoire. That's where he keeps it all."

Obsession and "keeps it all" could only mean one thing—a mistress. Maybe even a favored hooker.

Avrianna slipped the key into the door's lock and opened it. Chuck followed her into the office. From the looks of it, everything appeared normal. Diplomas and plaques adorned the walls behind the desk, and bookcases packed with law books stood on either side of a large window. On the opposite wall the dark-wood armoire beckoned to her. What secrets did it hide? Once, she had found a blown-up sex doll in a judge's quarters. You just never knew what you were going to find.

"Would you like the honors?" Avrianna asked Chuck.

"Why not?" Chuck positioned himself before the armoire. He took hold of the small, round knobs. "One…two…three." He flung them open. Nothing kinky hid behind those double doors. The interior was covered with papers, maps, and photographs.

Frowning, Avrianna stepped closer to get a good look at the contents. All of the photos were blurry still-shots taken from security footage. In one, she could see half a woman's face. A thin, dark, finely arched brow, an eye surrounded by layers of black that stretched to a point on her temple, and half a mouth complete with glossed lips. Another image was a partial view of a woman's body from the neck to the waist. Black leather shone on a woman's petite form. A pale hand poked out of the end of a long sleeve, and in that hand was a throwing dagger in the shape of a swirl.

Avrianna squinted at a photo with what looked like electric green lines floating in the air, but what upon closer inspection turned out to be hair, bright green hair. A sliver of light in the corner showed an ear and a jawline. It appeared that this image was snapped when the woman was turning around, with her hair flying out from the motion.

Written in bold, permanent-marker were three letters: DIZ.

Initials, perhaps.

A piece of lined notebook paper contained a list of names beneath a header that read, "Kills."

Edward Ashley

Mark Cavner

Xander Robertson

Benji Sanzio

ME?

Avrianna examined the maps of the United States and New Vida's islands. Red dots marked where—she assumed—those kills, and others, had occurred.

They weren't dealing with any normal murderer. They were dealing with someone unafraid to kill on either side of the Veil. A universal killer. And that woman had sniper capabilities that made her elusive during her deadly pursuits. Except, Benjamin Holmes had caught her trail, somehow and for some reason.

"What do you think?" Chuck said while studying the armoire's interior.

With her fingernail, Avrianna lifted a piece of paper tacked over another. The one underneath it was a pencil drawing of a spiral bullet identical to the one that had blown through Holmes's brain.

"I think we found our girl." She let the paper settle back into place. "Or Holmes did…and that's probably what got him killed."

"It's as if he was researching her," Chuck said.

She nodded. "And tracking her."

"I told you, she was his obsession."

They turned to find Sassy in the doorway.

"This is why his wife divorced him last year and his only son quit the law firm."

"Do you know why he was obsessed with her?" Avrianna asked.

Sassy shook her head. "He didn't want to tell me, said it was safer that way."

And, yet, Sassy knew about the things he had on this lethal woman. Sassy might've even snuck in and taken a peek at the armoire's insides to really see what her boss was up to. Holmes might not have wanted to put his devoted assistant's life at risk, but he had done that anyway. If this woman knew about Holmes, there was a strong chance that she knew about Sassy, too. Spiral bullets or no, if this woman came for Sassy, she'd have another thing coming. Avrianna would like to see what this assassin would do when faced with burning orbs, Avrianna's own special weapon.

She turned to the entrance. "Hey, Sass, could you get me a cup of coffee?"

"Sure." Sassy twirled on her three-inch heels.

Keeping her voice low, Avrianna spoke to Chuck. "I think Sassy should be placed in protective custody."

Chuck tucked his hands into his pockets. The lines of his face were tight. "I was thinking the same thing." He glanced toward the door. "But you know that's not going to fly with her."

Avrianna let out a breath. He was right. Sassy would not agree with protective custody. She needed a cozy bed, fuzzy slippers, beauty supplies, and her closet.

"You know what you have to do, kid."

She peered at Chuck, aghast. "No."

"Yup."

"I refuse."

"You gotta."

"Nuh-uh."

"Uh-huh."

She let out a groan. "You can't make me."

He continued to stare. His eyes said it all, "You have no choice."

"Shit," she hissed under her breath. "Fine. I know, I know." She let out another groan before calling out Sassy's name.

Sassy came back with a coffee cup in her hand. "Yes, sweetie?"

"Your safety is paramount at the moment. We have to make sure that this woman doesn't know about you." She jabbed her finger over her shoulder at the opened armoire. "So, until further notice, you're going to be staying at my place. We'll go to your house later so you can pack a bag."

Sassy gave her a blank stare. "A bag? As in one?"

"Yes."

"Not happening. I'll need one bag just for my cosmetics."

Avrianna tipped her head back in exasperation. "Your life is at stake. You can live off one bag for a while."

"No, I can't." Sassy set the coffee cup on her boss's desk. "You have perfect contours and have never had to worry about dark circles or bags under your eyes, for which I will never forgive you, but I need the help of a ton of makeup and other potions to make me look halfway normal. I'd rather her kill me while I'm looking drop-dead gorgeous than looking like the crypt keeper." Sassy crossed her arms. "If I can't have all the stuff I want at your house, then why don't you protect me at my house?"

"Because no one in their right mind would break into *my* house."

Sassy stuck out an index finger. "She would."

There Sassy was right.

"Fine," Avrianna groaned. "I'll come to your house instead." And she hoped she'd be able to catch this murderess sooner rather than later.

Investigators boxed up the items from the inside of the armoire then left to start their research into each piece of paper and photograph, to try to figure out just who this woman was and whom she could be after next. Fortunately for them, they didn't have to worry about what to do with Sassy in the meantime.

Avrianna chewed on her bottom lip. "Now what?" she whispered to Chuck.

"Two words. Ride. Along."

Avrianna shook her head. "Oh, no. I draw the line there. I can't bring her on ride-alongs. We have to go to Mr. Holmes's house and talk to his estranged ex-wife."

Chuck lifted his hands. "If we leave her alone, she's a sitting duck."

She glanced at Sassy as she fluffed her hair with her hand and flirted with a male investigator. "Peacock," she muttered. "She'd be a sitting peacock."

"Hey, Sass." Avrianna waved her over.

"My, my, you sure work with some sexy men," Sassy said while fanning herself.

"Down, girl."

Sassy grinned. "I'll try."

Avrianna winced. If Sassy was this way now, what would she be like tagging along for the whole day wherever they had to go? You could bet there would be men, and men were Sassy's weakness.

"Today is your lucky day. You always say you want to spend more time with me. Well, this is your chance to get a first-hand look into what my job is like."

Sassy clapped her dainty hands. "I'm so excited! But what about my car?"

"We'll have someone bring it to the police department. It'll be safe there. It'd be better if it looked as though you're not home."

"Uh. Okay."

"One condition." Avrianna eyed her foster mom.

"No. More. Flirting."
Sassy pouted.
"I mean it."
"I suppose I could resist."

Don't Touch the Gun

First up, they had to tell Ms. Haley the bad news about her ex-husband. On the driveway, outside a one-story house painted a pale yellow, Avrianna parked her car behind Chuck's and faced Sassy, who sat in the passenger's seat with her ankles crossed.

"Stay in the car."

"But—"

"No. You can't be around when we let someone know a loved one has been murdered, or when we question people. Got it?"

Sassy let out a soft sigh. "All right."

"Thank you." Avrianna got out of the car and shut the door. She met Chuck as he rang the doorbell. "I'm going to call Veena to come and take over babysitting."

"Quitter."

Avrianna shot him a look before the door opened. A woman stood there at the entrance in blue jeans and a flowery blouse. Her feet were bare, and her toenails had chipped blue paint on them. She peered at Chuck and then at Avrianna. Her lax features hardened. Her mouth became rigid, pursed, and deep crevasses between her brows formed as she frowned. Hostility radiated off her.

Avrianna nudged Chuck discreetly, signaling for him to take point.

"Ma'am, I'm Detective Davis. This is my partner, Detective Heavenborn. We would like to talk to you about your ex-husband. May we come in?"

"*You* may," she said to Chuck, then she narrowed her glare on Avrianna. With a sweeping gaze that started from Avrianna's boots and ended with the top of her head, where the sun gleamed on her bright, silvery locks, Ms. Haley added, "*She* may not."

Annoyance had Avrianna's hands forming into fists. It wasn't proper to deck civilians, especially those who may be grieving for a loved one in a matter of moments. But, damn, did Avrianna wish she could slap the disgust off that woman's face.

"Detective Heavenborn is my partner. Wherever I go, she goes," Chuck said.

Ms. Haley sniffed. "Fine." She opened the door wider and stepped aside. Avrianna followed Chuck in, squeezing past Ms. Haley, being sure not to so much as brush the woman with her shirt's sleeve.

In the living room, Ms. Haley indicated at the couch while she took a chair across from it. When Avrianna started to lower onto a cushion, she noticed Ms. Haley start to rise, with her hand out as if to stop her, but she didn't. Instead, she sat back down, wringing her hands. Avrianna had a feeling Ms. Haley would've laid newspaper down on the cushion, treating Avrianna like a filthy dog that she didn't want to ruin her couch.

"So, what has Ben done now?"

"Ma'am, Mr. Holmes's body was found at the Veil. He was murdered."

Ms. Haley leaned back against her chair. "She finally did it, then."

Avrianna and Chuck exchanged glances.

"Who do you mean?" Chuck asked.

"The assassin, of course."

Avrianna arched a brow. "How much do you know about her?"

Ms. Haley met Avrianna's eye and kept it. "Nothing really. Ben didn't want me to know much. I do know that she killed his brother, though."

"His brother?"

Ms. Haley snorted. "Don't know about him yet? And you call yourself a detective. My father used to say women shouldn't be in the police force."

Avrianna clenched her teeth. To hear another woman say that made her blood boil.

"Or, at least, he was right in your case. They tried to bar you from the police academy and from joining the Aurora Police Department, didn't they?"

Avrianna forced a smile that would look like a death threat on a rabid dog. "They did," she said through her snarl. "And they failed. Both times."

Lucky for her, Chuck had stepped up when it was time for her to get a partner, when no one else wanted to do it. She never knew why he did it, but ever since, he'd been like a father figure to her, always looking out for her.

Even in that moment, Chuck had her back. He took out his notepad and poised his pen. "What is Mr. Holmes's brother's name?"

"Simon Holmes. He was an anti-money laundering analyst. Ben believed his brother stumbled onto a money laundering scheme and the people involved hired a hitwoman to take him out. Everything Ben did was in order to find out who killed his brother, and when he found out, he became obsessed."

Obsessed. Sassy had used the same word.

"All he talked about was this unknown, mysterious, lethal woman. Day and night. It's why we divorced. I couldn't take it anymore. Couldn't share my marriage with a faceless gunwoman." With that last word, she sent Avrianna a withering look, because Avrianna was a "gunwoman."

A knock on the door had Ms. Haley rising from her chair.

"No, allow me." Avrianna got to her feet.

Ms. Haley balked. "It's my house. I don't want you opening the door and scaring away one of my neighbors."

"It's for your safety."

This gun-toting woman may save your life by

scaring away whoever is at the door.

Ms. Haley put a hand to her throat. "You…you don't mean to say that this…this hitwoman could be out there, looking for me, do you?"

"No, but I'd like to open the door to be sure."

"O-okay." Ms. Haley sat back down, looking as if she was going to be ill.

Avrianna unfastened the button to the clasp securing her sidearm and lay her hand on her piece, ready to pull it out and use it to save the life of a woman who condemned Avrianna's very being.

She approached the door slowly, angling her body so that if someone fired a shot, she'd be a smaller target, although, it wasn't necessary because a bullet couldn't hurt her. Police academy lessons stuck, though, even if she didn't need to take the precaution, herself.

At the door, she peeked through the peephole to see Sassy on the other side, applying a layer of pink lip gloss to her lips. She screwed the wand back into the container of gloss and smacked her lips.

Avrianna rolled her eyes and removed her hand from her weapon. "False alarm," she said over her shoulder and then proceeded to unlock the deadbolt.

Sassy smiled when Avrianna opened the door.

"You were supposed to stay in the car," Avrianna hissed under her breath.

Sassy crossed her legs and bounced in place. "But I have to pee."

Avrianna sighed. "Fine, get in here." She ushered Sassy inside. "You'll go to the bathroom, and then go straight back out to the car. You won't say a word to

Ms. Haley."

Unfortunately, Ms. Haley came around the corner. She halted in the hallway, the line between her brows deepened. "Sassy, what are you doing here?"

"They picked me up from the office, concerned for my safety. I was waiting in the car for them, but I have to use the ladies' room. May I?"

"Um, sure."

Sassy turned to Avrianna. "See? She doesn't mind."

"Just hurry up."

"You're so bossy. When did you get to be so bossy?"

"Since I got my badge. Badge means I get to be bossy. Even to you."

"Um. You might want to check that last part." Sassy planted her hands on her hips. "I trump the badge. Every time."

"Not in my business you don't."

"Humph."

"Do the two of you know each other?" Ms. Haley's question had Avrianna and Sassy facing their audience.

Before Avrianna could supply an answer that wasn't too revealing, Sassy said, "Duh. She's my daughter."

That statement had Ms. Haley's eyes widening.

"Well, not biologically, of course. No one is."

Avrianna closed her eyes.

"But we love her just the same. I was her aunt through adoption, and then I later became her foster mom."

"I-I had no idea."

"Ben knew."

Ms. Haley crossed her arms. "Well, he didn't tell me."

"Ah. That's okay. Now you can see us side by side. Don't we look alike?" She hip-bumped Avrianna and ended up hitting Avrianna's holstered weapon.

"No," came Ms. Haley's clipped reply.

Ms. Haley was right. They looked nothing alike. Sassy had honey-brown eyes, and Avrianna had unnatural green eyes that made people like Ms. Haley think she wasn't human. Sometimes, she thought they were right. Her sharp features and flawless skin were said to be too perfect, alien even. No, Avrianna didn't look anything like Sassy. She didn't look like anyone alive. Or dead.

"Oops," Sassy said. "I moved your gun's purse."

"It's called a holster."

"It looks like a purse. I'll fix it for you." She started to straighten the holster, but Avrianna slapped her hand away.

"Don't touch the gun."

"It's crooked." Sassy went to try again.

Whack. "Don't."

"But—" Sassy's fingers zeroed in on the leather case once more.

Whack.

"Fine." Sassy started to turn away but stopped. "Aren't you going to snap the button back on?" She poked the button on the strap.

Smack. "Don't."

"Safety first, Avrianna."

Whack.

"Okay, but do you know there's grease or something on it? Right there."

Smack.

"Aren't you going to wipe it off? I'll get it for you." Sassy licked her finger and went to clean off the smudge from the back of the polymer gun.

Avrianna slapped away Sassy's fingers once more before rounding on her. "Don't. Touch. The. Gun."

Sassy sighed. "Fine."

"Don't you have to go to the bathroom?"

Sassy perked up. "I almost forgot. My bladder is about to burst. Where's the ladies' room?"

Ms. Haley didn't so much as blink. Her face was a mask of shock. She pointed her thumb over her shoulder. "End of the hall."

Sassy hopped to it, slipping past Ms. Haley, who inched to the side so that her shoulder pressed into the wall. No doubt she now thought Sassy was tainted by Avrianna's freakish nature and didn't want any of it to rub off on her.

"Well, I think we're done here," Chuck said and stashed his notepad and pen.

"We'll leave as soon as Ms. Miller rejoins us."

Sassy returned a moment later, and the three of them left for Mr. Holmes's house. Parked on the side of the road among CSI vans and cop cars, Avrianna turned in the driver's seat to give Sassy her instructions. Before she could say a word, Sassy said, "I am not waiting in this car again. That crazy bitch could be out there. A bullet can go through a car window, as you well know."

Chomping down on her bottom lip, Avrianna

looked at the back window. Though resistant to regular bullets, she wasn't so sure about spiral bullets dispensed from a sniper's gun. She drummed her fingers on the steering wheel. DIZ could be anywhere, lurking in a shadow, sprawled out on her belly atop a neighboring house's roof, perched at the top of a tall tree, with her gun balanced on a branch, peering at them through the scope, the backs of their heads in her sights. If DIZ wanted to watch the spectacle and pick out targets that could know about her or discover her, she'd be there. And Sassy and Avrianna would be at the top of that list—Sassy as someone who could've been in her dead boss's confidence, and Avrianna as someone who aimed to bring DIZ down.

"Okay. You can come inside, but don't touch anything. We're pulling evidence from his house. We don't need your fingerprints on anything."

"Aye aye, Detective."

"That's not what cops say," Avrianna began. "Oh, never mind. Come on."

At the threshold, Avrianna opened her metal case and pulled out blue shoe covers to slip over her boots. She handed a pair to Sassy.

"These don't go with my outfit." She held them back out to Avrianna. They dangled between her thumb and forefinger as if they were dead fish.

"Put. Them. On."

Sassy stuck out her tongue. Holding onto Avrianna's arm, she tugged the blue mesh covers over her high heels. When she finished, Avrianna passed her a pair of gloves.

"Look at that. The gloves match the booties,"

Avrianna said.

"Ick, but they're latex. You should get nitrile gloves." She wiggled her fingers into the gloves with a grimace. "I don't know how you wear these things."

"I do it to protect the evidence." Avrianna pulled out a final crime scene accessory. "Here. Last thing."

Sassy recoiled. "Absolutely not. You put that hideous hairnet away."

Laughing, knowing Sassy wouldn't stand for it, Avrianna stuffed the hairnet back into her case.

Inside Mr. Holmes's one-bed, one-bath house with blue-gray walls, Avrianna ushered Sassy into the living room and deposited her in a corner away from the investigators canvasing the space. "Stay here. Don't talk to anyone."

Sassy mimed locking her lips with a key and made a show out of planting her covered stilettos in place. During the next half hour, Avrianna went through drawers, checked pockets of the pants and coats hanging in the closet, thumbed through books for slips of paper Mr. Holmes had been trying to hide, and unzipped the covers on the couch cushions.

In the living room, Avrianna, Chuck, and a few investigators crowded together beside the black coffee table.

"He must not have brought his obsessive work home," Chuck said.

"We could check to see if he has a safety deposit box," an investigator offered.

Avrianna nodded. "Do that."

"We're also checking his work files in case he labeled one to throw someone off."

"Good."

"You could check the safe behind that painting." That suggestion came from behind them.

Avrianna turned to see Sassy standing in the exact spot where she had left her. Sassy's hands were clasped in front of her, holding her purse by the strap.

Avrianna frowned. "What safe?"

Sassy pointed over Avrianna's shoulder. "The safe behind that painting."

Intrigued, Avrianna went to the far wall. Standing to the side, she lifted the corner of a discreet ocean painting and peeked behind it to see a metal door with a keypad lock in its center. Eyebrows lifted, she turned back to Sassy. "How'd you know this was here?"

"I am…*was* his assistant. I was here when it was put it in."

"You don't happen to know the—"

"Eight-three-four-six."

Without a word, Avrianna pressed the numbers into the keypad. A beep sounded and the red light turned green. She pulled open the door. Inside, the safe almost looked empty, but sitting on the bottom was a black laptop. She lifted it out and handed it to an investigator to bag as evidence.

"Well, that's it," she said to Chuck. "I'm going to get Sassy out of here."

"Good luck, kid."

She gave him a look that said "thanks, I'll need it," and then she went to Sassy. While removing her gloves, she said, "We're going to stop at my house so I can get a few things. Then we're going to your house."

"For a slumber party," Sassy squealed. "I'm going

to call the girls."

Avrianna's eyes bulged in their sockets. "The girls" consisted of all the women that Avrianna considered family—Deja, her adoptive parents' real daughter; Grandy, her adoptive grandmother and Sassy's mother; Lexie, her best friend since foster care; Simone, Aurora Police Department's medical examiner; Evony, Avrianna's stylist for undercover operations, and Emerson, Evony, twins and good friend of both women. Veena, Sassy's daughter, wouldn't be able to come, though, because she was currently living on Earth, in the "Real World," being a bad ass lieutenant in New York City. Although Avrianna loved them all, and would fight and die for them, slumber parties were not her thing. The idea of one put genuine fear in her. To her, it very much sounded like torture.

"Absolutely not. I'm over for my job, to keep you safe. I cannot do that with a houseful of women running around in pajamas with separators between their toes and opened bottles of nail polish everywhere."

Sassy clapped her hands. "Manis and pedis!"

"No. No. No…and no."

Sassy pouted.

"No."

Marshmallows

Avrianna let Sassy into her house. The lights were off. When she flicked the switch on the wall to turn on the living room ceiling fan and light, it illuminated the sparse surroundings. A couch and a chair, where she enjoyed her morning cup of coffee, were the only sources for sitting in the living room. On the coffee table sat two remotes. One for the TV and one for the DVD player. She didn't even have coasters. Above the couch, on the beige wall, hung a single painting, a map of New Vida and its seven islands—Aurora, Houston, Avalon, Nation, Tamara,

Medallion, and Zakuska. On the kitchen counters, where the granite was the one bit of art, sat an old-fashioned coffeemaker with a glass pot, a microwave, and a toaster. She didn't even own a blender or a waffle maker.

Sassy looked at the space and shook her head. "I could really spice this place up if you let me. Some candles for the coffee table, a few colorful throw pillows, and fake potted trees in the corners for the illusion of life in this dreariness."

"I like my house just the way it is," Avrianna said. "It suits my needs."

"Your work needs, but what if you meet someone?"

Avrianna arched a brow. "Whom would I meet? Everyone already knows who I am, and no one in their right mind would want to date me. They're afraid. If they aren't afraid, they hate me. Besides that, I don't want to date. I'm happy alone."

The corners of Sassy's mouth turned down. "Are you really?"

She wouldn't admit this to anyone, because she hated to share her feelings, to show her vulnerability, but during the late, long hours of nighttime, while lying in bed and struggling to fall asleep, she thought about what it would be like to be loved by someone and tried to imagine what that person would look like. Sometimes she saw flashes of dark hair and pale eyes, but they were only dreams…yearnings…impossibilities.

"Yes," Avrianna muttered. "I'm going to get my things." She didn't want to think about what would never happen.

From under her kitchen sink, she dug out a plastic grocery bag, and then she carried it into her room. She folded a pair of dark jeans and a black T-shirt and laid them inside the bottom of the plastic bag. On top of them, she set a black sports bra, boy shorts, and ankle socks. In the bathroom she stuck her toothbrush in a sandwich bag and added it to her clothes with her deodorant and hair brush. Finished, she knotted together the handles to the plastic bag and met Sassy in the living room.

"Okay. I'm ready. Let's go."

Sassy eyed the plastic bag. "That's it? That's all you're bringing?"

"It's all I need," Avrianna said. "A change of clothes, my toothbrush, deodorant, and hair brush."

Sassy stared at her with wide eyes and her mouth hanging open. "No makeup?"

"Nope."

"That is…the scariest thing I've ever heard." She shook her head. "You got the jackpot of genetics, girl."

The only thing was, they didn't know where her genetics came from. Some speculated extraterrestrials, which could explain her powers, but she didn't know. No one did. And that was part of the problem. She had been found floating in the ocean, off the coast of Aurora. No plane had crashed. No boat had sunk. She was just there, floating without assistance from anything. No raft. No basket. All she had was a strangely water-resistant white baby blanket wrapped tightly around her. Etched in the cotton of the blanket was her full name. That was all anyone knew about her.

She was Avrianna Heavenborn, and she had been found floating in the Aurora Diamond.

"Hold on." Sassy laid a hand on her arm. "What about your perfume?"

"I don't wear perfume."

Sassy put her hand to her chest. "What?"

"Never have."

"You use baking soda for laundry detergent and a simple bar of soap. How do you smell so good?"

Avrianna shrugged.

"Are you telling me that this lovely aroma"—Sassy waved a hand in front of Avrianna to waft the scent toward her—"that you've had since you were a teenager wasn't your signature perfume but…you?"

"I guess so."

Sassy leaned forward and inhaled. "Do you know what you smell like?"

Uncomfortable, Avrianna inched back. "No."

"You smell like peppermint leaves, lavender, and vanilla got together for a classy tea party, but then a sensual peach blossom showed up, unannounced, and their tea became a sultry foursome. And, just when you think that's sexy enough, an orange blossom walked in on them and joined in on the fun. Vanilla became pregnant as a result of their orgy and spawned a sparkling and sweet and intoxicating lovechild."

Avrianna blinked. "That's really graphic for a smell."

"That's how *you* smell."

She squirmed. "Well, I don't want to."

"Too late."

Shit. Did everyone think she smelled like a

fragrance orgy? She hoped not!

Deeply uncomfortable, she drove Sassy home, but as soon as they stepped inside, she locked the door and pointed for Sassy to stay right there. In Sassy's ear, she whispered, "If someone else who isn't me comes into the hallway, turn around and run to your neighbor's house."

"You're scaring me," Sassy whispered back.

In response, Avrianna looked her in the eye and removed her sidearm from the holster at her hip. Cradling the gun in her hands, aiming it in front of her, she took careful steps, one foot in front of the other, as she moved through the house. She checked in every corner, closet, behind curtains, inside the shower, and under Sassy's bed. When she was satisfied that a murderess was not lurking anywhere in the house, garage or attic, she returned to Sassy and stuck her weapon back in the holster. "All clear, but we should keep the lights off so it looks as though you're not home."

Sassy's shoulders lowered. "Good. Now we can have fun."

Avrianna winced as Sassy took off her feather boa and flung it on the back of a chair. She kicked off her high heels, leaving them in front of the door and hurried off into the kitchen, bare footed. Avrianna picked up Sassy's shoes and tossed them to the side. The last thing she needed was for Sassy to trip over them and fall while making a mad dash out of the house to safety.

Sassy came back out of the kitchen with a bag of marshmallows, two metal skewers, and a stove lighter. She carried everything over to the coffee table where she sat on the floor, with her back against the couch. One at a time, she lit the half-dozen candles of various sizes and colors that were scattered over the surface of the coffee table. Then she stuck a marshmallow on the end of a skewer and held it over a candleflame.

A smile dawned on Avrianna's face as she walked toward the kitchen and peeked carefully between the blinds. The backyard was cast in darkness, but the moon was full and shining its celestial light upon the world. Everything its light mated with created shadows. Shadows that moved with the wind. Shadows that grew and shrank. Shadows that could really be a stealthy assassin. She focused her gaze on the darkness.

Warmth burned in the center of her eyes as they lit with their power. Bright green light reflected in the window's glass. With her powers activated, she could see everything in the night as if she were wearing night vision goggles.

The shadows vanished. No one was there in the darkness. At least not in that area, and not right then.

She went to the living room. Kneeling on the couch, she inched the curtain to the side with the tip of her finger, enough to see out the side. No one hid between Sassy's house and the neighbor's house.

With her hand resting on her sidearm, she stood by the front door to peer through the side window. When she turned around, something soft plopped against her forehead. At her feet lay a marshmallow. She looked at Sassy. "Did you just throw a marshmallow at me?"

"Yes, I did. You're scaring me. Stop pacing and looking out the windows."

"I'm doing my job. I'm here to protect you, not to

roast marshmallows."

Sassy pouted as she stuck another marshmallow onto her skewer and set it in a candle's fire. A corner of the marshmallow burst into flame. The marshmallow turned crispy black, and Sassy turned it to roast the other side. As soon as she turned it, the flames extinguished where they had been eating the sweet marshmallow, burning it to ash. With the other side now aflame and becoming charcoal, Sassy lifted it and blew out the flames. The smell of burnt sugar floated through the air, bringing back childhood memories of moments just like this with Sassy and Veena.

Using the tips of her fingers, Sassy delicately removed the roasted marshmallow from the skewer. The burnt surface caved beneath her touch. She brought it to her mouth and licked off the stickiness left on her fingers. Sighing, she put another marshmallow in its place.

"Look, Sass, I'm sorry, but I am here for a reason, and that's to keep you safe. This woman could be anywhere, and she is extremely dangerous. We don't know who she is going after next. We also don't know where she is. We don't even know what she looks like. She's that elusive. I have to stay on the lookout, which means checking our surroundings and having my gun with me at all times."

Avrianna blinked when another marshmallow bopped her between the eyes. She could still feel its powdery imprint on her skin.

"You saying all of that isn't helping me to feel any less frightened." Sassy hopped to her feet. "I need a drink." She shuffled past Avrianna into the kitchen.

Getting drunk wouldn't help matters, especially if Sassy had to make a run for it, but Avrianna bit her tongue. She'd let Sassy have a couple of shots and then she'd remove the bottle.

A moment later, Sassy returned with a bottle and two shot glasses. "Good thing I have marshmallow-flavored vodka."

Avrianna rolled her eyes. Only Sassy would have such a flavor.

Back on the floor, with her legs tucked under her, Sassy poured two shot glasses to the rim with marshmallow-flavored vodka. "Let's cheers to sexy killer women," Sassy suggested while she raised a shot glass in the air.

"I am not toasting to that."

"Party pooper." Sassy clinked her shot glass into the one sitting on the coffee table, the one meant for Avrianna. Then she downed the vodka in one swallow. She immediately poured another and put it down the hatch.

While she had her head tipped back, Avrianna thought she heard a floorboard creak down the hall. She took a step back, in direct line of the hallway, and lifted her gun from its holster, but she kept it at her side, pointed to the ground.

"Whoa." Sassy shook her head from side to side with her face scrunched up. "That is some good stuff."

Avrianna quickly stored her gun back in its place and turned toward Sassy. However, she couldn't stop her gaze from shifting toward the end of the hall.

"Get over here and take your shot before I do."

"I can't, I'm—" Her words were cut off when yet

another marshmallow hit her in the exact same spot as the previous two. "You really need to stop doing that." Three marshmallows now littered the ground at her feet. "I have to say, though, you have surprisingly good aim."

"Where do you think Veena gets it from?"

Avrianna smirked. She should've said "me," since she was the one who taught Veena to shoot, but Sassy did have amazing precision with eyeliner pencils, though, so it could be true.

"Come and roast some marshmallows with me."

Avrianna let out a sigh. What harm would it cause to roast a freaking marshmallow with the woman who raised her when she had no one left? If Avrianna could do anything, making Sassy happy would be one of them. She joined Sassy on the floor, on the opposite side of the coffee table. Just so Sassy wouldn't drink it, Avrianna picked up the full shot glass and knocked it back. She shivered at the taste; it wasn't her choice of liquor, that was for sure—she'd prefer bourbon or whiskey. Neat. No silly flavors, just good, old-fashioned booze.

She picked up the other skewer and selected a marshmallow from the opened bag. Part of her felt silly roasting marshmallows while she was technically still on the job, but she had to admit to herself that it felt good.

"Do you remember we used to do this when storms would knock the power out?" Sassy asked.

"I remember the marshmallows always tasted like scented candles."

"Well, we're in luck. These aren't scented."

Avrianna smiled while she let her marshmallow turn into a blaze. Then she blew it out with a puff. She ate the marshmallow right off the skewer. The outside was crisp and tasted like ashes, but the inside was warm and sweet. She picked up another marshmallow, but paused after she pushed it down onto the skewer. Staring at it, she recalled a time when she was roasting marshmallows with Sassy and Veena.

"I remember how I once used my powers to roast the marshmallows." She lifted her index finger, and green flames snaked up and down the length of it, from knuckle to the tip of her nail. The flame grew, stretching past her nail, like a flame extending taller than a candle's wick. "And you and Veena weren't afraid to eat those marshmallows." She looked into Sassy's gentle eyes. "You weren't afraid that you could've been consuming something radioactive. That maybe you and Veena could've died from it."

Sassy gasped. "How could anything you do be dangerous or toxic to us? We love you, and we know you love us."

A lump formed in Avrianna's throat. She swallowed. "But my blood melts, and my tears burn. There *is* something wrong with me. My blood type isn't like yours, isn't like anyone's. There are things in it that shouldn't be there."

"That doesn't matter to me or to anyone who loves you."

Avrianna nodded. She quietly roasted her marshmallow. After she ate it, she looked at Sassy, who was lining marshmallows all along her skewer. She had three of them on it and was shoving on a fourth.

"Thank you."

Sassy looked up. "For what, honey?"

"Just…for being you."

Sassy lowered her skewer. "And thank *you* for being you."

Diz the Assassin

Early in the morning, a knock sounded on Sassy's front door. Avrianna got off the kitchen stool where she had been sitting and drinking coffee. Her hand, as if on its own, settled over the sidearm she still wore. She looked through the peephole to see Veena standing there. Avrianna wasn't sure who she expected to see. Perhaps the inside of a barrel of a gun, but definitely not Veena. She opened the door.

A silver, rolling, hard-sided suitcase stood beside Veena. She had on faded jeans and a worn feather jacket over a vintage rock T-shirt. Her wavy, burgundy hair was pulled into a ponytail. Large sunglasses covered half her face.

"What are you doing here?"

"Chuck called me yesterday to tell me what was going on. I took a flight from New York to Arizona, hopped on a bus, and then waited for them to open the Veil."

Avrianna held the door open for Veena while she yanked her rolling suitcase up the doorstep. "Can you get my other one?"

"Other one?" Avrianna turned to see a second, identical suitcase sitting on the welcome mat. She stepped out to get it and was amazed at how heavy the thing was. "What in the world do you have in this thing?"

"Shoes."

Avrianna tripped over one of the suitcase's wheels. She straightened and gaped at Veena. "Shoes?" She pointed. "This thing is full of shoes?"

"Yup."

"And what do you have in that one?" Avrianna pointed at the suitcase Veena had rolled up beside the chair where Sassy had flung her feather boa the night before.

"Clothes."

Avrianna hid her grin. Like mother like daughter.

"What I want to know is why Chuck called me and you didn't." Veena put her hands on her hips and scowled at Avrianna.

"I didn't want to worry you, or put you in danger, too."

"Please." Veena rolled her eyes. "I'm armed and dangerous." She turned and lifted her jacket to show two guns nestled at her back.

"How'd you get those through the airport? How'd you get them through the Veil?"

Veena smirked. "I have my ways."

"See. And this is why I worry about security. If this assassin can come in with a gun and spiral bullets, and you can come in packing heat, what else is making its way into our world?" She paused. "*Who* else?"

Veena shrugged. "Don't change the subject. You should've told me right away. She's my mom, too."

"More your mom than mine."

"Hey, don't say that." Veena frowned. "You know mom loves us equally."

Avrianna wasn't so sure about the equally part. After all, Veena was her blood daughter. Avrianna was just her adopted niece. But she did know Sassy loved her. Otherwise, she wouldn't have taken Avrianna in when she had needed a home.

"I know. You're right," she said hurriedly. "I did plan to tell you about the situation, but yesterday was a hectic day. It's actually good that you're here. I'll be able to do my job, so I can find this woman, and you can keep an eye on Sass while I work."

"That's why I'm here. Chuck made it sound as though you'd need the help."

Avrianna nodded solemnly. "When it comes to Sass? Definitely."

Veena chuckled. "I am relieving you of duty."

"Bless you child."

That had both of them cracking up with laughter.

"What a treat. Both of my girls are here with me." Sassy came out of her bedroom wearing a silk nightgown. She put an arm around each of them. "Breakfast?"

"I'll make it," Veena said. "Lord knows neither of you can cook worth a damn."

Avrianna crossed her arms. "Hey, I can make a mean bag of popcorn."

Veena's eyes widened. "You make jokes now?"

"It's a recent occurrence."

After a pancake breakfast, Avrianna went in to work. Chuck found her at her desk where she was reading through the evidence reports from the investigators about the content of Holmes's laptop. Holmes believed DIZ got her hits from an area of the dark net where assassins logged on and accepted kill orders from billionaires and mobsters around Earth, from Italy to New York and every corner in-between. They got paid millions for their kills. And apparently DIZ was a favorite, always in high-demand. But before yesterday, she had only done her jobs on Earth, so Holmes thought he was safe. How could a woman like her cross through the Veil? After all, it was heavily guarded.

Avrianna shook her head in disgust. If only he had known the bullshit the US government put them through, making it easy for criminals to sneak to their side. Holmes should've been safe here. Every citizen in New Vida should be safe, but from the moment the Veil was discovered on Earth, they became screwed. None of them were safe now and likely would never be.

"You look like you want to kill someone."

Avrianna looked up at Chuck. She clenched and unclenched her hands and decided against going into yet another rant about the state of their world. "Just please tell me there's a way I can find this part of the dark net where assassins accept hits."

Chuck grinned. "Well…"

Her jaw dropped, and she sprang to her feet. "No, shit."

"Our best has been looking, and an eighteen-year-old kid found it. They've been monitoring things from a secure laptop all night."

"Show me."

"Right this way."

Downstairs, a group of IT experts crowded in front of a sturdy, black laptop. A young man sat in front of it. He had a battered baseball cap on his head and wore a long-sleeved black T-shirt. On his hands, he wore fingerless, leather biker gloves.

"Make way." Chuck clapped his hands. "Come on, move."

The crowd parted.

The kid behind the laptop gaped at Avrianna. In his mouth, she could see a wad of blue gum smashed against his bottom set of teeth. She took the chair someone had abandoned next to him, turned it around, and sat down facing the laptop's screen. "Show me what you've got."

The kid jumped. "Okay."

The screen was black with white text. It looked a little like an old-fashioned Internet chatroom, if it weren't for mobsters naming people they wanted dead and listing how much they'd pay to have it done.

Whenever an order came in, an assassin would respond, claiming it. If more than one assassin wanted the job, the person who put out the hit would announce that whoever got the deed done first would get paid.

"Holy shit," Avrianna breathed.

"No kidding," the kid said.

"Can these people be tracked down?"

He shook his head. "We've tried, but they're bouncing their IP addresses in over a hundred locations on both worlds. It's impossible to pinpoint them. Just when we think we're close, the IP addresses scramble."

"Any sign of DIZ?"

"None."

Avrianna pursed her lips. "She's out there somewhere," she whispered. "She'll be on. Sooner or later. It's what she does. And I'll get her. Because it's what *I* do."

She settled in for a long day monitoring the correspondences that came through. A lot of the time, nothing happened. She wondered how many assassins were sitting in front of their secure laptops, waiting for an order to come in. Was DIZ one of them? Surely, by now, the woman was in a safe place somewhere, relaxing after her hard work of scaling a skyscraper and killing a man. Was she in a fancy hotel enjoying her blood money, a crappy motel slumming it to be invisible, or in a safehouse part of an underground network of assassins? The possibilities were endless. The woman could even be snoozing in a car in the police parking lot. After all, the closer you were to your enemy, the blinder they became.

The chomping of a piece of gum broke through her

thoughts. She took a deep breath in an attempt to halt herself from snapping at the teenager sitting next to her. He chewed with his mouth open, letting everyone hear his gum smacking between his teeth. Finally, she couldn't take it anymore. "Kid! Gum."

He jumped. "Oh, do you want a piece?" He dug into his jean's pocket and pulled out a packet of bent gum.

She turned to him, seething. "No. But if you continue to chew your gum like that, I'll make it so you can't chew anymore. Got it?"

The kid squirmed in his chair. His Adam's apple bobbed as he swallowed hard, and she had a feeling he had swallowed the wad of gum.

She stifled a chuckle. "Much better."

For lunch, Avrianna ate lo mein noodles from a carton with cheap wooden chopsticks in front of the laptop. Beside her, the kid crunched on an eggroll, which he kept dipping into a container of duck sauce. Flaky crumbs scattered across the laptop's keyboard every time he moved. Avrianna did her best to ignore it.

Two hours and a fresh cup of coffee later, an order came in that had Avrianna choking on her coffee. She set aside her cup. "Two million, Christopher Edwards, New Vida, Aurora." That was a prize significantly larger than any other so far that day.

Avrianna sat forward.

Within seconds, a reply posted.

—Diz: Consider it done.—

Avrianna smiled at the black screen and those

white letters. Not initials as she had thought, but a name made of three little letters—Diz.

Diz, Benjamin Holmes's killer.

Diz, the universal killer.

Diz, Avrianna's next bust.

While Chuck tailed Christopher Edwards all day, keeping close tabs on him, Avrianna tried her own hand at hacking to discover Diz's location, but the kid was right, when she thought she finally narrowed it down to the final IP address, it suddenly vanished and a hundred new ones popped up in its place, pinging here and there and everywhere, even on Earth. She finally gave up.

If Holmes's research was correct, Diz liked to attack at dark. So then at dark, Avrianna and Diz would meet. Face to face.

Chuck called at a quarter to eight. "We have officers at his house. They spoke to his wife and are making sure she doesn't contact him. We don't need him being tipped off and acting weird. He has to follow his routine to the letter. If he knew, he'd mess up."

"I agree."

"I've got good news. He gets off work at eight o'clock, and every evening before he comes home, he goes to the liquor store five minutes away."

"And that's where she'll do it."

"And that's where she'll do it," he agreed. "You have twenty minutes."

Avrianna ended the call without a parting word. She sprinted out of the police department and to her car. A text came through as she buckled her seat belt. It was from Chuck, sending her the name and address of the liquor store. From her location, it would take her exactly twenty minutes to get there. She'd have to drive fast to make it in time, and she'd be cutting it close.

With her dashboard lights on, she broke every speed limit from there to the liquor store, but traffic was heavy. She laid on her horn and let every colorful curse word that came to mind spew forth from her lips. Still, she was in a traffic jam a block from the liquor store. With five minutes to go.

Letting out another curse, she swerved into the first parking lot that she came to and shot into a free space. Then she yanked the key free and rushed out of the car. She didn't even bother to lock it but cut across the street and ran full force down the sidewalk. At the corner, she leapt off the sidewalk, over a shrub, and landed on the asphalt on the other side. The liquor store stood in the middle of a shopping center. She aimed right for it, but her gaze ricocheted from rooftop to rooftop. Where would Diz be hiding? Where would she be preparing to take her shot?

Avrianna rushed past parked cars and jumped over concrete curbs. The liquor store was half a parking lot away. The glass door opened and a man stepped out. He unscrewed the cap to a mini bottle, brought it to his lips, and tipped his head back while he downed the contents. With just one more aisle to go, she pushed her legs to go faster. Her innocent was right there. Just feet away. She had to get to him, had to protect him. No matter what.

She sprang onto a plot of landscaping with small trees and plants. Mulch kicked up at her feet. She hopped off it onto the pavement in front of the stores. A truck zoomed in front of her. It blared its horn, and the driver slammed on the brake, causing the truck to lurch to a stop in front of her. She collided into the side of it. Frustrated, she smacked the truck's cab. Then she shot around the tailgate to the other side. Her innocent still stood there. Staring at the truck that had blocked her from him.

"Go back into the store," she yelled as she ran to him. "And get down!"

He turned to her, frowning. "What?"

"Go inside!" She reached out her hand toward him, ready to yank him back into the store and cover him with her body.

Less than a yard from him, his neck snapped forward, and a hole appeared in the middle of his forehead. The bullet passed with centimeters to spare above her head, following the part of her hair. Blood splattered onto her face. And the man dropped onto his knees. When he slammed into the ground, his hair brushed the tips of her boots and blood pooled around her feet.

Avrianna's gaze, burning with anger, lifted to the rooftop directly in front of her. There, a dark form stood. Dark except for one thing—her hair. When Diz turned, her bright green hair, the same color glowing from Avrianna's eyes, fanned out around her.

Then she disappeared from sight.

Avrianna snatched up her radio and shouted into it, "Rooftop of Jupiter Tools. Diz is on the rooftop of Jupiter Tools!" She peered at the man at her feet. "Man down. We need a bus at Celestial Liquor. I repeat, man down. Diz got her mark."

She clipped her radio back on her belt. While staring at the man she was meant to save, she gripped her hands into white-knuckled fists. Green flames burst from them. The blood of an innocent stained her face.

She had failed.

Chuck joined her. "She got away."

Of course, she did.

"No one even so much as caught a glimpse of her."

Seething inside, she tilted her head to him. Her eyes still burned. "I did."

Avrianna cleaned Christopher's blood from her face and stayed at the crime scene until his body was bagged and sent on its way to the morgue.

Chuck hesitated beside her. "Are you okay?"

She looked at him. Although her hands and eyes were no longer burning with her rage, that venom still coursed through her veins. "I'm fabulous," she said and turned away. She walked back to her car, with her heart pounding an angry rhythm in her chest. Her breaths were short and controlled, and her jaw was clenched tight.

Inside her car, she sat alone in the silence. That silence implored her to release, to let go, so she leaned forward and screamed her fury. It felt as though her vocal cords were on fire, for the sound that came out wasn't quite human, but something else. Something…other. The sound of her rage was almost demonic.

When it left her body, she collapsed against the seat, spent. And yet, deep inside, that anger flickered, with the potential to erupt into an infernal if tempted.

Dizlock Forest

Once home, Avrianna went for the cabinet in her kitchen where she stored a couple bottles of liquor. Some days, working the job, she needed something strong. The only problem was, alcohol didn't affect her as it did everyone else. She'd never before been drunk. Not even buzzed. Even when she was desperate for alcohol to make her forget the things she saw and heard on the job, it wouldn't do it for her. The sting of the liquor doing down her throat didn't even register for her, but there was something soothing about it, so she poured herself a high-ball glass of bourbon and took it in one swallow. She poured herself a second and added a single ice cube before going to her favorite chair.

She set her radio on the coffee table next to her gun, and on the chair's armrest, she put her cell phone. Off duty, but ready for anything, she leaned back and sipped the bourbon. She wondered how Diz was celebrating her latest kill.

Did Diz celebrate with her beverage of choice? And what would that be? Absinthe to go with her green hair? A dirty martini? Perhaps a Death in the Afternoon cocktail, a blend of Absinthe and champagne? Bloody Mary? Avrianna was betting on a Psycho Killer cocktail, because if the shoe fits…

She took a swallow of bourbon.

How else did Diz celebrate?

Roll around on a bed full of cash?

Expend leftover energy with a hooker or two?

Snort something illegal?

Or plot out her next kill?

Avrianna couldn't get the flash of green hair she'd seen out of her head. The color of Diz's hair felt like a personal slight, considering green was the color of Avrianna's power. Had Diz done that on purpose, knowing once she killed on New Vida soil she'd have to deal with Avrianna?

A brisk knock yanked her out of her thoughts. She got up, high ball glass in hand, and went to her front door. A glance through the peephole showed her sister Déjà. Brunette hair framed her olive face. Brown eyes looked straight ahead, as if she knew Avrianna were looking at her through the peephole.

Avrianna wasn't in the mood for company, but she opened the door anyway.

"Hey, Déjà."

Déjà eyed the glass in Avrianna's hand. "Your day that good?"

The single ice cube clinked in the glass when Avrianna raised it. "Yup." She widened the door to let Déjà enter. "Do you want one?"

"No, thank you." Déjà plopped onto the couch. "It must suck that alcohol doesn't do anything for you."

"Yeah, well, I appreciate the taste." Avrianna lowered onto her chair. "It's either this or wail on a punching bag, but I don't have one and Light-Year Gym evoked my membership when I accidentally broke an exercise machine." She paused, considered the glass in her hand. "Actually, they didn't ban me until I broke the second one."

Déjà's dark brow lifted. "You broke exercise equipment? How?"

Avrianna gave an innocent smile. "I outran a treadmill. Fried it. And then I snapped an all-in-one home gym system. In several places."

"Damn."

"Yeah."

"You should get your own equipment and make a home gym."

"I'd probably have to replace everything weekly." She shook her head. "It's okay. I'll run my anger off later." She liked to run at night, when no one could see her, especially if her anger had her running so fast that she blurred.

"Grandy called. She said she saw you on the news

at a crime scene where some dude was killed by a sniper. She said you had blood on your face."

Avrianna sipped her bourbon. "Not my blood."

"I figured that."

Sighing, Avrianna set her glass to the side. "I was right there. A foot away from him. And then…and then he was no more."

"I'm sorry."

She shook her head. "Let's talk about something else. How is it at the museum?"

"Fine." Déjà shrugged. "I'm still not able to acquire art for it. I've been doing some freelance work, though. I've helped a couple of artists put on shows. They were fun. You know…I invited you to both showings."

Avrianna winced. "I know. I'm sorry. I couldn't get away from work. And…I don't think the artists would've wanted me there, anyway. I would've ruined their shows."

"That's not true."

Avrianna looked her in the eye. "Please. I'm like the plague. If I had showed up, guests would've up and left, and we both know it."

Déjà broke eye contact, revealing she did, indeed, know it.

"I saw the pictures you posted of both, though. They looked successful."

"They were."

Avrianna smiled. "The museum may not be panning out how you had hoped, but you're doing something right working with local artists and planning their events. And, one day, if you find an artist who likes neon green, I'll show up to support you. I'll even wear a dress."

Déjà's eyes widened. "Okay. Now I'm going to make that happen."

Avrianna laughed.

"You laugh now, but just you watch. I'll have the last laugh, and I'm going to get a ton of pictures of you as proof to show Grandy and Sassy and all the girls."

The smile vanished from Avrianna's face. "That's cruel."

Déjà did get the last laugh. At least that night.

After Déjà left and Avrianna called Veena to check in, she changed out of her jeans, swapping them for black cotton workout pants. Then she stripped out of her top, leaving on only her sports bra.

With the darkness of the night concealing her, her sneakers pounded on the asphalt. Rock music blared in her ears and encouraged her to run faster. The glimpses of Diz—electric green hair, an arched brow, and black eyeliner painted into a cat eye—dogged her steps, forcing her to pick up her speed. It wasn't so much that she felt Diz behind her, but rather in front of her.

She raced past streets, ignoring stop signs.

A step out of reach.

Her hands balled into fists. Power surged in her veins. A sheen of green light spread over her skin as she ran harder. Cars, trees, and mailboxes blurred past her. If someone were to look out a window, all they'd see was a streak of green blazing down the street. They'd know it was her, but that didn't stop her, didn't slow her.

The only thing that could was the vibration in her

pocket. She skid to a halt, tugged the earbuds out of her ears, and answered her phone.

"Detective Heavenborn."

"Detective, we've got the results back from dust fragments taken from the shoe prints. They tested positive for residue from alspir trees."

She tilted her head to the side. "Alspir trees?" Trees that twisted toward the sky in corkscrews; the only ones of their kind anywhere in the universe.

"That's right."

There was only one place in New Vida where alspir trees grew, and the name of that forest was a slap in the face delivered by Diz herself. Predictable. How could they not have thought of it before?

Dizlock Forest.

"Does Chief Logan know? Has he asked the Justices for access to the satellite to view images of Dizlock Forest?" The Justices, seven neutral individuals appointed decades ago to make fair decisions regarding issues that could impact New Vida. If you wanted to do anything in New Vida—start corporations or open certain facilities, cut down trees or clear land—you needed their approval.

"He's doing that now," Chuck said. "Emergency meeting."

She nodded. "I'm on my way."

She ran back to her house, changed into fresh jeans and a black T-shirt, and rushed to the Aurora Police Department. When she arrived, Chief Logan was returning from his meeting with the Justices.

"Sir." She fell into step with him. "What did the Justices say?"

"They granted us access to the satellite to scan Dizlock Forest."

"Sir, one more thing. If a dwelling is found, I would like permission to go with SWAT to apprehend Diz."

Chief Logan halted. "You're not SWAT. You're a homicide detective."

"I know that, sir. I also know that Diz is my murder suspect, and I have weapons that not even SWAT has."

Chief Logan considered her. She met his eye straight-on. "Okay, but you have to follow Sergeant Chastain's orders."

"Of course."

"I will let Sergeant Chastain know you'll be assisting them."

"Thank you, sir."

She rushed to the tech lab where imaging and thermal scans of Dizock Forest using the satellite had just gotten underway. The scans broke the forest into acres and then into smaller square footage. She paced back and forth from each screen. As she passed them, she searched each one for a blimp of a heat signature, for anything that shouldn't be there. She was passing one of the middle screens when her eye caught something. Her feet rooted in place. She spun around, fully facing the screen.

"Go back on this one. I saw something."

The image inched back, fraction by fraction.

A black shape peeked out from thick tree canopies. It was a corner of a larger object, possibly rectangular.

She pointed. "There."

The image pixelated as it zoomed in.

She eyed the image and nodded. "It's a cabin."

A cabin on protected land where building anything, even a shed, was prohibited. Diz had built a safe haven in the one place no one would think to look for her.

"We found her."

Avrianna strapped on a bulletproof vest for appearances. No one, not even Chuck, knew she was bulletproof, and she intended to keep it that way. She was buckling the strap to her helmet under her chin when Chuck came up to her, wearing a bulletproof vest and helmet, too.

"What are you doing here?" she asked.

"I got clearance from Chief Logan to back up my partner while she tags along with SWAT to an assassin's secret lodgings." He lowered his voice. "What I didn't say was that I think my partner is homicidal and wants to kill said assassin."

Avrianna fixed her radio to her belt. "I'm not homicidal."

"Look me in the eye and say that."

Her gaze flicked up to his. She glared at him, but she didn't speak.

"That's what I thought."

Whatever. She shoved her firearm into its holster after checking the cartridge.

"Load up," Sergeant Chastain shouted.

Avrianna and Chuck hopped into the back of a SWAT van. They rode in silence to the edge of Dizlock Forest before disembarking and trekking on foot for two miles. Every step they took was a cautious one.

Their eyes were peeled for trip wires, mines, and sensors that'd tip Diz off to their approach, even sticks that could snap underfoot.

The cabin came into view.

SWAT spread out, surrounding the cabin, caging in Diz so she wouldn't have anywhere to escape. Avrianna hung back behind a tree with Chuck and Sergeant Chastain. Everyone waited for the sergeant's word.

"In position," came the voice of a SWAT officer on the other side of the cabin.

Sergeant Chastain raised his radio to his lips. "Everyone, move in."

SWAT advanced from all sides, with Avrianna among them. She held her gun in front of her and followed behind the heavily-armed and heavily-armored SWAT members. Chuck was close at her side.

She watched SWAT close in on the door to the cabin and picked up her pace, wanting to have their backs. She sprinted a few yards ahead, out into a small clearing between the cabin and spiraling trees. The closer Avrianna got to the cabin, the more a strange tingling sensation developed at the back of her head, in her brain stem.

She pulled to a stop.

Chuck glanced over his shoulder and stopped, too. "What's wrong?"

She shook her head, not sure, but the hairs on the back of her neck were at attention, and that was never a good thing. Uneasy, she called upon her powers. Her eyes warmed as they brightened. She eyed the cabin while her vision cut through the layers, allowing her to see through the door. One by one, like an X-ray slicing through skin and muscle to the bones buried deep within, she was able to see past every interior wall. She scanned the cabin. Kitchen appliances. A fireplace. A bed. A dresser. A small couch. A coffee table. Her vision zeroed in on the coffee table and what sat atop it. A box. No, not a box. It was metallic. There were wires. And a timer.

Her eyes widened. "There's a bomb."

Instantly, her powers snapped off.

SWAT officers were feet away from the porch.

Thinking of their safety, she yanked her radio from her belt, compressed the button, and shouted, "Pull back! Pull back now!"

"What are you doing?" Sergeant Chastain roared. "You don't have the authority to tell my men to pull back."

"There's a bomb," she shouted.

"You can't know that."

She rounded on him. Fury had her eyes searing. Green beams of light reflected off his helmet. "Yes, I do. Pull your men back now."

He lifted his radio, and while peering right into her eyes, he said, "Continue." Then to Avrianna he said, "I'm writing you up for insubordination!"

"Do it," she snarled.

Then she launched toward the cabin and the SWAT officers unknowingly approaching their deaths because they were following orders. The wrong orders.

"Stop! There's a bomb! St—"

The cabin exploded.

Glass, wood, and bricks shot out in every direction with rolling flames. The force of it lifted Avrianna off her feet. In mid-air, she thrust her hands toward the explosion, hoping to contain it. Green light poured from her palms and formed a wall. The wall slammed into the blast directly in front of her. She pushed all of her strength into it to keep the flames back. The green shield had just reached the edges of the cabin when gravity wrapped around her and she started to fall. Her body slammed into the ground. The back of her helmet bounced off a rock. The moment of impact knocked the breath from her lungs and had her dropping the shield.

She sat up quickly to see the entire cabin a burning inferno.

Screams at the back had her blood running cold. They were the screams of SWAT officers who had been advancing from behind; her efforts to contain the blast hadn't helped them.

She sprang to her feet and raced around the side of the cabin. As soon as she rounded the corner, her feet skid to a stop.

Several officers were covered in flames, flailing their arms, running around frantically in an effort to escape the flames that ate away at their uniforms and flesh.

She launched into action.

When her right foot hit the ground, green flames burst around her boot. Her left foot struck the ground, and green flames encircled it, too. Those flames snaked up her shins, braiding around each other. Over her knees and up her thighs. Around her hips. With each stride, the flames crawled up her body. They looped around her stomach, back, and chest. Swirled about her neck like a scarf. Washed over her head like an ocean wave. Twisted down her arms and swallowed her fists. Every step she took left behind a footprint of green flames in the dry leaves and green grass. She raced toward the officers, burning from head to toe in flames.

She reached the closest officer, whose back was a cape of flames as they ran, desperate and consumed with fear. The officer spun around in a circle. She caught their shoulders. "I've got you!"

The orange and yellow flames feasting upon their back flowed to her hands and up her arms, joining with the harmless green flames that surrounded her. As soon as the flames extinguished from the officer's uniform, she released their shoulders and whirled around to search for the next one.

An officer ran blindly—a human torch.

She sprang forward. One, two, three large strides, and then she hurled her body through the air. She collided into the officer and wrapped her arms around them. As the two of them fell, the flames igniting the officer were attracted to her fire. The flames completely left the officer's body in favor of her fiery cocoon.

They hit the ground.

"You're okay," she said, although she didn't know that for sure, and jumped to her feet.

A few yards away, another officer lay on the ground. Burning.

She raced to them and slid over the ground. At their side, she plunged her hands into the flames. Her palms flattened to their back.

"Come on, come on," she hissed while her powers sucked up the flames.

A scream had Avrianna turning her head to see an

officer swatting at the flames on their legs that were spreading higher and higher.

She reached an arm out toward them, palm out, and called the flames toward her. Starting from their boots, the flames spiraled out, stretched through the air, and connected with the center of her palm. Flames continued to pour into her aura from both the officer lying face-down at her side and the officer whose legs had been burning.

The last flicker of fire from the officer a distance away hopped off the tip of their boots and zipped toward Avrianna. When it touched her fire, becoming green, too, the final flame from the officer beside her also went out.

She dropped backward.

Her shield of protective fire vanished in soft puff of smoke.

Breathing hard, she looked at the officer at her feet. They were burned over most of their body. Silent. Unmoving. She didn't think they were alive.

Her hands were shaking when she searched for her radio, but she must've dropped it because it wasn't there. "Medic," she whispered. "We need a medic."

They needed four medics. More, even.

But she didn't have to request them, because there was already a flurry of activity around her. SWAT officers surrounded their fallen comrades. A medic joined Avrianna, checked the officer, met Avrianna's eye, and shook their head.

Just like that, there was nothing left to do.

The medic left.

Avrianna got to her feet, staggered backward.

She peered around as the other three officers were bundled up in sterile burn blankets and transitioned onto stretchers. One was already gone. Another didn't look likely to make it. Two might have a chance. But that was not good enough. This could've been avoided.

She searched for Sergeant Chastain among the chaos. He stood off to the side, shouting orders. She marched over to him. He met her eye when she planted herself right in front of him. In a low voice, she said, "I'll be telling the chief about this. If I have to, I'll tell the Justices, myself."

"Are you threatening me, Detective?"

She didn't blink. "I'm threatening your career."

With that, she spun on her heel.

She didn't know if what she had to say about Sergeant Chastain would result in his firing or even a suspension or just a slap on the wrist or, more likely, nothing at all, but she'd try. For those four officers, she'd try.

Chuck hurried over to her. "Avrianna!" He forced her to a stop. "Your helmet is cracked." He unclipped the buckle beneath her chin and removed the helmet from her head.

Sure enough, a crack stretched from the base of the helmet to the top. She took it from him. "I'm fine." She took a step but stopped when someone called out to her.

"Detective!"

She turned to see a SWAT officer jogging toward her. Instinctively, she braced for the verbal attack of an officer coming to defend their sergeant.

"Detective." He stopped in front of her. "I'm team leader of one part of this platoon. I told my team to standdown after I heard your call on the radio. I was the only team leader to do so. I saved my team because of you, so I want to thank you for what you did." He glanced over his shoulder. "I also want to tell you that Sergeant Chastain made a bad call."

She studied the leader in front of her. "What's your name?"

"Sam."

She nodded. "Good luck, Sam."

He started to leave but turned back. "For the record, whenever my team gets a call, you're more than welcome to join us."

She smiled. "I appreciate that."

When Avrianna was a police officer, considering her next steps, she had contemplated joining SWAT, but when the opportunity to become a homicide detective came, she'd taken it because she'd felt there was a bigger need to bring peace to victims and to their loved ones. Now, she wondered if she'd made the wrong decision. After all, she was bulletproof. For all she knew, indestructible. She could've put that to good use as a SWAT officer. She could have these men and women's backs every single day.

If only she could do it all.

7

Cat the Assassin

Avrianna stayed behind, after the cabin burned completely down and the flames snuffed out. While crime scene investigators canvased the charred remains, she scanned the ruins from several feet away. Nothing remained. Nothing had survived. All the furniture had been reduced to heaps of charcoal. The appliances were metal husks barely holding together. Not even the fireplace stood. The explosion had ripped it apart, brick by brick. The investigators wouldn't be able to find a thing in the wreckage. No clue or shred of evidence that Diz had been there. Except for the fact that someone had planted that bomb for them.

Rage swarmed in Avrianna like magma about to erupt. Diz had laid the perfect trap for them, the promise of capturing her inside a secluded cabin. And she set the trap with a bomb that could've killed four SWAT teams, nearly half their platoon. Avrianna had received the word that one of the three SWAT officers who had been evacuated to the hospital had passed away. Diz was responsible for killing two civilians and two officers. On Avrianna's watch. That burned her with rage.

On. Her. Watch.

Avrianna would never forgive herself for not catching Diz sooner.

Hands in fists, she about-faced, vowing to make Diz pay.

Back at the department, Avrianna sat behind her desk, back rigid, shoulders tensed, jaw clenched. She needed a way to get close to Diz. Except, Diz was an elusive assassin. No one knew who she was. No one had ever laid eyes on her. Not even the people who paid her millions to kill knew who she really was. She could be anyone. The closest anyone had ever gotten to her were her victims, separated by a spiral bullet, a moment from death. Although her victims never had a chance, they were connected to Diz, whether they wanted to be or not.

Avrianna sat up straighter.

That connection was her way in, but not in the usual sense, not from a detective's standpoint using a victim to hunt down the killer, or even using Diz's target to try to catch her before it was too late, as it had been for Christopher Edwards.

No. Avrianna needed to target Diz's target, too. She needed to become an assassin, competing for the same mark.

She got up, went over to Chuck's desk across from hers, and rapped on it with her knuckles. "I have an idea. Follow me."

Without another word, she headed straight for Chief Logan's office.

"Your idea involves the chief?" Chuck asked from behind.

"His permission."

"His per—" Chuck pulled up short. "Avrianna, what are you thinking?"

"You'll see."

She didn't stop to see if Chuck still followed her but knocked on Chief Logan's door. His brisk reply told her to come in. She opened the door and stood at attention in front of a large, cluttered desk where Chief Logan lounged in a leather swivel chair.

Chuck stepped up beside her.

Chief Logan studied them. "What can I do for you, detectives?"

Avrianna didn't dally. "Sir, I have an idea for how we can catch Diz."

Chief Logan laid down his pen. "I'm all ears."

"We use the dark web where assassins claim their marks. We wait for Diz to pick her next target, and when she calls dibs, we do the same, ensuring that we'll be in the exact same place as her, at the exact same moment, hunting the same target. Except, for us, that's her."

"For this to work, we'd need one member of our team to go undercover as an assassin."

"Yes, we would, and I'm hoping that you'll agree to let me do that."

Chuck rounded on her. "What?"

"I see you didn't run this by your partner first," Chief Logan said.

"No, sir, I didn't. I got the idea a moment ago."

"Well, now we can see what he thinks of it. Chuck?"

Avrianna faced her partner.

He glanced at her briefly before addressing the chief. "Sir, I don't think it's a good idea. Avrianna is, understandably, enraged, but I'm afraid her motives aren't entirely innocent. I'm not sure what she'll do when she comes face to face with Diz."

Avrianna clenched her jaw. "I will do my job. Nothing has ever stopped me from doing my job and doing it right. My partner may not have faith in me—"

Chuck cut her off. "I don't have faith in you? I'm looking out for you."

She met his eye. "Then do that by having my back."

Like now.

She turned back to Chief Logan. "I am the safest option for this task, sir. We lost two SWAT officers already. We can't lose anyone else. Diz can't hurt me."

"So, what? You're immune to spiral bullets now?" Chuck asked.

Avrianna ignored that question, but inside she thought, *yes.*

She didn't break eye contact with the chief. "Sir, I can pass for an assassin."

"Now *that* I can believe," Chief Logan said.

"I will bring Diz down." She cast a quick glare at Chuck. "In handcuffs."

Chief Logan stared hard at Avrianna.

She waited for his verdict.

"Okay. You have my permission to go undercover to catch Diz. Do whatever is necessary."

"I will. Thank you, sir."

She led the way out of the chief's office and down the hall.

"Avrianna, hold it." Chuck caught her elbow and tugged her to a stop. "You really don't think I have faith in you?"

"You don't think I can take Diz down without what? Setting her aflame with green fire? Melting her with laser vision?" Which she didn't have.

"I've never treated you like you could do any of those things."

He was right; he never had, and it wasn't fair of her to accuse him of that now.

"Tell me the truth…" She pushed. "You don't think I can arrest her without hurting her…without making her pay for what she's done?"

"No, I don't."

Avrianna seethed inwardly.

"And not because of what you think. I believe that because *I* would want to make her pay. Every officer in the department wants to make her pay for the lives we've lost. And you are stronger than all of us combined, so it'd be easier for you to exact vengeance on her. None of us would blame you for it, but that's not who you are, Avrianna."

No, it's not.

"Except, the look I've seen in your eye ever since Diz killed Christopher Edwards makes me wonder if you could do it. Kill her, I mean."

She nodded slowly. "So…you really don't have faith in me. Good to know."

She spun on her heel.

"Avrianna, wait. Come on!"

But she didn't turn back, because even though she knew she wasn't the kind of officer who would ever use her badge to exact vengeance on anyone, she didn't have much faith in herself to not kill Diz if the opportunity came.

Avrianna sat in front of the department's laptop that they had used to enter the dark net before. The IP address was protected from discovery, just as all the users who used the dark net protected theirs to evade capture. She waited by herself, watching the chatter, the hits as they came in, assassins snagging them, bragging about their kills, and claiming their money. For hours she looked over the symbols as they scrolled across the screen. Was Diz sitting in her hiding place and watching the same exchanges unfold, patiently waiting for a hit worth accepting?

Avrianna could only hope.

She ate lunch in front of that laptop. And dinner. She even brought the laptop home to monitor the feed after everyone had clocked out and gone home themselves. Lying on her couch, with the laptop resting on a pillow, she leaned her head back and kept an eye on the comments, although the dark net was pretty dead tonight.

Pun intended.

She had been on stakeouts before and could pull all-nighters while working a case, but staring at a black screen for hours upon hours was beginning to bore her. If only she weren't alone doing this. Chuck had stayed away the rest of the day. Veena was busy keeping an eye on Sassy and doing mother-daughter things. She couldn't call anyone else, because this was top-secret law enforcement business. Still, she wished she had someone. Someone to watch the screen with. Someone to talk to and joke with to pass the time. Someone...anyone...

The old pang of loneliness struck her. Yes, she had family and friends and Chuck, but she still felt so alone. She didn't have anyone to share her life with and likely never would. After all, who in their right mind would want to share their life with her? There was so much about her that was unknown, even to her. Scientists and reporters still hounded her. People stared and pointed everywhere she went. Law enforcement officers didn't trust her, not even ones in her own department. Whoever would be brave enough to link themselves with her would be just as hounded and targeted. Possibly despised, scrutinized, and disrespected.

How could she put someone through that?

She couldn't.

Wouldn't.

Her family and friends felt the brunt of that

already. She tried to shield them from it the best she could, and threatened anyone who dared to consider treating them horribly. Threaten her with malice, fine, but no one better do that to her loved ones.

Avrianna was feeling down from her train of thoughts when she noticed a kill order pop onto the screen.

Michael Jones, New Vida, $2 million.

Avrianna sat up straighter, with her fingers poised over the keyboard. Surely Diz wouldn't pass that up. Two million dollars was worth coming out of hiding for.

And Diz didn't disappoint.

—Diz: Consider it done.—

Avrianna quickly tapped out her reply.

—Cat: You'll have to beat me to it, Diz.—

—Diz: Who the hell are you?—

Avrianna smirked.

—Cat: I thought you could read. I'm Cat.—

—Diz: I've never seen you here before.—

—Cat: That's because I usually get my marks in

other ways.—

—Diz: I've never heard of you.—

—Cat: There's a reason for that.—

And because Avrianna wanted to make Diz mad…

—Cat: You, on the other hand, I have heard of, but not in a good way. You've gotten messy, Diz. They're saying your name all over my police scanners. Everyone in New Vida knows you're here.—

—Diz: I guess I missed my welcome party.—

Avrianna glared. Diz was cocky, but she wouldn't be for much longer.

—Cat: You think it's funny to put our entire operation at risk? If you're not careful, soon enough, no one will want to hire you.—

*—Diz: *yawn*—*

Avrianna squinted her eyes.

—Cat: I've got news for you, Diz. New Vida is my territory. You've already taken two marks that should've been mine. I'm not going to let that happen again.—

—Diz: Yeah, and how are you going to stop me?—

Wait and see, Avrianna whispered.

—*Cat: Let's play a game of Cat and Mouse. Let's see who can get to the mouse first. If it's me, I win. If it's you, you'll become the next mouse in my trap.*—

—*Diz: Not unless I get you with a spiral bullet first.*—

Avrianna smirked.

—*Cat: We'll see who the better assassin is.*—

—*Diz: Yes, we will.*—

Avrianna contacted Chief Logan with the name of the next target so investigators could gather as much information as they could about him. They needed to find him before Diz, and Avrianna needed to get to him before a spiral bullet could take his life. That was the trick, wasn't it? She needed to be faster than a speeding bullet from a professional killer's weapon. She wasn't Super Woman, but she damn well could catch a speeding bullet in the palm of her hand; she'd done it before.

At first light, Avrianna made a phone call.

"Hey, Evony, I know it's early, but I need your help."

Avrianna and Evony had known each other for years. Their friendship started one day when Veena introduced her to Evony. The moment Evony saw her, she declared, "That hair color is like a unicorn's mane." She grabbed a chunk of Avrianna's locks to inspect them closer and shared her deepest desire to cut Avrianna's hair one day.

That day still hadn't come, but Evony could help in another way.

"That's one way to wake me up." Evony's voice, although deep and slathered with sleep, was alert and intrigued. "What do you need?"

"A disguise."

"What kind of disguise are we talking about?"

"I need you to make me look like an assassin."

Evony gasped. "A sexy, kick-ass assassin?"

"Sure."

"Yes! How soon do you need it?"

Avrianna looked at the time on her phone—six o'clock in the morning. "Now."

"Only for you will I open my shop three hours early. I'll meet you there."

Avrianna drove to Evony's beauty shop located in a strip mall. Only one other car was in the usually-packed parking lot. Evony got out of a small teal-colored car. She wore skin-tight white pants, knee-high lace-up boots with three-inch heels, and a black long-sleeved shirt with a deep scoop neck that showed off her cleavage. Today she had styled her hair into a single long, thick braid. Her wide lips were painted a glossy nude to compliment her tawny skin tone. For having been pried out of bed extra early, Evony sure didn't look it. She looked amazing. Next to her, Avrianna felt rather frumpy in her jeans and plain black T-shirt and boots that needed to be shined.

Avrianna followed Evony into her shop. Rows of chairs for hairstyling, a beauty bar for cosmetics, sinks for hair washing, dryers with large hoods, and tables for nail art filled the space. In the back, there were changing rooms, mirrors, and a walk-in closet with wardrobe options for clients looking for a head-to-toe makeover. When it came to Evony's skill, most of clients wanted the full treatment because Evony was the best, and she owned the best beauty shop in all of New Vida.

"We definitely need to hide your hair." Evony looked her up and down. "With your complexion, you'd make an excellent redhead." She opened white, floor-to-ceiling double-doors to a set of cabinets. Inside, black mannequin heads were lined up neatly in rows atop several shelves. This cabinet was full of red wigs, from coppers and gingers to auburns and mahoganies. "Let's try this fiery auburn. There's more red in it that I think you can pull off."

Evony fixed a cap to Avrianna's head and then situated the auburn wig into place. "Oh. Nice." She brought some loose waves forward to drape over Avrianna's shoulders and frame her face. "Very pretty. Hot even." She winked thick lashes over dark brown eyes. "Take a look."

Avrianna faced a mirror. Seeing herself with rich, red hair was a shock. For the first time in her life, she appeared normal. Well, as normal as someone could get with eyes that nearly glowed even without the assistance of supernatural powers.

"Do you like it?"

"I do. What do you have in mind for my outfit?"

"I figured we'd go with something a little G.I. Jane." Evony disappeared into the walk-in closet and returned a moment later with a pair of dark gray camouflage pants, a black long-sleeve shirt with holes in the soft cotton, and polished combat boots.

Avrianna took the hangers and the boots by their tied strings. "I'm surprised. I wouldn't think you'd have these in your closet."

"I dress people of all styles, from glam to grunge."

"That's why you're the best."

"I love it when you flatter me."

Avrianna laughed. She dressed in the camouflage pants and long-sleeve shirt, and then laced up the boots.

"Try tucking in the shirt, and let's put on this belt." Evony passed her a leather belt with a silver dragon buckle on it.

Avrianna threaded the belt through the loops of her pants.

"Better. And this." Evony held out a metal choker that, too, looked like a dragon, with its tail in its mouth. "There. You look mysterious, hot, and badass. I'll do your makeup now. Have a seat." She showed Avrianna to a chair in front of a vanity brimming with cosmetics. The way she applied makeup, it was like an artist creating a masterpiece on a canvas. Indeed, Evony was an artist, and Avrianna's clean face was her canvas—for contouring, blush, eyeshadow, eyeliner, mascara, lipliner, and lipstick. Her hand was steady as she painted and drew and lined and dusted.

For the finishing touch, she added a fake tattoo below Avrianna's left eye of the ancient Egyptian vulture hieroglyphic, the symbol for the letter A—for

Avrianna.

When she finished, she turned Avrianna toward the mirror, and Avrianna couldn't recognize herself in her own reflection.

"What do you think?" Evony asked.

Avrianna nodded. "I think I'm ready to hunt an assassin."

Evony blinked. "Whoa. Really?"

Spiral Bullets

Avrianna hunkered low on a rooftop beneath a black sky speckled with stars of every color. The moon was waning, casting very little light. Good for her, and for Diz. A cool breeze ran its invisible fingers through her auburn wig. She kept her eyes peeled, scanning the nearby rooftops. On one of those rooftops, Diz would appear. On one of those rooftops, Diz would make her kill.

Down below was the business hub of Asteroid Bank, where Michael Jones worked. He worked until nine o'clock on Tuesdays, completing paperwork and counting money, or whatever it was that wealthy bankers did. As it turned out, Michael Jones owned Asteroid Bank, the first bank opened on New Vida. He reaped the financial benefits, making him a prime target for anyone looking for a payday. And someone wanted to cash in that check. Unfortunately for Michael, Diz had that check…in the barrel of a sniper's gun.

A movement on a rooftop to her right caught her attention. She turned her head to see a figure moving through shadows. The figure made its way across the rooftop, like a black cat slinking down a dark alleyway, pursuing a mouse. Avrianna's lips quirked. Except a bigger cat, with a higher vantage point, had that alley cat in its sights.

The figure stopped at the end of the roof and lifted an object onto the parapet.

Rather than risk being spotted by using her powers to see through the darkness, Avrianna lifted a pair of night vision goggles to her eyes.

"There you are," she whispered.

Diz took her place behind her weapon. A pale hand emerged. A thin finger curled around the trigger guard in preparation.

Avrianna brought her radio to her mouth and whispered, "Diz is here. She's on the rooftop of Orbit Technologies."

"Got her," came the voice of one of their trained snipers.

"Any sign of Michael Jones?"

"Not yet," Chuck's voice came out low through the speaker.

They hadn't talked since Avrianna had asked Chief

Logan for permission to go undercover. It was the longest they'd gone without speaking. Avrianna didn't like it, but she chose to put their partnership woes on the backburner. Taking down Diz was far more important at the moment. Afterward, they'd have time to patch things up.

"It's nine o'clock," Chuck said. "Michael should show up any minute now."

Avrianna eyed Diz. She wondered if Diz could sense she was being watched. If she could, she probably wouldn't stay out in the open. Unless she ignored the feeling on purpose, wrongly under the impression that the eyes she felt on her belonged to someone who she could defeat without any effort.

Funny, but while watching Diz staring through her sniper's scope with such dedication and focus, Avrianna couldn't help but notice their similarities. Avrianna stared through night vision goggles at Diz with dedication and focus. They both had patience to sit and wait for their prey. For Diz that was her kills. For Avrianna that was criminals. Both of their names were notorious throughout the universe, and they both were good at what they did. Except, Avrianna was better.

"Mr. Jones is walking outside," came their sniper's voice.

Avrianna perked up.

On the rooftop to her right, Diz's finger settled over the trigger.

"He's on the sidewalk."

Avrianna got to her feet.

"He's making his way across the parking lot."

Avrianna backed up several feet.

"He's nearing his vehicle. Detective, what's your order?"

"Avrianna, what are waiting for?" Chuck asked. "We can take her down."

Avrianna rocked back on her heels. "No," she said to no one but herself and the wind. "I can." Her eyes blazed to life with her powers, and she launched into action.

She ran toward the parapet. A few feet away, she flipped forward into a handstand on the edge of the parapet and shoved off it. With her powers enhancing her hearing, she heard Diz's finger pin the trigger and the gun eject a bullet. She rotated in the air, reached out her arm, and caught the speeding bullet in the palm of her hand. The wind whistled in her ears as she fell to the low rooftop of the adjacent building. Her boots punched the concrete parapet, and she twisted around to look up at Diz.

She held the spiral bullet, perfectly intact, in the air between her thumb and index finger. A smile meant to taunt stretched her lips.

Diz swung her rifle in Avrianna's direction. The assassin didn't wait a second before firing off a bullet.

Avrianna shot forward.

The bullet sailed behind her, an inch from her spine.

She sprinted along the parapet, narrowly missing each bullet Diz sent her way. Her gaze latched onto a fire escape on the side of Diz's building. She angled her body, positioned her foot on the edge of the parapet, and pushed off it. A second later, she collided into the fire escape. Her hands gripped the rusted metal, and she locked her leg around the ladder before she could fall. She ascended the fire escape quickly.

When she reached the top, her eye connected with Diz's through the sniper scope. The impact of a bullet hitting her in the middle of her chest made her flinch. The sound of metal on concrete met her ears. She looked down at the crumpled spiral bullet. The corner of her mouth tilted upward. Her gaze flicked back to Diz. Smirking, she straightened, stepped onto the parapet, and then hopped onto the rooftop.

The woman in front of her was a full head shorter than Avrianna. She wore skin-tight leather from neck to ankle. Black lined her eyes and stretched toward her temples. Her hair was sleek black with thick neon green highlights. Her lips were a soft coral. She could be any woman who liked the punk look. Except, she wasn't just any woman. She was a murderer who hid behind a sniper's gun.

Diz lowered her weapon. "You're not an assassin. You're *her*."

Avrianna took a step. "Her who? Go on." Another step. "Say it. Who am I?"

"Avrianna Heavenborn."

"You're not wrong." She let her hands erupt with neon orbs.

"So, you're here to arrest me?"

"I'm here to arrest you in whatever means."

Diz dropped her gun and removed two long silver spiral daggers from behind her back. "You'll have to kill me."

Avrianna's eyes brightened. "I can do that."

Diz yanked her arm back and threw a dagger.

Avrianna caught it.

The tip poked a hole through her cotton T-shirt.

Her grip tightened. Green flames encircled her hand and feasted on the dagger. It melted into a stream that puddled at her feet.

"If you want to stop me, you'll have to try harder than that."

She ran at Diz.

In a few feet, she tackled Diz to the ground. The two of them rolled over each other, their limbs tangled, elbows and knees jabbed, bruising. Diz managed to get her remaining spiral dagger between their bodies, and she shoved it into Avrianna's stomach.

Eyes wide, Avrianna gasped.

Diz leered. "That wasn't so hard, after all."

Avrianna's eyes fell into slits. Her mouth closed into a sneer. "So gullible." Her gaze shifted to her stomach, drawing Diz's eye. In the center of her stomach, a neon green whirlpool of light had formed, and the spiral dagger had sunk into it, causing it to melt and leaving her organs unscathed.

"You're out of weapons now, Diz."

"No, I'm not." Diz slipped brass knuckles with spiral points onto her fingers.

A snort left Avrianna. If Diz wanted to fight her fist to fist, then they'd fight.

Fist to fist.

Diz swung out.

Avrianna tilted backward.

Diz's brass knuckles slipped past Avrianna's chin by mere centimeters.

Each move Diz made to land a punch, Avrianna

countered effortlessly. She spun and dipped, twisted and pivoted, twirled and dodged. Her feet danced on the concrete, her body flowed. It was a dance. A dance between two lethal women.

Diz tried twice as hard, twice as frustrated to hit Avrianna, and expended her energy twice as fast. When she stumbled and wobbled, weak and off balance, Avrianna thrust her fist into a fierce upper cut. Her knuckles plowed into Diz's chin. The force of the impact had Diz flying into the air, flipping head over feet. She slammed into the rooftop on the other side of the building.

Groaning, Diz got to her knees.

In the blink of an eye, Avrianna was behind her. She wrapped her arms around Diz's neck and applied pressure to Diz's throat.

Diz seethed.

A voice in Avrianna's head told her to kill Diz. Take Diz out so she wouldn't be able to kill another person, so there wouldn't ever be the chance of Diz escaping. She could do it so easily. She positioned her hands around Diz's head. With just a twist, Diz could fall down dead. Never again would she be a threat to anyone, anywhere in the universe.

Do it.

Her grip contracted.

Kill her.

Her eyes blazed.

Do it!

Avrianna let out a scream as she battled with the urge to eliminate an assassin who had killed countless people out of greed.

DO IT! DO IT! DO IT!

With the war waging inside, she released her powers. When Diz fell unconscious, Avrianna let her fall from her arms to the rooftop floor.

She dropped to her knees, panting. How close she had come to taking someone's life shook her to her core. It wouldn't have been out of self-defense or to save someone in immediate danger—since Avrianna had already eliminated Diz's threat to Michael Jones. It would've been out of hatred, anger, vengeance. If Avrianna had done that, she would've been crossing a line that she had vowed to never cross.

Hands shaking, she removed her handcuffs and shackled them around Diz's wrists. Then she lifted her radio to tell Chuck and the other officers that it was over.

"Diz has been apprehended," she said. "I repeat, Diz has been apprehended."

Epilogue

New Vida

S WAT circled Diz, weapons at-the-ready, while they escorted her into the police department where she'd be held before being transferred to New Vida Prison. Avrianna leaned against her car, watching it all unfold and making sure Diz didn't attempt escape. Part of her wanted to trail after them all the way to Diz's cell, but she told herself that SWAT had everything under control and could take it from here on out. She had to have faith in the rest of the department to contain Diz.

From a few feet away, Chuck stood back. She

could sense that he wanted to approach but didn't know what she'd do if he did. Sighing, she turned her head to look at him and waved her hand, signaling that it was safe for him to come closer.

His shoulders lowered instantly. His relief washed over her, leaving her swamped in a pool of guilt. She'd treated her partner, who had only been looking out for, horribly. From the very beginning, that was all he'd ever done. She didn't like having to admit she was wrong, but she did know that when she did wrong, it was her responsibility to set things right. And Chuck deserved that.

He stepped up beside her and faced the department as the doors closed behind Diz and her armed escorts. "Good job, kid."

"Thanks." She shifted toward him. "I'm sorry."

His brows bunched together. "For what?"

"For accusing you of not having my back. You were right about everything. I was taking Diz and everything she'd done too personally and wanted to make her pay." She peered at the starry sky and took a deep breath. "Up there. On the rooftop. I almost killed her. I *could* have killed her." She met Chuck's eye. "I wanted to. Part of me needed to. It would've been so easy. Fast."

"So, why didn't you?"

"Because that's not why I went into law enforcement. That's not what will help New Vida. And…that's not me."

Chuck nodded. "When I said those things, it wasn't because I was believing the worst in you. I have always known what a great cop you are. I was worried, though.”

“I know. I know you were. I’m sorry for causing you to worry.”

“And I’m sorry for making you think I didn’t trust you or have your back.”

“Those thoughts were all my doing. Not yours. You have had my back from day one. Minute one. I am honored to have you for a partner.” She glanced at her feet. Her heart told her to tell him what he meant to her as a father figure, but the words got stuck in her throat. Sharing her feelings was tough for her, but one day she’d tell him.

“One thing, though,” he said. “Next time, don’t keep me out of the loop, especially if you want to do something as crazy as pretending you’re an assassin.”

She laughed. “Deal, but you have to admit, I make a pretty good one.”

He scanned her from boots to wig. “If you ever go rogue, you’d be the assassin of all assassins.”

“You’re probably right about that. Luckily, that’s not me, either.” She held up a finger. “Now, assassinate assassins, that I could do.”

“You’d wipe out the entire dark web of assassins in no time.”

She grinned. “Now wouldn’t that be fun?”

Cosmic Killer

Chrys Fey

Rookie

Six Years Ago

Every rookie is eventually called to the scene of someone's murder, and it's not something they ever forget.

Avrianna parked her marked car in front of two-story home with a picket fence. The mailbox's red flag was sticking up, waiting to attract the mailperson so its contents could be sent off. Along the road and driveway, the lawn was edged to perfection. A child's bike lay on its side in the grass. She took in all these details on her way to the door. And more. Details that not many people would pick up on, like the brown mark on the house's stucco where a wasp nest had once been, the faded chalk stick family on the concrete, a yellow golf ball nestled in red mulch beneath a patch of daffodils, blending in with fallen yellow petals.

Ever since Avrianna was a child, she'd learned to notice what others didn't, what others would overlook or ignore. She had to. Deciphering what could be a threat became a necessity early on when people wanted to hurt her—experiment, torture, taunt. And she needed to know what was safe. What could be used as a weapon? Pretty much anything. Even that yellow golf ball would be lethal in her hands. A mind like that helped her with her job as an officer for the Aurora Police Department in New Vida, a planet lightyears from earth but joined to earth by a portal acting like an umbilical cord. The Veil, discovered in the Grand Canyon, was how New Vida's existence became known, how New Vida became exploited, how New Vida was now a place that required law enforcement.

On her way to the front door, Avrianna walked alone. She didn't have a partner, as all rookies usually did. No one had wanted to be saddled with a freak who could burst into green flames and melt metal with her hands. Officers had protested against her hiring. Several quit. But because of her outstanding scores and record, she was given the opportunity to join the force and try to help her home. Except she had to do it alone.

Fine. She preferred it that way. She certainly didn't need anyone to protect her.

In her starched unfirm, with her badge on her chest and her firearm at her hip, she knocked on the white door. It opened to a man wearing gray sweatpants and white sleeveless shirt with a shaved head. Tears reflected in his brown eyes, but even through those tears, Avrianna detected a shift upon seeing her. His eyelids twitched. His jaw flexed.

"They sent *you*? Is this a joke? My wife was murdered in our bed and they sent not only a rookie but a cast out among her own?"

She wouldn't let this man's words get to her; she had a job to do. "Are you Dee Underhill?"

"I am."

"And you found your wife, Sally Underhill?"

"I did."

"May I come in?"

He scanned her from her silvery-blonde hair slicked into a neat bun to her shined black boots. No, he wasn't objecting to her appearance. Just to her.

"I'm here to help. Let me do my job."

He sighed and widened the door for her to enter.

As she passed him, she caught the smell of antibacterial soap. Her gaze flicked down to his hands. Clean. Trimmed nails. A silver wedding band. She activated her powers for the briefest of moments, using her vision like a microscope and blacklight at once. Droplets of water along the silver band from freshly washed hands.

Dee hadn't noticed the use of her powers.

She looked toward the living room. Schoolwork lay on the coffee table with the name Chadwick Underhill scrawled across the top.

Next to the door stood a white dresser with family portraits chronicling a child's growth. In each photo, Dee towered next to a woman with blonde hair, who sat in a chair. First, she held their son on her lap, but soon he became too big and he took the place on the other side of her, mimicking dad. Beside the most recent photo was a bundle of keys.

"How old is your son?"

"Twelve."

"Is he home?"

"Sleeping over at a friend's house."

For the better.

"Is your bedroom upstairs?"

He started toward the stairs.

"Sir, I need you to stay downstairs. I need to preserve the crime scene."

"I've already been in the bedroom."

"And possibly had contaminated it." Or changed it in some other way that'd impact their investigation. She couldn't allow him to do more. "Stay downstairs."

"She's dead!"

His shout made her jerk.

"What the fuck do you expect to do now, huh? She's dead! You're too late."

She shook her head. "No, I'm not."

He stared.

"I'm not too late to find out who did this. I'm too late to bring her justice. I'm just in time. Now you need to let me do my job. Please stay downstairs."

Tears leaked from his eyes, and he lifted his hand, indicating for her to go on.

"Which room is it?"

"Second on the right." His voice was choked.

As he turned away, he swiped a lone tear from his cheek.

Being careful to walk in a straight line and not touch anything, she made her way up the stairs. First, she passed one room on the right. A peak inside revealed an office. A room on the left was set up as a guest room.

The second door to the right was open. She glanced toward the door directly across from it where light poured out—a bathroom. The sink basin was wet from recent use, and a bottle of orange antibacterial soap sat beside the faucet. It's smell still scented the air, the same scent she'd detected on Dee. A suit jacket and pants hung on a hanger on the door.

Dee had told dispatch that he'd come home and found his wife dead in their bed. Except, he was in clothing meant for relaxation and sleep, his suit already off, his hands washed. That didn't indicate he'd come home and found his wife immediately. He'd had time. Time to change. Time to clean up. Possibly time to kill. Time to ruin evidence.

She peered farther down the hall at a door with a sign posted on it announcing the owner of that room belonged to one individual and one individual alone— Chadwick. A boy who'd just lost his mother and didn't even know it yet.

She stepped into the second bedroom on the right and flinched to a stop.

Sally was sprawled out on one side of the bed with her throat slit. Blood soaked her pillow and the bed beneath her shoulders.

"Fuck."

There was no doubt about it; Sally was dead. Murdered.

Avrianna lifted her radio and asked dispatch to send crime scene right away.

After getting confirmation, she walked, one foot in front of the other, to the side of the bed to get a closer look. The slit in Sally's throat didn't run from ear to ear but sliced through a few inches below her chin. That wound told Avrianna two things. One, the killer hadn't stood where she'd stood in order to take Sally's life, because if they had, they would've had a better reach and that line would've stretched farther. And two, the killer had been on top of her, possibly holding her down, limiting their range of motion.

Her gaze shifted lower.

Sally wore a red nightgown. One strap was pulled down below her right breast. The hem was bunched around her hips, exposing her.

The bed next to Sally was rumpled. The pillow angled, the bedsheet folded back. Someone had very clearly been on that side of the bed.

Avrianna called upon her powers. Her eyes warmed, and bright green light lit up the room. Using her powers, she scanned Sally from head to foot and paused when she noticed what she'd feared—streaks of semen on the inside of her thighs.

She sucked in a breath and snapped off her powers.

Someone'd had sex with Sally moments before she'd been murdered.

Maybe even moments before they'd killed her themselves.

Dee claimed to have only arrived.

Arrived and found his wife dead.

More disturbingly, Sally's eyes were wide open.

She'd looked her killer in the eye. She didn't appear to have fought. Her body was in a relaxed position, likely sedate from the sex she'd engaged in. The bed didn't appear thrashed in, except perhaps from the throes of passion. Even her hair appeared mussed from sex and not danger. She hadn't felt threatened, revealing the possibility that the person who she'd had sex with had ended her life, maybe right after she'd come. Had he kissed her before he'd done it? Had he still been inside her? Details Avrianna hoped she'd never now.

Turning carefully, she followed her footsteps back to the foot of the bed. From there, she searched the room. Another suit—jacket and pants—lay in a rumpled heap on the opposite side of the bed from Sally, presumably Dee's side. She approached the clothing and squatted down to examine the jacket's visible tag. A custom-made suit with Dee's name stitched on the inside. The pants' legs were stretched out on the carpet. Perhaps discarded by Dee in a rush to make love with his wife.

A peek in the master bathroom showed an uncapped bottle of perfume. Used to entice her husband to spend some time with her in bed after a long day at work?

Avrianna stepped back out into the hall and paused at the threshold to the guest bathroom. The tag on the inside of the jacket was visible and identical to the one on the floor in the bedroom. Another custom-made suit for the man of the house.

Downstairs, she found Dee sitting on the couch, clasping his hands. "Mr. Underhill, can you describe to me what you did when you got home?"

He ran his hands over his face. "Unlocked the door, put my keys down"—he pointed toward the white dresser—"I went upstairs, took a leak in the guest bathroom, changed out of my work clothes into this"—he waved his hands in front of himself—"then I walked into the bedroom I share with my wife and found her dead. There was so much blood. I didn't know what to do. I ran down here and called the cops. And they sent me a fucking rookie."

She let that last bit go. "Did you wash your hands?"

"After I took a piss? Yes, I washed my hands. Would you rather men touched their dicks to use the bathroom and not wash their hands?"

She let that slide, too. "How far into your bedroom did you go?"

"I don't know. Maybe four steps before I saw all the blood and froze."

"And you didn't touch her?"

"No. As I said, I saw her and ran down here."

"What about the suit on the floor by the bed?"

His brows lowered. "What suit? I told you I changed in the bathroom."

"Why the guest bathroom and not the master bath?"

"Because I get home late and don't want to wake Sally."

Present tense. As if Sally were still alive.

"Was anyone else here when you arrived?"

"No. Whoever did this was long gone."

A knock at the front door sounded before Avrianna could ask any more questions.

She put up a hand to still Dee when he started to rise. "That's probably crime scene. Stay here." Hand resting on her firearm, she opened the front door to members of the crime scene unit. One additional cop accompanied them.

While the cop stood guard near Dee, she headed upstairs with CSI. To one of them, she pointed to the bathroom. "Take a picture of the suit hanging on the door."

The investigator did as instructed.

"And the sink with the bottle of soap visible."

The investigator lowered their camera. "Why?"

"Because he'd washed his hands."

"How do you know?"

"Take a whiff."

The investigator inhaled.

"Smell the antibacterial soap?"

"Yes."

"He washed his hands. The smell is on him. Please take the picture."

The investigator snapped a couple of shots of the sink with the soap bottle.

In the bedroom, one investigator was photographing Sally's body as another placed markers for evidence. She indicated at the suit on the floor. "Mr. Underhill claims he changed out of his suit in the bathroom, but then there's this suit right here. Next to the crime scene, and the victim hadn't been alone in bed."

The investigator who'd taken the photos of the bathroom sink documented the suit on the floor with several photos at varying angles.

"There's an uncapped bottle of perfume in an otherwise pristine bathroom where everything is in its place, and there's semen on the inside of her thighs."

The investigators glanced at each other, passing on silent words. In their eyes, she could tell they also had the same assumption as she did—murder of a cheating spouse, a crime of passion. They'd likely seen it many times. This was Avrianna's first.

She peered back at the suit on the floor. Something on the sleeve caught her attention. It gleamed dark and wet in the fluorescent lighting. "Excuse me, could I have a pair of gloves?"

"Sure." The investigator reached into their kit and gave her a pair of blue latex gloves.

"Thank you." She wiggled her hands inside them and then squatted down beside that suit again. Gingerly, she picked up the jacket to inspect the sleeve. Something glistened. Several spots, in fact. On both sleeves and across the front. She dabbed a fingertip to one of the spots and pulled back to see red. "Blood." She twisted the jacket slightly so the other spots could catch the light. "Blood spray. He'd been wearing the jacket when he'd killed her. Bag this carefully."

She watched the investigator bag the jacket. Then she went downstairs. One look to the officer standing there had him removing his taser from the holster at his side, preparing in case Dee didn't want to cooperate.

She paused in front of Dee. "Mr. Underhill, can you stand please?"

He got to his feet. "What's going on?"

"Turn around and put your hands behind your back."

"You're fucking kidding me, right?"

She settled a hand on her taser and removed her cuffs with the other. "Do not resist. Turn around and put your hands behind your back."

"Fucking bitch." But he turned, and he put his hands behind him.

She restrained him one cuff at a time. "Dee Underhill, you're under arrest for the murder of your wife, Sally Underhill."

Dee let out a laugh.

"You have the right to remain silent…" She read him his full rights and led him to her squad car with the other officer following.

Before Dee ducked inside, he shot a glare. "You'll regret this."

She pushed on his shoulder. Once he was inside, she slammed the door. "Not likely," she said while making her way to the driver's side.

Dee didn't say anything else on the way to the police department where she handed him over officers to be booked. He didn't look over his shoulder, but she heard him say, "Remember what I said."

She figured she'd always remember him and her first murder scene, but she doubted she'd ever see him again.

"Officer Heavenborn."

She turned.

"Chief Logan would like to see you in his office."

"Thank you, sergeant."

She went straight to Chief Logan's office, expecting him to want a rundown on what had transpired at the crime scene before she'd arrested Dee.

The officers she passed sneered and scowled and edged away from her as if brushing elbows would give them her own personal brand of cooties.

At Chief Logan's office, she knocked on the door.

"Come in."

She opened the door.

Chief Logan sat behind a cluttered desk, holding a to-go cup coffee in one hand and a pen in the other. He had a slight paunch from sitting at a desk all day, and a balding spot in the middle of his scalp from too many years on the job.

"Ah, Officer." He waved her inside.

She stood at attention in front of his desk.

"You arrested Dee Underhill today for the murder of his wife."

"Yes, sir. I did, sir."

"Do you know who Dee Underhill is?"

"No, sir."

"He is a prominent business man. A gun manufacturer. Underhill & Co. His company is the top producer of guns in New Vida. And you arrested him."

"Sir, with all due respect, I would've arrested him even if I'd known who he was. All evidence pointed to him being the number one suspect in his wife's murder."

Chief Logan nodded. "And that is how I know you're a good cop. You can't be bought. A name or reputation won't make you back down and not do what is right." He leaned back in his swivel chair. "The crime scene investigators said you took charge of the crime scene, told them what pictures to take, noticed things they hadn't, and found the blood on Mr. Underhill's jacket."

She didn't move nor speak.

"Someone with that eye, that intuition shouldn't be a street cop. They should be a detective. And someone who can stomach that crime scene and put two-and-two together so quickly should be a *murder* detective. You walked off your first murder crime scene and got yourself a promotion."

She frowned. "I don't understand."

"I'm promoting you to detective."

Crystal Bullet

Six Years Later

"He escaped."

Avrianna stared at Chief Logan from her place in front of his desk. "I'm sorry, sir. Who escaped?"

"Dee Underhill escaped prison last night."

It was a name she hadn't heard in years, since Dee had been on trial, convicted of voluntary manslaughter, sentenced to life in prison.

She could sense Chuck, her homicide partner, eying her and her reaction, so she kept herself calm. "Wasn't he in maximum security?"

"He was."

"Theories?"

"None."

She frowned. "How is that possible?"

"He was last seen in his cell, and then he was gone. The prison went on lockdown when the guards realized he wasn't in his cell. They've searched every inch of the prison and its grounds, and they haven't found him. They viewed the security footage outside his cell, and no one had gone into his cell. The man vanished."

"He couldn't just go poof."

"Except all evidence supports he did. You arrested him. I thought you should know, and I want you and Chuck to investigate his disappearing act. This entire department is on the hunt for him, and I need to two of you to run point on this."

Avrianna nodded. "We'll do everything we can."

Chief Logan bowed his head. "Get to work."

Avrianna and Chuck left his office.

"You okay, kid?" Chuck asked.

She shrugged. "Peachy. A man who used to produce the most guns in our world and murdered his wife after having sex with her escaped prison without a trace. Yeah…I'm just peachy."

First, they visited New Vida Prison. Warden Mosh, with not so much as a strand of brown hair out of place, met them at the doors.

"Warden."

"Detectives."

Avrianna bowed her head. "May we view the security footage?"

"There's nothing on the security footage."

"We'd like to view it all the same."

Warden Mosh exhaled through his nose, hinting at annoyance. "This way." He spun on his heel.

Avrianna and Chuck followed.

"You make friends everywhere," Chuck whispered.

Avrianna spoke in a higher-pitched, falsely sweet, excited voice. "*Best* friends."

Chuck roared with laughter.

Warden Mosh looked back at them with a glare.

Avrianna only smiled.

In a room lined with security footage, Warden Most showed them to a screen.

Avrianna and Chuck sat in side-by-side chairs to watch the footage from the moment Dee was escorted to his cell after getting some fresh air to the moment the guard found him missing—twelve hours later. They sped up the timing, searching for any presence at that cell door. None. They kept an eye out for the camera getting covered or the feed transforming to static. Nothing.

But then Avrianna caught something.

"Wait." She snatched the computer mouse and dragged the marker backward.

The feed replayed.

Silence.

Stillness.

And then a black streak blurred across the screen.

"Did you see that?"

Chuck nodded. "Yeah."

She rewound it again.

That black streak moved from the right of the screen to the left, toward Dee's cell.

She watched the feed closely.

That black streak returned, now moving from left to right, away from Dee's cell. So quickly. There one second and then gone the next.

"What is that?"

Chuck shook his head. "Your guess is as good as mine."

They showed the footage to Warden Mosh, who waved a hand. "That's a fly. There's a lot of flies in that part of the building. We have a hard time getting rid of them. Sometimes they land on the camera lenses. They get into everything. A real nuisance."

Avrianna considered what she'd seen. That black streak could've been a fly darting back and forth, being a pesky little insect. On film, insects always looked like blurs and streaks, so it made sense.

"What do you think, kid?"

She shrugged. "Likely. The feed doesn't glitch. And his cell door stays closed. Let's keep watching."

They resumed the video.

When they reached the moment when the guard came to get Dee for his next dose of fresh air and discovered the cell empty, they paused it.

Avrianna sat back. "The door stays closed the entire time, and there were no sudden time jumps to indicate the footage had been tampered with. Unless a fly broke Dee out and he turned into a fly himself, there's nothing here."

"Then how the hell could he have gotten out?"

She lifted a hand and looked toward where Warden Mosh leaned against the wall, drinking an espresso from a tiny cup, with his pinky finger raised. "May we see Dee's cell?"

Mosh sighed. "This way."

He led them down halls and their checkpoints to maximum security.

In Dee's cell, there was a cot with a Bible resting on it and a crude toilet, which was secured to the wall. They checked the concrete walls and floor for holes, even scratches, but they'd turned up zilch. Dee hadn't even made marks on the walls to indicate the days, weeks, months, years he'd spent there. A photo of his wife and son was still taped to the wall beside his cot, where he probably gazed at it while lying there, regretting, pondering, hoping.

Avrianna stood in the middle of Dee's cell with no clue as to how Dee escaped. "I guess we won't be able to answer how he got out. We just have to find him."

Back at the department, she and Chuck joined a debriefing on the plans for the manhunt for Dee—news and radio bulletins, a scrolling message across all national television channels, front page news in print and on websites, facial recognition ready to alert them to the possibility of Dee's presence, and every officer on duty out on the streets searching for any glimpse of Dee. Everyone had to be a part of the search, including the public. With citizens on notice, they could have Dee in no time.

Except forty-eight hours later, there was no sign of Dee anywhere.

Worse, Avrianna and Chuck had gotten nowhere.

She stared off into space, considering the people they'd questioned and were surveilling—his son, his parents, close relatives, and known acquaintances from his days as a mass gun producer. Even if someone knew where Dee was, it was clear no one would volunteer that information willingly. Only someone on the inside would be able to get close enough to convince or trick that information from their lips.

She tapped her fingers on her desk. Maybe that was what it would take. Someone on the inside. Someone with a background in weapons.

Idea in mind, she snatched up a pen and began to sketch a drawing of woman with dark hair and bangs and a leg brace from ankle to knee.

She slid it over to Chuck.

"What's this?"

"That's Crystal. She's an expert in creating rare bullets. Bullets made from diamonds. She's my next disguise."

"Disguise for what?"

"To lure Dee out or…maybe I can get in wherever he may be."

After a moment, Chuck laid down the sketch. "I hate to say it, but it may be our only option." He met her eye. "Get to it, kid. It's the only plan we have."

Smiling, Avrianna hopped to her feet to visit Evony, the mastermind behind Avrianna's many disguises that had helped them close cases and catch bad guys.

Evony's beauty salon was packed, as it should be if you wanted the best service, the best products, the best looks. But whenever Avrianna stepped inside, Evony dropped everything, even stopping mid-shampoo for a client and getting one of her stylists to finish, in order to assist Avrianna with her outlandish requests that always delighted Evony. This time was no different. She handed a curling iron, still attached to a woman's hair, to the stylist next to her.

"Avrianna!"

And Avrianna was swept up in Evony's brown arms in a friendly hug. Not much of a hugger, Avrianna did her best to show it didn't bother her and that she was happy to see Evony, too, because she was. Evony was one of her best friends, and she hadn't seen Evony since she'd turned Avrianna into an assassin.

"Hey, I'm hoping you can help me with a new disguise."

"Of course, I can. Come on back."

In the back was her "laboratory" full of wigs, contacts, cosmetics, and clothing.

"What do you have in mind this time?"

Avrianna showed her the sketch.

"Hm. I have a wig just like this. I can hem any pant leg to go with the brace, but I'll have to send someone out find a brace somewhere. I don't have one."

Before Avrianna could open her mouth, Evony was back in the-sized shop, ordering one of her stylists to go to a medical shop to buy a medium leg brace. No questions asked. Just do it. Then she hustled back to Avrianna.

"What kind of outfit are you thinking of? You drew what looks like a corset." Evony grinned. "Please tell me I get to fit you into corsets." She tugged on a rolling rack. "I have dozens."

Sure enough, the rack was packed with every style of corset—from leather to lace to frilly and in every color.

"I actually *was* thinking of a corset. No one would ever look at a woman in a corset and guess that I'm her…or she's me…or whatever."

Evony waved her hand with a flourish at the rack. "Take your pick, honey."

Avrianna checked out the options. She'd never worn a corset in her life. So, she had no idea what she was looking for or what made a good corset, but when she spotted one covered in rhinestones, she lifted it off the rack. "This one. My disguise…her name is Crystal. She makes diamond bullets, and I have a feeling that she's the type who likes to make a statement."

"Yes, she does!" Evony took the rhinestone corset. "Okay. I'm seeing it. This corset with pleather pants." She plucked a pair of pleather pants off another rack without even looking at it. "Is she a heel or sneaker girl?"

"Ankle boots."

"Oh, sexy." Evony spun to a closet and flung open the doors. She selected black leather ankle boots. "We want that corset to shine, so the shoes need to support the look, not draw attention to them. Alright. Let's get you in this, and then I'll do your makeup."

Avrianna dressed behind a curtain. The pleather pants were skintight, and the corset

squeezed her A-cup breasts, giving them the appearance that they were bigger than they really were. She swept the curtain to the side. "What do you think?"

Evony gasped and laid a hand to her chest. "I think

everyone will want to bang you."

Avrianna grimaced. "Not the reaction I want."

"Or is it precisely the reaction Crystal would want?"

Evony had a point.

Avrianna sat so Evony could do her makeup—smoky eyes and a red lip.

"What color contacts were you thinking?"

"Dark brown."

Evony fetched a contact container, and Avrianna put them in. Her vibrant green eyes didn't even show through.

"You've mastered creating contacts for me."

"I've also been creating a line of jewelry for you with hidden cameras." She showed Avrianna a display of necklaces. "Do you think any of them will work?"

Avrianna studied each one. When she saw a silver cross, she pulled it off the display. Over the past two days, everyone they'd spoken to had said how religious Dee had become in prison. The Bible on his cot supported that. A cross could appeal to him, assure him that she was a friend, not a foe. "This one."

"Interesting. Okay." Evony hooked it at around Avrianna's neck. "And now the wig." She removed a black wig from a mannequin's head, fitted it onto Avrianna, and fussed with the bangs. "You look good with bangs, girl. Not many can truly pull it off, although everyone at some point wishes they could."

In the mirror, a woman she'd never seen before peered back at Avrianna. She didn't recognize herself, which was the goal. But even with her other disguises, she'd always been there, if you looked closely enough.

With Crystal, though, it was as if she had actually transformed into someone else.

The stylist Evony had sent off to buy a leg brace returned.

"Thank you," Avrianna said.

The stylist smiled. "Happy to help with one of Evony's creations."

Evony assisted Avrianna with getting the external brace on and then marked the pleather pants where she'd have to cut them to create a new hem. While Evony did those alterations, Avrianna called Chuck.

"Hey, I need a favor."

"Name it."

"For my disguise, the leg brace proves more restricting than I anticipated. I'm going to need something to help me get around, and that Crystal could use as a weapon if necessary."

"Like a cane?"

"Yeah, could you help with that?"

"Sure. I'll hunt something down and bring it to Evony's."

"Thanks, Chuck."

Evony finished the pants, and Avrianna put them back on again. The hem was perfect. "I was thinking…do you want to try your hand at creating scars?"

Evony's eyes widened. "You are making my day!"

So, Evony created prosthetic skin, which she layered delicately onto Avrianna's leg. One after the other. Avrianna didn't tell her how many scars. She just let Evony do her thing. When Evony was satisfied, she set to painting them to match Avrianna's skin and to give them the look of healed skin in shades of pink. The process took two hours, but they'd be able to reuse the prosthetic skin later.

Evony had just finished when a knock sounded. The door cracked open and Chuck called out, "Knock-knock, is it safe to come in?"

"It's safe."

Chuck entered and jolted to a stop. "Holy shit. Is that you?"

"Nope. I'm Crystal." And she said it in a different voice. Deeper. More seductive.

"Shit. Crystal scares me a little."

She chuckled. "Good."

He pulled his arm out from behind his back to reveal a tall, titanium staff. "Will this work?"

She took it and leaned on it. "Stylish and yet practical."

"I also have this for you." He opened his hand to reveal a 9mm bullet unlike any she'd ever seen before. The primer and case were steel, and the projectile, was a diamond carved into the shape of a bullet.

"Where'd you get that?"

"Pulled some favors. I figure you could use it as a prop, a sample of your goods.

It has gunpowder in it, and will actually fire if tested."

She pinched it between her thumb and forefinger. "This is amazing."

"I also got wind that a group of Dee's old buddies from his Underhill & Co days go to Vega every Friday night to drink expensive vodka, snort whatever they can get their hands on, hook up with women, and broker weapons deals."

"What kind of deals?"

"They're trying to start up an import, export business."

Illegally ship weapons into New Vida and Earth.

Not what they needed.

Not at all.

"So, guess where you're going tonight," Chuck said.

"I'm apparently going to party with smugglers."

Vega

Vega was dimly light for club dancing and dirty dealings. Music throbbed through the place. As Avrianna made her way through the crowds, people groped her and ground up against her, as if just being there gave them an open invitation to her body. They didn't have any such invitation, and when one guy kept blocking her path and trying to gyrate against her, she flicked up the bottom of her staff, nailing him right in the balls.

He went down.

And she stepped over him.

She heard Chuck's laughter in her ear thanks to the hidden earpiece.

"Another practical use," he said.

Well, she did say Crystal may have to use it for a weapon. If she had to, she fully intended to use her staff like Gandalf.

She located an empty spot at the bar and wedged herself next to a stool.

"What can I get you, beautiful?" a female bartender asked.

"Vodka martini, please, with your best vodka. Extra olives."

The bartender gave her a martini glass proving with two stirring sticks piled with fat olives. For that, Avrianna gave her a generous tip. While standing there and sipping the strong martini, her gaze skimmed around the room, pausing at each VIP room. She'd memorized the photos of Dee's old buddies and searched for them among the people bending over tables with a finger to one nostril, getting blow jobs on the club's couches, and popping expensive bottles.

She recognized one of them—the VP of Underhill & Co. who'd worked under Dee.

That was her guy—Vaughn Wagner.

Thankfully, he wasn't snorting anything, and his pants were zipped.

Martini in hand, she took a step at a time up the stairs to the second floor where the VIP rooms were. No one was there to stop her, so she made it to the top unbothered. Beyond their velvet ropes baring access to their exclusive spaces were a few random tables along the rails. She chose the table directly across from

Vaughn. Standing to the side of the table, she made sure he could see her and all her rhinestone glory. With that corset setting off thousands of flashes of light, as well as her staff, she was easy to spot. Still, she made sure that when he looked at her, he'd be intrigued. She pulled the diamond bullet from the space between her cleavage and began to play with it on the table, spinning it on its tip. She did this again and again, hoping he'd notice.

And he did.

"Excuse me?"

She tilted her head toward the voice.

A man in a suit stood beside her table. "Mr. Wagner would like you to come into his VIP room."

She glanced at Vaughn. "Tell Mr. Wagner that I'm not interested in giving him a blow job." And she resumed spinning the diamond bullet.

"No. You misunderstand. He wants to talk to you."

"Sure, he does."

"He does. About that." He pointed at the bullet. "Please."

She peered toward Vaughn again.

This time, he raised a hand and called her over with the flick of his fingers.

She decided to obey that order and walked over to the rope.

"Be careful," Chuck whispered in her ear.

She'd be careful, but from here on out, there was no telling what'd happen.

The man who'd been speaking to her unhooked the rope to allow her entrance.

Vaughn sat up straight from his relaxed position.

"I'm Vaughn."

"Crystal."

"Now, that's fitting." He indicated at the seat next to him. "Please."

"Because you're so polite…" She lowered onto the couch, stretched her right leg out in front of her because of the brace, and rested the staff next to her as a barrier between her and Vaughn.

"You're the most fascinating person here, and I like to know fascinating people."

"Well, you're in luck, because so do I."

He grinned. "What were you playing with over there?"

She held the bullet out to him.

"May I?"

"Sure."

He plucked the bullet from her palm and inspected it closely. "This is exquisite. Can it be used?"

"Of course, I designed it myself. It can fit any gun with 9mm bullets."

Vaughn held out his hand to the man who'd approached her table.

She watched the man remove a gun from behind his back.

Vaughn took it, released the mag, and slid out the remaining rounds one at time. Mag empty, he slid the diamond bullet into place. He then popped the mag into the handle of the Glock. "Amazing. I'd love to fire it, but—" A press of the button on the side of the handle had the mag releasing again. "I can't exactly do that in a club."

"That may be frowned upon."

He tossed the diamond bullet in the air, caught it, and then held it between his thumb and forefinger again. "Do you have any idea what you have here?"

"Why don't you tell me?"

"Billions."

She laughed as she snatched the bullet back. "For one little bullet?"

"No, for as many as you can produce."

"Well, there's a problem there. Diamonds of that size aren't exactly cheap. If they were, this corset wouldn't be covered in rhinestones."

His gaze lowered to her corset and her breasts. Apparently, it didn't matter how small they were, as long as they were presented in such a way. And then if you added some sparkle, you had men drooling like Vaughn was about to.

He swallowed. "I could help with that." His gaze flicked back up to her eyes. "My boss would be interested in this. Very interested. He'd pay you to make these. In fact, I have a feeling he'd offer you an exclusive deal to make crystal bullets for him and him alone."

"And who is your boss?"

He smirked. "I can't exactly tell you that."

Because he was on the run?

She raised a brow. "I don't want to get into work with someone I don't know."

"He has to be protected at all costs."

"You're making it sound like he's The Godfather of weapons."

Vaughn winked. "He is."

"Oh. Now that's intriguing."

"He'd be intrigued by you and that crystal bullet, that's for sure. I can guarantee a lucrative deal for you if you offer him exclusive rights."

"To crystal bullets, not to me."

His teeth flashed in a quick grin. "Of course."

"Before I agree, I need to know this Godfather of Weapons' resume. What makes him a big deal? Aside from a man in a suit with a bodyguard chilling in Vega telling me that he is?"

His grin widened. "He'll like you."

"Then he has impeccable tastes but that doesn't help me."

"He has connections to Underhill & Co."

She blinked. "*The* Underhill & Co?"

"The one and only."

"The gun industry hasn't been the same since Underhill & Co stopped producing pistols and revolvers." Good for her and the safety of her world, but not for people hoping to profit off it. Like Vaughn. Like Dee. "The guns now are inferior at best."

Not true. People with guns produced by other companies still killed others just the same.

"Agreed. So, what do you say? Do you want to join forces?"

"How could I refuse an offer like that?"

"Excellent. Is there a way he could reach you?"

She hadn't thought of this. Stupid. Fortunately, she had a burner phone that she'd used when undercover before. She didn't have the phone on her, but she had the number memorized, so she gave it to Vaughn.

"He'll be in touch."

She smiled. "I hope so. Now, if you'll excuse me,

I'm going to freshen up in the ladies' room and get a fresh martini, because I left mine at the table out there, and if my fellow ladies have taught me anything, it's not to drink anything you left unattended." She rose. "Thank you for inviting me over. I'm looking forward to hearing from the big man."

Vaughn raised a glass of amber liquor in a salute as she left.

On her way down the stairs, Chuck's voice returned in her ear piece. "Let's hope they really do call you."

Except all the hoping wouldn't make it come true. Because a call never came. Not the next day. Not five days later.

They were back at square one.

Mission

The chime of Avrianna's cell phone pulled her out of her dream of black plains and bleak skies. She groped for the device on her nightstand, picked it up, and tapped the green icon. "This is Detective Heavenborn."

On the other line, the gravelly voice of Chief Logan came through. "Detective, you and Chuck need to get the police department as soon as possible."

Avrianna sat up in bed, fully alert. "Was Dee found?"

"Unfortunately, no."

"Was a body found?"

There was a pause on the other end before Chief Logan said, "This isn't that kind of call."

Avrianna frowned. Her work involved murder, investigation, and nailing suspects for their insidious crimes. There was always one body involved. Sometimes, more than one. Once, half a body.

"I can't say more over the phone. Come to my office immediately. This can't wait."

The call ended.

Avrianna stared at the phone in her hand a moment. Sure, she'd been woken up in the middle of the night before for her job. In fact, nighttime was the most active time for murders and other crimes to take place, but never had Chief Logan given her so little information and implied their phone lines weren't safe.

She tossed back her comforter and sprang out of bed. Strange call aside, when your chief ordered you to come to their office, you dropped everything, even sleep, to get there as soon as possible. She snatched a pair of black pants and a black button-up shirt from her closet and tugged them on over her boy shorts and tank top. In the bathroom, she brushed her teeth with brisk movements and a little too much minty paste. Then she quickly pulled her silvery-blonde hair into a ponytail.

One of the perks of being Avrianna Heavenborn was that she never looked tired. And she never got sick. Her eyes were clear, without a single red line of exhaustion in the white. The green of her corneas was even brighter than her silvery hair, which shimmered in the fluorescent lighting.

After making sure she hadn't left any white

toothpaste around her mouth, she slung her badge around her neck and fastened her holstered sidearm to her belt.

The drive to the Aurora Police Department was a peaceful one. Only a few other cars occupied the roadways. With businesses closed and everyone at home in bed, New Vida appeared serene. Avrianna knew better, though. Her world was rank with evildoers, making it hard to survive. That was the reason why she had joined law enforcement. One day, she hoped to make a real difference.

Outside the department, she caught up with Chuck as he entered through the automatic doors. He glanced at her. "Did the chief tell you anything about why he wants us here?"

"Not a thing," she said.

They walked side by side past darkened offices. A janitor came out of one of them, pushing a cart full of cleaning supplies and carrying a bag of trash. They nodded at him as they continued to the end of the hall and the light shining through the gaps around the door ahead.

Chuck rapped his knuckles against the door.

"Come in."

Chuck twisted the handle and opened the door wide for Avrianna to step through. As she did, she took a quick survey of her surroundings. Chief Logan's office appeared normal. It was not in disarray, and no one else occupied the space with him, which she took as a good sign. Atop his desk were piles of paperwork and stacks of files. She wondered if he wanted them to work on one of those cases.

"Avrianna, Chuck, thanks for coming. Please close the door."

Chuck shut the door at their backs. Then he stood beside Avrianna. They stared at him. The chief's clothes were wrinkled. Creases on his right cheek indicated that his head had been resting on a pillow not long ago.

He lifted a hand. "I don't know how else to say this but to come right out with it. I need the two of you to go to Area 51."

Avrianna blinked. Surely, she had misheard him. Perhaps he had said, "Aurora Air One," the airport. After all, Area 51 wasn't even on their world!

"Sir." Chuck shifted. "Do you mean *the* Area 51 on Earth? The military site believed to be a top-secret base for alien and UFO investigations?"

Chief Logan gave a brisk nod. "One and the same. We've been tasked with the mission to retrieve an item that New Vida gave to US custody years ago for data discovery. And we're to bring it safely back here for our scientists to do further examinations."

Avrianna couldn't believe what Chief Logan was asking her to do.

"Sir…respectfully…you want me, a woman who was found floating in the middle of the ocean as a newborn, to go to Area 51?"

Chief Logan stared, apparently not understanding her concern.

"You want me, a woman who people believe to be an *alien*, to go to Area 51? A woman who has been experimented on by scientists here on New Vida, and who has unexplained powers?" She glanced between him and Chuck. "Is this a joke?"

Or worse yet…a trap?

Could everything she'd ever done and gone through been leading up to this moment for when the people of New Vida finally found a way to get rid of her? And what better of a way to do that than to lock her up in Area 51?

"This is not a joke," Chief Logan said. "Because our world doesn't have a government system or special agents, the Aurora Police Department was selected for this mission, what with us being the largest department on New Vida and all. And…I'm sorry, Avrianna, but out of all of my officers, you're the only one I trust with something like this. You know how to keep a secret."

His words made her fidget in place. Yes, she had many secrets, and she knew how to keep them, including what all her powers were and the sorts of things she'd gone through as a child when the people of New Vida realized she was different. Except, she couldn't help but think Chief Logan hinted at something more, such as her origins—where she came from and what she was. Unfortunately, she didn't have a clue on either of those points. What she did know was that she had a human body, and had lived as a human every day of her life. So, as far as she was concerned, she was human, damn it! But did Chief Logan think otherwise? Did he suspect she was keeping her origins a secret? Did Chuck?

If she were keeping that information a secret, she had good reason. No one else in all of New Vida had powers, and, when a few of her skills had been discovered, everyone in her world had suspected her to be an alien. Consequently, they had put her through hell. If they ever had evidence she really was one…

She shuddered at the thought.

"Detective, I understand your apprehension," Chief Logan said. "But this is not a joke."

"What about searching for Dee Underhill? Isn't he our top priority?"

"He remains top priority, but we've been stalled out for days. Nothing will change in the few hours this will take."

Except, everything could change in a few hours.

"You and Chuck are the only ones right for this job."

"Why couldn't one of the Justices retrieve this package?"

The seven Justices had been put in place to protect the world and to look out for the good of the people. To do anything worthwhile, you needed their permission.

"The US government spoke to the Justices about this matter, and they chose our department for this task. When I told the Justices the two of you would courier the package between worlds, they agreed with my decision."

Avrianna pursed her lips. She'd never had any trouble with the Justices in the past, but if anyone wanted her gone, going through the Justices would achieve that.

"So, what is this package?" she said.

Chief Logan shrugged. "No idea. We're not to know the contents, only pick it up and deliver it."

Avrianna nodded. She was skeptical, but this was her job and she had never failed to close a case, catch a bad guy—Dee excluded—or complete a mission, and she wouldn't start now. "Okay. I'll do it."

"So will I," Chuck said.

On their way out, Chuck elbowed her softly. "This is bizarre."

"No kidding." It wasn't odd to have to set a case aside to complete an order issued by your chief, or to have to work on a new case. What was odd was the order itself. To go from searching for Dee to having to courier something between worlds from the infamous Area 51? Yeah, bizarre.

But she'd do it so she could get back to looking for Dee. She'd been thinking she should go back to Vega as Crystal, remind Vaughn about her and her crystal bullets to get Dee to contact her. They *needed* Dee to call her.

Antsy from having to put Dee on the backburner, she drove straight to the Veil, the portal that linked Earth to New Vida. At two o'clock in the morning, the Veil was shut down to traffic—no cars honking while they came and went, no exhaust choking the air, no annoyance. Only a pair of guards in a small post off to the side remained. As Avrianna approached the massive crystal arc, a humming vibration tickled her eardrums. The electricity dancing in the air made the hair on the back of her neck stand on end.

They showed their badges and their clearance papers, signed by the seven Justices, to the guards on duty. Those papers stated they could leave New Vida during those hours, when no traffic was usually permitted to come through on either side. As soon as the guards confirmed the validity of the papers,

Avrianna faced the Veil. Trapped inside the crystal arc, the portal was equivalent to an opal curtain of glistening magic. Gentle waves of cosmic energy flowed from it.

"You ready for this?" Chuck asked.

"Born ready," she confirmed.

Together, they took out their IDs, raised their hands above their heads, and took a step through the portal. The Veil felt cool and silky, with the gentle spark of static.

A single step and Avrianna left her world behind. The sleeping cityscape of New Vida morphed into the shadowed rock formations of the Grand Canyon, and before her stood eight armed U.S. Marines. The soldiers were in full combat gear and aiming semi-automatic guns at them.

"Easy," Avrianna said with her hands still in the air. "We were invited."

Chuck held out his ID. "I'm Detective Davis, and this is Detective Heavenborn.

You can check our credentials."

A soldier crept forward, hunched down and still aiming his weapon. He snatched their IDs from their hands before backing cautiously to his men. Two soldiers looked them up to be sure they were who they said they were. While they did that, the rest of the soldiers eyed them with zero trust. Hell, the feeling was mutual. The people from Earth took whatever they wanted from New Vida, and she suspected they illegally let their criminals into her world so they wouldn't have to deal with them anymore. That alone had Avrianna glaring at them with contempt, and that's when she realized they weren't pointing their weapons at the two of them. They were pointing their weapons solely at her.

The corner of her mouth tilted up. Little did they know that none of their bullets would be able to penetrate her flesh.

"Okay," one of the soldiers said. "You've been cleared." He handed them back their identification. "I'm Sergeant Willis. We'll be escorting you to Area 51. This way."

They followed him to a helicopter.

"In," he barked.

Avrianna scanned the helicopter. It was military-grade, massive, and had machine gun mounts. She climbed in, took the farthest seat, and fastened the harness. Chuck sat down next to her, and the rest of the soldiers piled in after them. They each held their guns ready, with the butts against their shoulders and the muzzles pointing at the floor between their feet.

The helicopter roared to life, the blades beat against the air, and it lifted off the ground, soaring over the darkened landscape of the Grand Canyon. The motion of the helicopter had Avrianna's shoulders bumping into the side of the helicopter and into Chuck's shoulder. She had never been on a more uncomfortable ride, especially with the soldiers lined up in front of her not taking their eyes off her for a second. She endured it, though, during the flight from Arizona to Nevada.

Finally, a voice crackled in her helmet's mike. "We're approaching Homey Airport."

"Ten-four," Willis said. Then he removed a black

cap and a pair of sunglasses from a pocket in his tactical pants. He thrust them toward Avrianna. "Put these on. Now."

Avrianna frowned. "Why?"

Willis lowered the mike on his helmet and shouted to her over the ruckus of the helicopter blades. "Because we're tasked with bringing *you* safely back to the Veil. We don't need anyone at Homey Airport getting any ideas."

Avrianna blinked. *Shit*.

5

Diz the Assassin

I f a US soldier was concerned about the scientists at Area 51 becoming too curious when it came to her many mysteries, then she was in for a world of trouble. Feeling uneasy, she removed the helmet, tucked her hair beneath the cap, and hid her luminous eyes with the sunglasses, even though the sun wasn't yet up in the sky.

She couldn't believe she was doing this, willingly going to Area 51. The fear of not leaving iced her veins. Sure, she had abilities no one knew about that she could use to free herself if necessary, but they might have machines, cages, and weapons that could withstand even her hottest of powers.

The helicopter touched down with a bump, and a muffled exchange could be heard between the pilot and someone outside as the helicopter powered down. A momentary silence was followed by the helicopter's side door being shoved open. Two Air Force officers in desert fatigues stood there. One shone the beam of a large flashlight inside the cabin at them.

"Who are the detectives from New Vida?"

Chuck raised a hand. "We come in peace."

To illustrate the point, Avrianna showed the two soldiers the peace sign.

The soldier pointed the bright light at them. "Out."

The soldiers escorting them climbed out one by one. Avrianna was the last to exit. Immediately upon her boots touching the ground, Air Force officers forced her around and pressed her hands to the side of the helicopter. She clenched her teeth while they patted her down and ran a handheld metal detector over her. Other officers did the same to Chuck.

A hand clamped onto her shoulder. "Turn."

She rotated and came face to face with a stern-faced officer. "Remove your hat."

"Can't," she said. "If I did, you'd see my horns." She gave him a wide, toothy grin.

The soldier continued to eye her. "Remove your glasses."

Willis stepped forward then. "The glasses stay."

The two men glared at each other. After a tense moment, the officer faced her again. She tilted her head, silently challenging him to press the matter or to snatch the hat and glasses off her head. When he lifted his hand, her own hands fisted in response. But in his hand, he held the metal detector, which he waved around her head to be sure she wasn't concealing a weapon under her hat.

Once satisfied, he lowered the metal detector to his side. "Welcome to the Nevada Test and Training Range at Homey Airport. We will drive you to Sector Four."

Avrianna took the farthest seat again, but this time in the back of a tan Humvee. Not all of the Marines who came with them could fit, so a few of them had to stay behind. The vehicle took off right away, and the rocky ground caused everyone to jostle up and down and back and forth in their seats.

Several minutes later, they were released from the back of the Humvee, and

Avrianna peered up at the dark, looming peak of the Papoose Mountains. Without a word, they followed the two Air Force officers over the sand, along the base of the mountains. They walked several yards when the officers suddenly about-faced, causing them to halt.

With brisk movements, they passed out papers and pens. Avrianna took one look and arched a brow. The papers were Non-Disclosure Agreements.

"What you see from this point on, you do not speak one word about to anyone. Is that understood?" the stone-faced officer said.

Willis and his men confirmed this with one word. "Understood." They passed their signed forms back to the officer.

"Ten-four," Chuck said and handed over his completed form.

Everyone turned their attention to Avrianna. She scribbled down her signature. Then, just to annoy the officer, she mimed locking her lips with an invisible key. She even threw it over her shoulder for good measure. He scowled at her, not amused, before continuing on his trek.

Chuck elbowed her, attempting to hide his smirk.

She shrugged innocently.

Their group walked a few more paces before Avrianna spotted a line of nine sand-textured hangars. At first, she thought she was seeing things in the pre-dawn light, but sure enough, they were there, so well-hidden that you couldn't see them until you were practically upon them.

Not saying another word, not even glancing over their shoulders, the Air Force officers led them into the first secret hangar. It was empty. A Stealth didn't sit there. Nor a Lockheed U-2. Not even a crashed UFO was suspended in the space for examination. The sounds of their boots created a rhythmic drumbeat against the concrete floor as they walked the length of the hangar. At the back, everyone crammed into an elevator, and down they went into the bowels of the underground fortress. Avrianna half-expected creepy *Twilight Zone*-inspired music to come through the speakers during their descent, but the elevator was quiet except for the inhale and exhale of six men.

When the elevator door opened, a scientist greeted them, wearing black scrubs, a white lab coat, and blue mesh booties over his shoes. Instantly, Avrianna didn't like him. Memories of scientists from her world greedily experimenting on her for answers flooded her thoughts. How could she burst into flames? How could her eyes glow? How could she melt metal with her hands? The sickening things they had done to her may not have scarred her skin, but they certainly had scarred her mind. What would this scientist, and the others in this secret facility, do to her if given the chance?

The answer came to her right away

Everything. They'd do everything. And more.

The scientist stepped forward. "Welcome to Sector Four. I'm Dr. Newcomer." He tilted his head when he looked at Avrianna. "Why are you wearing sunglasses?"

"Migraine," she answered flatly. "I understand we are here to pick something up."

"Of course, right this way." Dr. Newcomer waved them to follow him down the corridor.

Solid metal doors, with large black numbers on their surface, lined the path. Each one required a facial scan, as well as a keycard to gain entry.

"What's inside these rooms?" Avrianna asked.

"That is Sensitive Compartmented Information."

"In other words, top secret?"

"Precisely."

"Uh-huh."

Her gaze moved from door to door as they passed. The temptation to use her abilities, to see what hid behind the doors, became almost too much to bear, but she restrained herself. If she unleashed her powers in front of her audience to uncover their secrets, they'd never let her go. But there was one thing she and Chuck deserved to know.

"And this package we're assigned to courier

between worlds…what is it?"

"That's classified as well."

She glared at the back of the scientist's head. "We have the right to know what will be in our possession."

Dr. Newcomer whirled around. "No, you don't."

Avrianna took another step, advancing on him. "Is it dangerous?" she pressed. "Could it harm us or our world once it is there?"

He took a skittish step in retreat. "No. It…it is non-lethal."

She lowered her voice so only he could hear her. "It better be."

Dr. Newcomer swallowed. "Right." His voice squeaked. "We're almost there." He turned on wobbly knees and continued down the hall.

Farther down, he stopped in front of a door marked forty-four. He leaned down so a scanner could detect his facial features and inserted a keycard simultaneously. A green light flashed on, and a beep sounded. He opened the door a fraction. "Only the detectives are permitted to enter."

Avrianna and Chuck exchanged glances. Neither of them knew what to expect, but unspoken words passed between them. Whatever was on the other side of that door, whatever happened, they'd have each other's backs.

They took a step into the room. The tile was pure white, and metal paneling covered the walls and cciling. A single round table sat in the middle of the room, and a rectangular apparatus, made of thick, see-through material, took up the surface of that table. Inside it sat a metal box with a handle. Dr. Newcomer pushed a code into the lock. As with the door, a green light flicked on, and a beep pierced the air. He opened the container and reached for the metal box within. It was the size of an old-fashioned lunch pail. What could be inside it of so much importance? A powerful mineral, a chunk of metal from a spacecraft, a vial of alien blood, a brain, or something that could kill an entire world?

Dr. Newcomer presented the box to them. Avrianna looked at it critically, not wanting to take it. Chuck moved to accept it, but the scientist yanked it away. "I was given strict instructions by New Vida's Justices to give it to Detective Heavenborn and Detective Heavenborn only."

Avrianna clenched her teeth. Of course, the Justices would specify that. Chuck didn't have her particular skill set if the package needed to be defended.

"Fine." She wrapped her fingers around the handle.

Dr. Newcomer, however, didn't let it go. "You swear to protect it?"

"It's my job," she said. "And I always do my job."

Satisfied, he relinquished the box to her. She gripped the handle as they walked back down the corridor to the elevator, through the hangar, over the sand to the Humvee, and during the ride back to Homey Airport. She didn't even so much as look at the box sitting on her lap until they were secured on the helicopter, flying away from Area 51. Now, she couldn't *not* look.

With the sunglasses concealing her eyes, she summoned her powers. Heat penetrated her pupils and spread to the edges of her irises. Beneath the dark lenses, searing green light glowed. She stared at the box while telling her sight to penetrate the thick metal.

A small metal chair had been built into the box, and strapped into it was a three-inch creature with gray skin, a face in the shape of an upside-down raindrop, and large black eyes. It looked up at the lid, and its gaze connected to hers through the layers of metal. A goofy smile formed on the tiny alien's face. Then it lifted its arm and waved at her. Gasping, she sat back and snapped off her powers.

Chuck leaned toward her. "What did you see?" he whispered.

"I don't know, but whatever it is, it says 'Hi.'"

6

Itsy-Bitsy Alien

Chuck's eyebrows came together as he frowned. "There's an animal in there?"

"No, not an animal." She glanced at the armed soldiers and lowered her voice. "An extraterrestrial."

Chuck's eyes widened. His voice came out in a rasp. "An alien? You sure?"

"It's the size of my finger, gunmetal gray, bipedal, and has a head too big for its body. Yeah, I'm sure."

"How do you think they got it?"

Avrianna shrugged. "The chief said it was the property of New Vida." As soon as she said it, she winced, regretting her choice of word. Humans shouldn't be anyone's property, and neither should aliens. Humans and aliens alike should be free.

"Then how did New Vida get it?"

She shook her head. "I don't know, but the better question is not how, but why." She tore her gaze off the metal box containing an extraterrestrial too tiny to be dangerous and looked at Chuck. "Why did New Vida give it to the American Government, and what in the world did they do to it in that horrid place?"

She didn't say so, but she could imagine. When her adoptive parents were at a loss about her "unique skills," they did what any worried parents would do, they sought the help of the medical industry. The problem was, the doctors and scientists they went to for help lied to them. They didn't have any way to cure Avrianna; because there was nothing to cure. All they had wanted to do was experiment. On her. And they never told her parents what they were up to. Why would they? If her parents knew, they would've protected her, and the doctors and scientists needed her to remain in their latex-gloved clutches. Without her, they wouldn't have been able to continue their experimentations—experimentations that still haunted her.

Blow torches.

Scalpels.

Needles.

And the things they did…what nightmares were made of.

The scientists at Area 51 could've done those same things to this little alien. They could've done so much worse.

"What are you thinking?" Chuck whispered.

She shook her head. "That no one, whether from Earth or New Vida or anywhere in the universe, should have to go through what this poor thing undoubtedly endured."

Chuck nodded. "What do we do?"

Avrianna directed her gaze out the helicopter's window and looked toward the horizon. "Our jobs."

For the rest of the flight, she didn't speak. Nor did she say a thing when they arrived at the Veil and the US soldiers there patted her down. She remained silent as Chuck drove to the Heptagon where the Justices resided. In the passenger's seat, she held the metal box on her lap and clutched it with her hands. She couldn't believe she was about to hand over an innocent being to the authorities so they could do God-only-knows what to it. Chuck's question came back to her and filled her thoughts. How was this little alien even discovered on New Vida? How did the Justices get their hands on it? And why did they give it to Earth's authorities and the scientists at Area 51? What had they wanted?

Chuck pulled into a parking space, and Avrianna peered out the windshield at the Heptagon. Inside seven Justices waited for the being inside a prison the size of a lunchbox. What did they want with it now?

As a detective, it was her job to uncover motives, but the Justices' possible motives behind wanting this itsy-bitsy alien back in their possession made her nauseous. Their motives couldn't be innocent, couldn't be anything good. Unless they intended to free it. But why would they do that?

She gazed at the metal box. New Vida had treated her horribly for thinking she was an alien because of her special abilities, and she looked human. Aside from her silver hair and neon eyes, of course. But the being inside the metal box in her grip was undoubtedly not from this world. Or Earth.

The people of New Vida would want the alien locked away forever. Even executed, just for being different. That realization made it all too clear to Avrianna that this little alien was doomed to endure a horrific ending, because she doubted the Justices knew how to send the alien back to its home planet, or even where it came from, and they surely wouldn't free the alien into their world. The alien wouldn't be welcomed or wanted. It would be hunted and targeted. People would claim to be frightened of it. The Justices would have no choice but to keep it under lock and key. A secret. A prisoner. That was no life for any being, regardless of its origins.

And she had to hand the alien over to that fate.

She got out of the car and entered the Heptagon.

Inside, she had to set the metal box down momentarily in order to pass through a metal detector. It didn't make a peep. She turned to find the security guard examining the box, trying to figure out how to open it.

"You can't open that." She snatched it from his hands.

"I must. You can't come in here with that unless it's checked."

"Buddy, you're a security guard. I'm a detective. I outrank you."

"Not here."

"Yes, here, because the Justice's want what's inside this container, and they don't want it opened by anyone. Nor do they want it out of my possession. So, if you have a problem with any of that, then you have to take that up with the Justices."

He apparently did have a problem with that and had the gall to take it up with the Justices. When he returned, his cheeks were pink and sweat beaded his brow. His vocal cords stuttered on his words as he told Avrianna she and the metal box were cleared and allowed to proceed.

"Ring you out, did they?" She smirked and continued into the building.

Instead of having to sit and wait for the Justices to call them into their chambers, a massive and circular space, they were brought in immediately. A small, rectangular table was positioned in the center with two chairs sitting side by side. In front of that table, along the wall, a high podium was built to distinguish the Justices' ranks above whoever sat in the tiny chairs, meant to make them feel small if the Justices staring down at them didn't already accomplish that. Seven distinct benches made up the podium, and the seven Justices occupied those podiums.

Avrianna stood behind one of the chairs and placed the metal box on the table.

Her hands trembled, so she balled them into fists at her sides.

"Detective Heavenborn, Detective Davis, thank

you for traveling to Earth to retrieve this item for us," Justice Valenti, a thin, bald man said.

Her gaze landed on the metal box. "This item," she whispered. Then she raised her gaze to the Justice who had spoken and said with more of a bite than anyone would ever dare to use, "This *item*?"

Justice Valenti fell silent.

But another Justice spoke up—Justice Dey, a woman with bronze skin and a thick accent. "Detective Heavenborn, you say that as if you know what is inside the container. Do you?"

Avrianna shifted her attention to Justice Dey. "If I do?"

"Detective Heavenborn, this is not a game." Justice Powell, a woman with umber skin and short braids, and the most powerful Justice of them all, spoke up. "Did you open the container?"

"No, ma'am, I did *not* open the container."

"Do you know what's inside it?"

Avrianna's gaze didn't flinch from Justice Powell's. "I do."

"How do you know what's inside it if you didn't open it?"

Avrianna inhaled slowly. As her lungs filled with breath, her eyes warmed, and green light reflected off the metal box. "Like this."

The Justices fell silent. None of them moved.

"Detective," Justice Dey said, breaking the silence. "That was forbidden of you to do."

"I didn't receive any orders but to bring this to you, which I have done. It was not relayed to me that I couldn't use my powers to see exactly what I was in position of, a right I believe I had. I do not apologize for what I've done."

The Justices exchanged glances.

"May I ask, what are your intentions for the being within this container?"

"You may ask," Justice Valenti said, "but we are not at liberty to tell you."

"Will you have it experimented on?"

"Avrianna," Chuck hissed.

He was urging her to stop with just the use of her name, but she couldn't stop.

Wouldn't.

"Will this being be harmed in anyway?"

"Harmed?" Justice Dey asked.

"Let me put it plainly…tortured."

"Watch it, Detective," Justice Valenti chastised.

Avrianna's cheeks warmed with humility and anger. She clenched her teeth. "So far, I have done my job, exactly what has been asked of me. I've brought the container and its contents from Area 51 to the Veil, into New Vida, and to the Heptagon, but that's as far as I can go with my duties."

"What do you mean, Detective?" Justice Powell said.

"I will not relinquish the container or the being inside it to you." Her gaze swept around the room, at each podium and the powerful individuals seated there. "None of you."

Chuck turned fully to her now. "Avrianna, what are you doing?"

She didn't answer him, because she wasn't quite sure what she was doing. All she knew was that she had to do this. Whatever *this* was.

Justice Valenti raised his voice. "Detective, you will be detained if you do not give us that package."

"Bars don't frighten me," she said.

"You will force us to call in the guards, who will handcuff you and haul you away."

"They could try."

"Detective!"

Chuck grabbed her arm and tried to pull her around to face him, but she did not budge. "Avrianna, think this through. Whatever you do will look badly on me."

And for that, she was sorry, but there were more important things at stake here than either of their reputations, and she was willing to risk both.

Her weapon's holster was empty; the gun locked safely in the glove compartment. She didn't even have her handcuffs, but what she did next, she did deliberately, slowly. Making a statement, she removed her badge from her belt and laid it on top of the table for all to see.

Peering at the metal box, she tilted her head toward Chuck and said, "I'm sorry."

For Chuck, she *was* sorry. He was her partner, and what she was about to do would erase that.

Chuck lowered his voice. "What? Why? Avrianna, what are you doing?"

"This."

She snatched up the metal box, whirled around, and raced right toward the floor-to-ceiling window to her left. Her boots pounded against the tile. She raised her arm to shield her face and leapt up. The glass shattered when her body slammed into it. Pieces of glass shot out and scattered onto the grass and cement on the other side. She landed on the sidewalk and ran for it. No, she hadn't planned this out, but she knew she had to get the hell out of there. Now.

Crystal Mountains

Avrianna cut across the street, slipping right through oncoming cars that honked at her. First, she had to get out of the city. Far away.

"Detective Heavenborn, freeze!"

She didn't fucking freeze. She didn't so much as falter.

Gunfire sounded.

People screamed.

Car tires squealed.

The bastards were opening fire in public, with

civilians around. She needed to get away from there. Away from them all.

She dove into an alley between buildings. Like most cities, Aurora was a maze. If she stayed on the roads, or even the alleyways, they'd soon catch up and surround her. For the sake of the itty-bitty alien, she couldn't get caught. Her one option was to get off the street. Literally. She leapt onto a fire escape and climbed up one handed. On the roof, she broke out into a run, aiming for the ledge and the next rooftop. She stomped her right boot onto the edge and launched into the air. Her feet slammed into the roof. She kept on going. Rooftop after rooftop.

It wouldn't take them long to deploy helicopters to search for her.

She had to get higher. A lot higher.

The highest point in the city, in all of New Vida, in fact, was the Crystal Mountains. The maintain range was on the western edge of the island, with peaks made entirely of quartz crystals. And she was heading right for it.

She relied on rooftops, running at full speed, springing from one to the other.

Down below, sirens wailed.

Every officer in the city would be after her in a matter of minutes with the orders to shoot her down. Apprehend her alive? She wasn't sure if they'd want to take that chance, given what little they knew about her.

With one rash decision—rash but right—she'd dismantled her entire career and quite possibly given herself a death sentence.

She wouldn't change that decision if given the

chance.

Yes, for one tiny alien she'd risk it all.

No one else would get that.

No would else would've done what she had.

But she wasn't like everyone else.

She wasn't normal.

And thank God for that.

She raced across rooftops until the city disappeared and no rooftops remained. Gripping the container to her chest, she said, "Hold on in there, little buddy." Then she sprang off the final rooftop toward the ground. With the container tucked into her body, she rolled over the ground before popping back to her feet and continuing her escape.

She was ahead of anyone pursuing her, but that wouldn't be the case for long. They had vehicles and choppers. They'd be on top of her soon enough.

The residential area was peaceful as she cut through yards and between houses. She hopped fences, avoided dogs, and performed flips to clear pools. With each neighborhood she raced through, she got closer to the mountains.

She breezed past a child playing basketball in front of a home, dodged a mail truck heading for the next mailbox on their route, and followed a trail in a path of woods behind a house. The path ended up ahead to a clearing. She aimed for it. A few paces to the end, she realized it wasn't a clearing. A canal was there. She wrapped her left arm around the container and leapt over murky water poked with cattails and coated with a sheen of green-ish yellow pollen. Halfway over the canal she realized she hadn't given her jump enough power.

She landed on the other side of the canal, a couple of feet from the water. "Damn it." Shoving the toes of her boots into the earth, she crawled her way up on her knees. Her right hand clawed around grass and dirt. "This would be so much easier if this thing had straps," she gritted between her teeth. If only the scientists at Area 51 had thought of that, but they had no way of knowing that the container they'd designed to imprison the smallest alien ever would be a part of a police pursuit because the person tasked with bringing it to the authorities would steal it.

She'd stolen something from the US government, from the Justices.

But they'd kidnapped, imprisoned, and tortured a live being first.

She dug her left elbow into the dirt and wiggled her way over the edge onto even ground. For a moment, she paused. On her knees, she took a breath. Her heart hammered. She'd committed a felony. Her own colleagues were after her—Dee was no longer their priority—and she had no damn clue what her plan was after she reached the Crystal Mountains. She was very clearly in over her head.

Eyes glowing, she peered at the container to check on her passenger. "Are you okay?"

The tiny alien looked up toward the lid and gave her that same big smile. Only this time, instead of waving, he gave her a thumbs up.

She chuckled. "Alright. We're not in the clear yet, so hold on." And she shoved to her feet. Up ahead was that clearing, beyond it was a stretched of woods at the base of the mountains. She broke out into a sprint. The faster she got to those woods for cover, the better. Anyone would be able to spot her making a dash across that field. She'd be easy to spot with her hair reflecting the light like metal. Suddenly she wished she'd kept on that damn hat the soldier had given her. Right now, that hat would come in handy.

The shrill of gunfire sounded.

Dirt flew into the air around her.

She pushed herself to run harder, faster.

The gunfire didn't cease.

The impact of bullets met her ears.

Dirt didn't shoot up at her feet.

They were too far away, but they wouldn't give up. She pictured them wading through the canal, tripping on whatever was in the water and slipping up the embankment to the other side. It'd slow them down, but it wouldn't stop them.

She made it across the clearing before gunfire could start back up again and dove into the woods. Earth crunched beneath her boots. Dodging trees, she ran through the five klicks of woods to the mountains. When she made it to the end of the woods, she skidded to a halt over rock and crystal fragments. She tipped her head back to inspect the incline. It was steep and rocky. In order to make that climb, she'd need her hands free. A large quartz boulder sat in front of her, so she hunkered in front of it.

She studied the metal case housing the poor, innocent alien. Fingerprint scanner on the lid. No locks. Just a handle. Whose fingerprint could open it? One of the Justices'? Perhaps Justice Powell, the most powerful one of them all? She considered her own finger. Her print wouldn't open it. That much she was sure of, but her finger could still free the little alien.

Summoning her powers, she focused on her finger.

A green flame burst from the tip. It burned hot enough to melt glass. She'd done this trick before, except not to free an alien trapped in a metal jail.

"I'll get you out of there," she told him through the metal. "Stay in that little chair until I have the lid off."

The alien nodded.

Pressing the tip of her finger to the top of the metal box, she used the green flame like a blowtorch. Steady. Steady. Steady. She drew a line across each side. When she made it back to where she'd started, she pulled her finger away. With extra care, she lifted the lid and dropped it to the ground.

The alien waved enthusiastically from his chair, and her heart went out to him.

"Okay. You can come out now." She lowered her hand into the box.

The alien scrambled off the chair and climbed onto her hand, where he sat in the middle of her palm.

She lifted him out and brought him close to her face so she could get a good look at him. Probably hundreds of years old, he looked like nothing more than a baby, and was freaking adorable. "Hi, there. I wish we had more time to chat, but we don't. I'm going to have you grab onto the tip of my finger so I can lower you into my holster. It's the safest place for you while I make this trek up the mountain. It won't be smooth, but it's the best I can do under the circumstances. Do you trust me?"

The alien raised his arms up—a sign of trust.

She hovered her finger above his head, and he latched onto it. "Hold on tight."

His body dangled from her finger when she lifted him out. On her knees, she brought her finger to her side holster and dipped it inside the space where her gun was usually stored. His hands released her.

She peeked in to see him standing at the bottom. "It might be better if you sat down, and just"—she raised her hands—"brace your hands on the sides."

He did as she'd instructed.

"Ready?"

He moved a hand from the inside wall to give her another thumb's up. Then he put his hand back into place.

"I'm going to get you out of here. I promise."

To hold up to that promise, she got to her feet and began the climb at a run. Or as much of a run as she could manage with the incline and crystal fragments making each step slip. Still, that mountain was their best shot.

Briefly, she wondered if she was following the same steps as Dee. Were they unable to find Dee because he'd fled to the mountains, too? If she encountered him on this mountain, he was no longer her priority, either. She'd look the other way. At least until the alien in her position was safe.

She couldn't hear anyone approaching, but she wouldn't pause to check.

The mountain she was climbing was known as Mount Elizabeth, and its peak was about three klicks high. People who hiked that mountain could take two, maybe three hours to reach the top. She had to cut that time in half. Hell, less than that. No one was as fast as her. No one was as determined.

She passed the one-mile marker—halfway there.

At the top, she didn't know what she was going to do. Her decision had been too rash to come up with a smart plan. All she knew was getting high up increased her odds of helping the little guy to escape. Once they were up there, she'd figured something out. The best bet would be to find a spot to set him free. They'd never be able to find him. He was too small, and he'd be able to blend in with the rocks and crystals. She just had to give him the best chance of survival. The peak offered that.

Suddenly, a force punched her in the middle of her spine, and her body slammed into the unforgiving ground.

Is That Three or Four Ks?

For a moment, she was stunned by the hit.
Breathless.
Then she sucked oxygen into her lungs.
"Fuck."
Staying low, she shifted onto her left hip and swept her hand over the ground. Her fingers touched warm metal. She picked it up to find a 7.62×51mm sniper bullet. The tip was crumpled from impact.

"So, SWAT is playing now. Welcome to the hunt, boys." She pushed to her knees. "You okay in there?"

The alien gave one of his thumbs-up confirmations.

"You're small but mighty, and I'm your guardian now. These"—she twiddled the bullet between her thumb and finger—"can't stop me."

She popped to her feet and hadn't made three steps before another bullet slammed into the back of her head. The impact brought her to her hands and knees. A shot like that? Anyone would think she was finished, but they couldn't be more wrong. She got right back up.

A third bullet collided into her back the second she straightened.

This time, she stayed on her feet, and she bolted.

A fourth bullet hit her. It caused her to stumble, but she stayed on her feet.

A fifth bullet aimed at her thigh made her fall into a tree. She grabbed it as a sixth bullet collided into her skull.

Gritting her teeth, fingers digging into the bark, she edged around the tree trunk.

None of the hits hurt her one bit. What hurt was that law enforcement was supposed to be her so-called family. Each bullet was a truth, though. They hadn't wanted her on their force. They'd made that clear from the start. And as they fired at her back, it was clear that they'd never had *her* back. Nor would they in the future.

All but Chuck. He was the only one who she could count on, and she'd betrayed him by what she'd done. Hopefully he'd forgive her.

With the tree at her back, she continued her climb. The trees became denser, obscuring the snipers' views. Bark exploded off trees left and right of her. A few grazed her arms and legs, tearing her clothes, but not so much as nicking her impenetrable skin. Nothing could do that. Not a bullet, blade, claw, or razor.

Nothing.

Absolutely fucking nothing could stop her.

Jaw clenched, hands in fists, she sprinted up that damn mountain, missing the bullets that snipers shot at her, blowing holes into trees and shattering crystal boulders. Eventually, she got out of their range.

The sun slowly sank in the sky, casting shadows across the mountain.

Those shadows were her friends.

She didn't stop until she came to the base of the crystal peak. There was nowhere else to go. You couldn't scale that crystal. Not even with the proper equipment. Going up there was a dead-end. She'd essentially put herself straight into a trap, but as long as the little alien got away, she didn't care what happened to her. She'd already been tortured in every way imaginable. Nothing that the officers searching for her could do would make her blink an eye. But if they tried any of that with her alien friend, not only would she blink an eye, she'd act, and they'd regret it. Dearly.

She lowered into a crouch and unbuttoned her holster from her belt. "I'm going to tip this to the side so you can walk out onto my hand." When she tilted the holster, the alien ambled over the leather and across the lines on her palm.

Back against the crystal peak, she pulled her knees to her chest. Then she leveled her hand to her knee so her alien friend could climb on. He stepped off her palm and plopped onto her kneecap. She smiled. "Hi there. I think you can understand what I say. I'm

Avrianna Heavenborn. Do you have a name?"

He flattened his miniature hands to her knee. A soft, wispy voice filled her head—alien telekinesis. *Qqqquirkkkk.*

"That sounds a little like 'quirk.' May I call you Quirk?"

He nodded.

"Quirk, can you tell me how you got here? I was told you were in my world first before our officials gave you to the U.S. government on Earth. How'd you get to New Vida?"

With his hands on her knee, he communicated with her using English phrases he must've pulled from her memory or picked up from his captivity.

Exploration. Universe.

"You were exploring the universe?"

Nod.

So, aliens were just as curious about the universe as humans were. Made sense.

"Were you looking for…um…alien life?"

Nod.

"And you found us."

Accident.

She frowned. "You found us by accident?"

Nod.

He passed her something through their connection—a memory, a vision.

Blackness, speckled with dots of light—stars—and swirls of color—gases and galaxies—and Quirk huddled in a fetal position inside an oval-shaped cocoon of shimmering substance. He was zipping along peacefully when his pod was suddenly smack-dab in the middle of a meteor shower of glowing green rock. A chunk of glowing green rock collided into his pod, shoving him off course at a dangerous speed. He went hurtling toward a planet—New Vida. As he breached the atmosphere, flames engulfed his pod. The next image she saw was his flaming pod pummeling into the ground. Inside a mini crater, he lay there, without his pod, unconscious.

"They found you after you crash-landed?"

Nod.

"How long was that? Do you know?"

An image of a newspaper, something he must've seen when he was first taken, flashed in her mind. She caught the date and did the math.

"Twenty-five years."

Twenty-five years ago, she'd been found floating in the Aurora Diamond. No explanation. No evidence for where she'd come from. Obviously, she looked nothing like Quirk, but could it really be a coincidence? The same time Quirk crash-landed on New Vida from a meteor shower phenomenon, she had also been discovered, a newborn with no family, just her name stitched onto the blanket wrapped tightly around herself. Was she the space version of Moses in the reeds?

Was she an alien?

Was she New Vida's Superman in a pod escaping a destructed world?

The questions, the mystery, the loneliness bombarded her from all sides. She hugged her legs to chest and peered at the little alien. "Do you know me? I mean…before we met…did you know me?"

He shook his head.

Still no answers.

Still a mystery.

Still lonely.

She sighed. "I don't know how else I can help you. I'm going to wait here until they come and put me in custody, but you need to go. Are you able to pull an *E.T.*?"

He tilted his head.

"Phone home?"

Blink-blink.

"Do you have a way to contact your people? To go home?"

Vigorous head nods.

"Then do it. Now. You have to get out of here before it's too late."

He clambered to his feet. Hands clasped above his head, he knocked his head back to gaze up at the sky, speckled with colorful stars unlike the ones seen on Earth. A golden glow formed around his hands. It grew brighter and brighter but stayed about the size of a pea. When it became so bright that she had to squint her eyelids, it shot skyward, straight toward the stars.

She watched it disappear into the atmosphere. Her gaze lowered to Quirk. "A signal?"

Nod.

"You really are small but mighty."

He gave her that goofy smile before sitting back down on her kneecap.

"How long do you think?"

Little shoulder shrug.

"Well, let's hope they're quick. We may only have

another thirty minutes before the people who want you for God-only-knows-what get here, and then I won't be able to protect you." Because she'd be surrounded with numerous guns pointed at her face. No, she couldn't be wounded by humans or weapons, but if Quirk weren't gone, she'd be tempted to fight them, and *they'd* be the ones getting hurt. She'd taken an oath not to harm anyone, even assholes in bulletproof vests.

While waiting, she thought about those assholes in bulletproof vests. So much corruption in her world because of America's influence. Once upon a time, her world had been peaceful. Until the Veil was discovered. Until America claimed their stake and colonized more land that wasn't theirs. Until they brought their greed and violence through the portal. The wealthy searched for more wealth beneath New Vida's surface. Criminals used her world to commit their evil deeds because New Vida didn't have America's resources. No databases. No security. They could get away with every manner of criminal activity. Even murder. That was how the American law enforcement system, with its sordid history, breeched New Vida. Vidians needed some way to defend themselves from what America brought into their world. Except, Avrianna didn't believe it'd been the best solution. She'd joined the force to help her world in the only way she could, but there had to be a better way, because that corruption had leaked into the justice system, just like with America.

There were bad eggs wearing badges and armed with semi-automatic weapons. Avrianna didn't doubt that those bad eggs were hiking Mount Elizabeth for her and an innocent alien who just wanted to go home alive. She didn't doubt that those bad eggs had tried to execute her with sniper bullets. She didn't doubt that the very department she worked for was choke full of those rotten fucking eggs.

"If only I could make a real difference and change the world," she muttered.

Quirk patted her knee. Except it wasn't in a "there-there" manner. He was trying to get her attention.

She focused on him. "Yeah?"

He planted his hands on her knee.

Snapshots flashed in her mind's eye.

A massive building of gold metal with sandy-colored windows, and a pyramid of reflective panels at the top that shot spears of peach sunlight in all directions.

A sign with the words *New Vida Reliance Corps* painted across it.

Herself wearing a badge that didn't say 'Detective' but 'Captain.'

A person with the softest of gray eyes.

She blinked and sucked in a breath. "What…what did you just show me?"

Your future.

She gaped. "My future, as in what you showed me will influence me into making that happen? Or my future, as in it would've happened even if you hadn't showed me all that?"

An image of a door with the number two on it stole her vision for a brief moment.

"Door Number 2? Clever."

Could she really create an agency that'd replace current law enforcement? Could she really save her world with it? How would she even begin to do something that grand? What even made her think she had the right to dream such an impossible dream?

Quirk's hand patted her knee again.

She smiled. Even though she hadn't spoken a word, she got the sense that he knew her thoughts and was giving her an encouraging pat, but she had to know. "Who was that? With the gray eyes? Who was that?"

Shoulder shrug. *Your future, not mine.*

She chuckled. "Good point." Being as gentle as possible, she laid a fingertip on the back of his hand. "Thank you for that…for showing me that I do have a purpose."

He put his other hand on her fingernail. *Thank* you. His gaze rose to the night sky. *It's time.*

"Time-time? I mean…" She glanced up. "It's time for you to go? They're out there?" She couldn't see anything but stars.

Quirk rubbed her finger. *Goodbye…friend.*

She smiled as her eyes misted. "Goodbye, friend."

He released her finger and climbed to his feet. With his adorable smile, he lifted his hand. While he waved at her, a thin beam descended from the sky and surrounded him. A second later, he vanished, and the beam winked out.

Head leaning against the crystal behind her, she studied the stars. The universe was so beautiful and vast, and where the hell did she fit into it all? A woman with no known origin, no blood family, and no clue what to do next to bring that future Quirk showed her into existence.

A twig snapping alerted her that she was no longer alone.

She raised her hands on either side of her head and stayed right there, immobile, waiting for them to come, surrendering to her fate.

9

The Heptagon

SWAT emerged from the trees and boulders and pinned her with red dots. Never mind the fact that she hadn't moved an inch or so much as flinched since she'd heard them approaching.

They shouted for her not to move.

They shouted curses.

They shouted, "Bitch."

All unnecessary.

Two of them broke from their pack, grabbed her, and slammed her into the ground despite the fact she wasn't resisting. One put a knee to her head with enough force that a grown man would've been shouting in pain and begging for him to stop. The other wrenched her arms behind her back with such force that abrasions would've formed on her skin if she had the sensitive skin of a human. Zip ties closed around her wrists, shackling her hands together so tightly that she'd be losing the feeling in them in a matter of minutes if anything like that could bother her.

Fortunately, their abuse couldn't harm her. That wasn't the case for everyone else, though, and that treatment was one thing she wanted to eradicate.

On their descent, she didn't say a word. She didn't so much as jerk to indicate any sort of resistance. She placed her footing carefully, maintaining a steady pace so they could keep her in their sights. The entire time, she considered what Quirk had shown her. How the hell would she manage that? Especially given the fact that she'd have to petition the Justices for approval to create such an agency. After what she'd just done, going against their orders like that and committing several felonies, how could they ever trust her to be in such a position?

Then again, on Earth, people who committed horrible acts were in high-ranking positions of government, and it'd been that way practically from the beginning. The good news was, she was nothing like them. She did things to help others. *They* did things to help themselves and themselves alone. Hopefully the Justices be able to see that and understand her motives, her hopes, her dreams, because it wasn't just a dream for herself but for their world.

At the base of Mount Elizabeth, a line of armored

cars waited. She was shoved into the back of one that several SWAT officers crammed into. They continued to aim their weapons at her. She didn't look at them, just stared at her boots and the gray, sparkling dust that caked them.

They drove her to the back of Aurora Police Department, yanked her out of the vehicle, and escorted her inside, weapons still drawn. No one was in the halls when they hustled her to the bowels of the building. In a matter of minutes, they had her in a cell, with the bars firmly in place.

Two SWAT officers remained while the others left.

She sat on a cot to wait for whatever they'd do next. Surely the Justices would demand to see her, put her on trial, sentence her.

Her gaze flicked from one officer guarding her cell to the other.

One of them took a step, aiming at her through the bars. "What the fuck are you looking at, freak?"

She let out a breath and dropped her gaze. Better to not look at them. A simple look could give them an excuse to fire. They'd say she'd looked at them aggressively, that she'd deserved it. The only good thing was that their bullets couldn't kill her, unlike others who weren't fortunate enough to be a freak like her.

She did know, though, that they wouldn't have done these same things to Dee. They would've put him in a secure cell in maximum, closed the door, and left. There wouldn't be semi-automatic weapons pointed at him while he lay on his cot.

"I want to see my partner!"

Avrianna popped to her feet at Chuck's shout.

The SWAT officers surged forward with their fingers on their triggers.

"I have clearance from the Justices. Now let me in. I said, let me the fuck in or the Justices will have all of your fucking badges!"

She'd never heard Chuck so angry before.

A beep sounded.

A door banged shut.

Footsteps punched the floor.

She looked to see Chuck marching down the hall.

He didn't look at her but stormed up to the SWAT officers. "Get those fucking guns off her and leave."

"We have our orders," one of them said.

"Your orders are to stand down and leave her the fuck alone."

The SWAT officers eyed him before leaving.

She stepped up to the bars. "Chuck."

He faced her. Still, he didn't look at her. He removed the bowie knife from his left-side holster. "Turn around."

She turned.

His fingers tugged at the zip tie. "Jesus, they put these on tight. Shit."

The zip tie snapped in half when he sliced the blade through the plastic.

As soon as she was free, she spun back. "Are you okay?"

He frowned. "Am *I* okay? Are you kidding me?"

"No." She grabbed onto the bars. "Are you okay? Did the Justices take your badge?"

"Kid, I don't care about any of that. I just care if

you're okay."

"I'm fine. Did they take your badge?"

"No, I still have my badge."

She let out a breath.

"Avrianna, what the hell were you thinking?"

"I was thinking that no being should be tortured or experimented on." He didn't know about what she'd endured at the hands of scientists, and if she had it her way, he'd never know. No one would. "I was thinking I couldn't live knowing that was happening." She studied her dirty boots. "I was thinking I had to do something."

Chuck released a breath. "I get it. You're braver than I am, but I wish you had told me, warned me."

"Plausible deniability, and I didn't exactly plan it. I didn't know I was going to do that until I was standing there in front of the Justices, listening to them. What happened after I…?"

"Broke through bulletproof glass and hightailed it across the island with an alien inside a metal lunchpail?"

She winced. "Yeah."

"They detained me. Questioned me."

She closed her eyes. "I'm sorry."

"They asked me if I was aware you were going to do that. I said no."

"See? Plausible deniability. They let you go. So, they believed you?"

"They did."

"Good."

He shook his head. "This isn't good, Avrianna. I heard officers say they'd shot you in the back…in the head…and you kept on going. How the hell—?"

"They're wrong. They missed."

He eyed her. "Trained SWAT snipers missed?"

"Yup."

"Okay. I'll let that go. Where's the little…um…?"

"Alien?"

Chuck nodded.

"His kind did a 'Beam me up, Scotty' on the peak of Mount Elizabeth."

"So at least you accomplished what you set out to do."

"At least I did. Do you know what they have planned for me?"

"I don't, but I will raise hell if they try to hurt you in any way."

She appreciated his protectiveness, even if it wasn't necessary. "Was there anything on the news about what I did?"

"Are you kidding? They can't let civilians know you broke E.T. out of the Heptagon. Can you imagine the panic and paranoia?"

She supposed he was right. "I guess I'll be here overnight, until the Justices are ready to see me. Can you do me a favor?"

"Anything."

"Don't mention this to Sassy." If her foster mom knew she'd been arrested and was sitting in a jail cell, they'd have a feisty middle-aged woman demanding to be let in to see her daughter or she'd rain holy hell on all of them.

Chuck looked horrified at the thought. "My lips are sealed."

She smiled at the thought of Chuck trying to calm

Sassy, but her smile quickly faded as reality sank in. "I'm sorry."

"For what?"

"You're my partner, and what I did impacts you. You may still have your badge, but being my partner hasn't been easy on you, and it will impact you long after we're no longer partners."

"When are we not going to be partners? You planning on retiring early?"

She lifted a shoulder. "I may not get my badge back. We may not be partners after this."

"Fuck that."

She lifted a brow. It wasn't often when Chuck let so many curse words fall from his lips. He only did it when he felt strongly about something, and she appreciated

that he felt strongly about her and their partnership.

"I know you may not like to hear it, but it's true. I don't think what I did is repairable."

"We'll see about that." And he whirled on his feet.

"Chuck."

He stomped away.

"Chuck!"

He disappeared around the corner.

A beep sounded, and a door slammed.

She leaned her forehead against an iron bar. "Shit."

When two SWAT officers returned to point their guns at her, she backed away, hands raised, and tried to do the least threatening thing—she laid on the cot and eventually fell asleep.

In the morning, even more SWAT officers joined her two watchdogs. Ten in total just to drag her out of her cell, strong arm her down the hall, and shove her into the back of a SWAT van. They caged her in on all sides while escorting her into the Heptagon. Moments later, she was cuffed in front of the Justices.

She didn't say a word, just waited for the hammer to fall.

"Detective Heavenborn." Justice Powell's voice carried loud, powerful, and angry. "Yesterday, you broke out of a high-security facility with New Vida property, evaded arrest, fled up a mountain, and *lost* said property. Did I miss anything?"

"No, ma'am, you did not. I did all of those things. Except, we're not talking about a dog or a cat. We're talking about an extraterrestrial being that cannot be anyone's property. Certainly not a *world's* property."

"You do not sound remorseful," Justice Dey said.

"I do not regret what I did. I'm a law enforcement officer. We're supposed to uphold the law. As such, I know when something is unlawful. And keeping that innocent alien in our position to do God-only-knows-what to him is one of the most unlawful things I've encountered as an officer. It is my duty to serve and protect. There were no limitations put on *whom* I should serve and protect. People of this world, surely, but even visitors. We have a portal that links us over lightyears to Earth. We serve and protect the people of Earth when they are here. They are not originally of this world. They come here through space travel. That alien you all were so eager to hand over to our scientists after letting Earth's scientists do inexplicable things to him is not originally of this world, either, and came here through space travel, too, so why did we treat him so differently?" She looked at each of them one at a time. "I chose to serve and protect that alien from *you*…from us. From New Vida. And, in turn, I prevented us from becoming cosmic killers. That is also in my job description. I *stop* killers. I prevent murder and harm from being done to others. I could not stand by to allow any of that to happen, so, no, I am not remorseful. Not in the slightest."

The Justices exchanged looks.

Avrianna continued. "I was able to reunite someone with their loved ones. Someone who had been kidnapped and tortured was able to go back home. As an officer, I've done that before. It is the most rewarding feeling, and I felt that again, when I helped that alien to go home, so, no, I am not remorseful. I am proud, and if you don't want an officer like that, then fine. Take my badge. I certainly don't fit in with the rest, except for my partner, Charles Davis, who had no idea what I was going to do. But if you're going to discipline me and take me off the force, then I won't fight you, because you're showing me what kind of officers you stand behind and what you support, and I don't want to work for a system…I don't want to work for *you*…if you can't see that what I did was within the bounds of what my job asks me to do."

She took a small step back. "That's all I have to say."

They were silent for a long, strained moment.

"We appreciate your candor," Justice Dey said.

"Yes, we do," Justice Powell said. "It's not often when someone puts us in our places, and every once in a while, we need that. And I think we would all agree that we don't mind that it was you, but *prefer* that it was you."

Avrianna frowned. "Why me?"

"Because we were reminded that you don't know where you come from, but New Vida is your home. Once, scientists treated you much like they would've treated the alien, and yet, you chose a career in protecting all citizens. One day, you might even have to protect one of those scientists, and we believe, after your display yesterday and your speech today, that you would."

It wouldn't be easy, but she would. She'd do her job. "I would."

"Which is why we are not going to take your badge and we're going to recommend that you go back to work, because we need officers like you on our streets."

"Thank you."

"Of course..." Justice Valente folded his hands together. "Any other disciplinary action would be up to Chief Logan."

"Understood."

Justice Powell raised her hand. "Please remove Detective Heavenborn's cuffs."

A guard stepped forward.

She angled toward him, hands raised, for him to unlock the cuffs.

He didn't look at her. The cuffs clattered, and he backed away.

Justice Powell's voice carried. "You're free to go,

Detective Heavenborn.”

“Thank you, Your Justices.”

They bowed their heads.

Not wanting to overstay her welcome or risk them changing their minds, she exited the Heptagon. Chuck was waiting outside for her.

“What are you doing here?”

“I followed your caravan of SWAT vehicles. Talk about overkill.”

She shrugged. “They had to take every precaution.”

“Against you?”

She shrugged again, but this time she didn’t say anything.

“What happened in there, kid?”

“They let me go.”

He laughed. “That’s obvious. What did they say?”

“That I’m free to go.”

He tilted his head. “Again, pretty obvious. What aren’t you telling me?”

“Nothing.” She sighed. “I…kinda put them in their place. Their words. And they realized that they want someone like me on the force who is willing to do good, even when others on the force will demonize me and say what I did was wrong.”

“You know I’d never demonize you, right?”

“I know. You’re the exception.” She pointed at his car. “Could you drive me to the department? I have to talk to the chief.”

“About?”

“My future.”

He nodded slowly. “Okay. Let’s go.”

They didn’t speak during the drive to Aurora

Police Department. Then he walked beside her through the halls, casting glares at anyone who dared to scowl at Avrianna. It wasn't necessary, but she appreciated his support. His show at having her back meant more to her than she would ever be able to form words to express.

Outside Chief Logan's office, he posted next to the door while she knocked.

"Come in."

Chuck gave her arm a reassuring squeeze.

Bracing for Chief Logan's ruling, she stepped inside.

"Detective."

She shut the door and stood in front of his desk. On the edge, her badge and firearm sat there, staring at her, pleading for her to make this right. "Chief."

Sighing, he leaned back in his chair. It creaked as he rocked back and forth. "I would like to give these back to you." He pointed at her badge and firearm. "But I can't."

She was bracing so hard that her spine felt as though it'd snap if she flinched.

"You are the best damn detective on this force, Avrianna, but I had to send our own men after you. I had to order our men to bring you in, whatever means necessary. That wasn't easy for me to do."

She nodded.

"I have to suspend you. Two months. Without pay."

Ouch.

But at least she wasn't being fired from the force. She'd never have a badge again if Chief Logan didn't give her a second chance.

"I understand, sir."

"When the two months are up, come back to my office, and I'll give these back."

Her gaze went to her badge and firearm, and she tried not to give them longing looks that'd embarrass Chief Logan.

"Until then, stay out of trouble, Detective."

"Yes, sir. Thank you, sir. I'll see you in two months."

She left his office and shut the door at her back. As her breath left her lungs, she deflated and tipped back into the wall beside Chuck.

"What'd he say?"

"I'm suspended for two months without pay."

He shut his eyes.

"By the time I come back, you may not want to take me back as your partner."

His eyelids sprang open. "Are you kidding? I'm not going to take a partner. I'll work alone for those two months."

"You can't work alone."

"I can."

No one could say that Chuck wasn't loyal, and she loved him for that.

"Well…" She straightened. "You should get to work. I…I guess I'm going to go home and…" She had no idea what she'd do at home. Her job was her life. She worked, she ate, she slept. Repeat. And most of the time, she barely slept. Sometimes, she skipped meals. "Do…something."

"Are you going to be okay, kid?"

"Sure." She'd thrown a bomb at her career in order

to save an extraterrestrial.
        She had no choice but to be okay.

Captain Heavenborn

The first few days of her suspension, she sat on her couch, drinking coffee and watching the news. Good stories came few and far between. Murders, missing children and adults, burglary, deadly car accidents, and every other manner of criminal activity dominated the news along with weather reports and flu numbers and gas prices. On the fourth day, she couldn't listen to anymore. She turned off the TV and flopped backward on her couch, resting her head on the armrest. Staring up at the ceiling, she tried not to think about the fact that Dee Underhill was still at large and she couldn't do a damn thing about it. If she went out on her own to search for him or investigated his disappearance in any way and Chief Logan found out, she wouldn't be facing a suspension. She'd have no hope of having a badge again. Then she wouldn't be able to do what she dreamed about doing—saving her world. And that future Quirk showed her would have no chance at coming true.

She bolted upright.

The flashes of that future came back to her. If that was her future, then the time was now. She leapt to her feet and hurried to her kitchen where she yanked open drawer after drawer, searching for paper. Cutlery clattered. Hot sauce packets jiggled back and forth. She found a pad of lined yellow paper beneath coffee filters and fast-food napkins. A pen she discovered in another drawer with reusable straws and a bag of licorice. After brewing a pot of coffee, she plopped down at her dining room table.

First, she listed what was wrong with current law enforcement, and there were many problems. Being on the inside, she knew the issues. She encountered them every day.

She wasn't going to sugarcoat a damn thing.

With that list torn out and spread across her table, she started a new list to address each and every one of those problems and how she'd personally correct them. She thought about discussions that had crossed over into New Vida from America about changes their citizens were demanding following tragic and inexcusable murders committed by law enforcement that ignited the nation. New Vida's law enforcement wasn't exempt from that. After all, it was a replica of America, with all of its horrific roots. It was time that New Vida severed its ties from that system, and she would listen to their citizens to create something better in *her* world. Maybe prove to America that it could be done, if only they wanted to change for the better.

A Crisis Aid Division, consisting of victim advocates and mental health agents. Because many tragic moments happened when officers responded to situations they were not equipped to handle. The division would have social workers and highly qualified therapist ready to go out in field if a call came in requiring their expertise to diffuse situations, especially if someone had a mental health disorder or could just simply be misunderstood for something normal, like being autistic.

Then there'd be Community Order Keepers, working closely with local community leaders. Those community leaders would be well-known business owners and neighborhood elders. With those leaders, the Community Order Keepers would attend calls for disputes and thefts and break-ins and other non-violent situations.

That left the Violent Crime Division, and that'd be for her officers. No… not officers. She'd never call her men and woman on the force an officer.

Defenders.

They'd defend New Vida.

They'd defend the innocent.

They'd defend the victims.

Then there'd be SWAT for high-risk situations.

Internal Affairs for, well, internal investigations,

because she was determined to make sure they never had any sort of corruption.

And, of course, the CSI Division for murder investigators.

But she didn't stop there.

New Vida didn't have all the security or investigative means as America, but in order to truly protect New Vida from crime, they had to step up their game.

Military.

Bureau of Investigation.

Coastal Defense.

Customs and Veil Protection.

New Vida Security.

Except her goal was to use these forces responsibly and not make the same mistakes as other nations. And that meant a huge change. Something no one else would consider...combining all of that under one umbrella...one agency—New Vida Reliance Corps. Eleven different divisions, but one team. One unit. That was the answer. No division.

But she didn't want to stop there, either.

Many crimes involved injuries and many calls ended with hospital trips. Aurora Hospital was sadly under equipped. It was the only medical care facility on the island, and it was more like a community hospital. She knew that because her best friend, Lexie, was a doctor there. Lexie vented about not having the funds for the equipment they needed, not being able to do pro bono surgeries, not having the staffing for emergencies, and having a building badly in need of repairs.

Avrianna dropped her pen and snatched up her

phone to call Lexie, her confidant in all things who she trusted to tell her if this was a bonkers idea or if she was onto something huge. Not just life-changing, but world-changing.

Today was one of Lexie's rare day's off, so she came over right away.

Avrianna was the farthest thing from a hugger, but whenever she saw Lexie after a stretch of time of no contact because of their busy schedules, she always gave her a hug. It was what they did since surviving the nightmare of the foster care system together. It was what they did since they'd forged an unbreakable friendship.

"Thanks for coming over. Can I get you anything?" Avrianna asked.

Lexie tilted her head. "Do you *have* anything?"

Avrianna gave a sheepish smile. "Coffee and…water?"

"Is that a question mark after water? You don't know if you have water?" Lexie teasingly turned on the kitchen faucet. "Ah. Tap. Look at that."

Avrianna laughs. "I meant bottles. I wasn't sure if I had the last one."

"That's okay. I'll have coffee."

Avrianna brewed a fresh pot, gave Lexie a cup, and topped off hers. Then she showed Lexie the papers mapping out her dream, explained every part, and sat nervously by while Lexie looked over everything once more. She valued Lexie's opinion more than anything, so when Lexie lowered the pages, Avrianna held her breath.

"Are you kidding?"

Her breath left her in a rush. So, bonkers it is.

"This is brilliant."

Avrianna blinked. "What?"

"Genius."

"I don't...what?"

"All of this." Lexie swirled her hand above the papers in front of her. "This is amazing. Hearing you talk about it, and seeing it written in ink, I can feel the possibilities. It's not impossible." She flatted her hands to the pages. "It's all right here. You need to bring this to the Justices."

Avrianna shook her head. "I can't."

"Why not? If you applied to them as a law enforcement officer, I'm sure they'd see how this could have a positive impact on our world."

"I'm not sure they'd want to listen to any idea I had. Last week, I sort of stole a tiny alien from them and broke through their bulletproof window and evaded SWAT and got put on two-month's suspension without pay because of it."

Lexie's jaw dropped.

"They didn't strip me of my badge." She rubbed her neck. "So, I guess that's good."

"You stole a tiny alien?"

Avrianna nodded. "Quirk."

"You named it Quirk?"

"No. That was the best translation of his real name that I could come up with."

"Oh, right. That's completely reasonable. Where the heck did you even get a tiny alien?"

"Area 51."

Silence.

"Okay." Lexie nodded. "I thought you were going to say something weird. Of course, Area 51. Where else?"

Avrianna chuckled. "I know how it sounds, but it's true. He showed me a vision of my future, and this"— she dropped her hands onto the papers just like Lexie had done—"is it. On paper. All thought-out to the best of my ability."

"And it's the best damn business personal in the galaxy."

"I still can't bring it to the Justices." She studied the paper in front of her with a sketch of the building she'd seen in Quirk's vision. "Unless I get backing. A hell of a lot of backing. From law enforcement, medical staff, citizens, and I'd need the biggest business loan in existence."

"Well, I'll back you. I would do anything to work at a hospital this grand."

"I appreciate that."

"How many names do you think you'd need for your petition?"

Avrianna shrugged. "Thousands."

"Well, one down."

The one that meant the most to Avrianna.

The next one would be Chuck. She invited him over the next day for coffee. He probably thought she was calling for updates on the hunt for Dee Underhill, but...for the moment, she had something more important on her mind, something that could help them to find and put Dee away for good.

She gave chuck a cup of coffee and her spiel.

Chuck sat back in his chair. "How the hell did you

come up with that in five days?"

One day, really, but he didn't need to know that.

"I had help."

"From?"

He also didn't need to know an alien had given her a vision of the future. "The point is the help I'm going to need moving forward. Help like yours."

"What do you need me to do?"

"Add your name to the list I plan to present to the Justices, for one."

"That's easy." He signed his name under Lexie's. "What else?"

"If this wild dream of mine actually comes true, I want you to be the chief of the Violent Crime Division."

His head went back, and he inhaled. "I'd be honored. What else?"

She smiled. "I need more backing. A lot more."

"I can help with that."

One by one, Avrianna approached her family and friends to collect their support.

Simone, medical examiner and one of Avrianna's closest friends.

Evony, disguise expert.

Emerson, Evony's twin and a renowned psychic who seconded Quirk's vision.

Veena, NYPD and Avrianna's foster sister.

Sassy, aunt and foster mother, who'd put her bid in to be Avrianna's assistant.

Déjà, Avrianna's adoptive sister.

Grandy, the most badass grandma to beat all badass grandmas.

After that, Avrianna sought security guards, cops, investigators, detectives, and SWAT officers—just not the ones who'd shot her—only the ones she knew wanted to do good.

Hundreds.

Then aids, nurses, doctors, and surgeons who'd made vows that NVRC could help them to uphold.

Hundreds more.

Followed by citizens. Business to business. Door to door.

Hundreds upon hundreds.

Finally, Avrianna had all the names she could get. Except one. The most important.

She knocked on Chief Logan's door.

"Come in."

She took a deep breath before stepping inside.

"Detective Heavenborn, this is a surprise. Your suspension isn't over yet."

"I know, sir. I'm hoping I could have a few moments
of your time."

"Of course."

She gave him the same speech as everyone else and ended it with passing him the pages and pages of signatures.

He flipped through it, no doubt spotting Chuck's name on the second line and a majority of his own officers after that. The pages dropped from his fingers onto his desk. "Is this your way of telling me that you're robbing me of my career, Detective?"

She flinched. "No, sir."

"But aren't you? When this…this NVRC is

constructed and most of my officers are gone, working for you, what will become of this department?"

"Police departments would transition to Reliance Advocacy Departments, with supporting roles to assist NVRC when needed."

"Doing what? The grunt work?"

She bristled and struggled to remain her composure. "No." And she did something she'd never done before. She didn't follow that with 'sir.' Disrespectful, but her respect was dwindling. "The departments would offer community-based assistance for non-violent crimes. And they'd worked closely with civilians to keep neighborhoods safe, offering night watches for neighborhoods that see a lot of break-ins after dark, safeguarding school children, looking after those in the poorer communities, who need security and not to be treated as potential criminals. They'd be repairing their fractured relationship with the people. They'd be making a difference and truly doing good deeds every damn day. No firearms. No pepper spray. No tasers. They wouldn't be looked at in fear anymore, but like friends to the people, because that's what they always should've been."

Chief Davis eyed her for several moments when she finished.

She didn't look away.

Maintaining that serious look, he said, "I'd like that very much."

She continued to stare.

He picked up his pen and added his name to the final line. Then he met her eye again. "I'm proud of you, Avrianna." The first time he'd ever used her first name since he'd hired her.

"Thank you, sir."

He held out the pages of signatures. "Now, get out of here and do some good."

"Yes, sir."

With all the support she could get, she took the signatures and her proposal to New Vida Bank to ask for the largest loan ever. One that she was informed they'd give her if and only if the Justices consented to the creation of NVRC. Now she had no choice but to approach the Justices.

In the same place she had stood when the Justices allowed her to keep her badge, after she'd previously stood there moments before breaking out with an alien hostage, she made her plea to the Justices. Her request was the biggest anyone had ever brought to them. Her request would make the most impact.

"Detective Heavenborn, less than a month ago, you almost risked your career to free an extraterrestrial being, and now you're asking us for permission to create a law enforcement agency unlike any this universe has seen?" Justice Dey asked.

"Yes, Your Justices, I am, and I hope that after my presentation, you'll see that NVRC is vital. Especially after one of the last things you said to me"—she locked gazes with Justice Powell—"was that we need more officers like me on the streets. Officers who have the same moral compass. Officers who want to do good. NVRC will be the home for such officers like myself, and these changes will do what you and I pray for…save New Vida."

Justice Powell nodded. "We will discuss this. Go

home."

Go home?

Avrianna stood there a moment, unsure of what to do, but if the Justices tell you to go home, then you go home.

And she didn't hear from them in weeks. A denial, surely.

On the second-to-last day of her suspension, a package was delivered to her home. She signed for it and found something she hadn't expected—a contract to become the owner and captain of New Vida Reliance Corps. With the help of Sassy, who'd be an assistant for lawyers for years, she read through the contract line by line. One stipulation, buried in fine print, was that Avrianna would need a partner for fieldwork.

No way would she be confined to a desk like Chief Logan. No way would she be strapped down to a partner. She loved Chuck. She truly did. But Chuck would be running the Violent Crime Division. He wouldn't have time to babysit her in the field. Nor did she need a babysitter. She had powers that meant she didn't need backup. She was her own motherfucking backup. If lying about having a partner for fieldwork meant all of this

would come to be, then she'd lie her ass off.

What the Justices didn't know, wouldn't hurt them.

The next day, they summoned her to the Heptagon.

"Detective Heavenborn, we trust that you've had time to look over the contract," Justice Powell said.

"Yes, Your Justices, I did, and I agree to your terms."

"Then I suppose we should now address you as

Captain Heavenborn."

Reliance Corps was thriving. The Justices had granted Avrianna approval to open a second New Vida Reliance Corps on the island of Houston to help with the areas devastated by crime there. She'd put Veena, her adoptive cousin and foster sister, in charge. Murder and crime rates had dropped throughout New Vida, but they were a long way from peace.

Even so, Avrianna was content. She'd forgotten about the pale gray eyes in Quirk's vision and had given up on searching for Dee, the man who had disappeared in thin air, long ago. She took down criminals and protected the innocent, just as her goal had always been. Sitting at her desk, closing another case, yes, she was content.

A knock on her door had her looking up from her laptop. "Come in."

The door opened.

"Captain." Chuck stepped in with a serious look on his face.

Her fingers stilled on the keyboard. "What is it?"

"He's back."

She frowned. "Who's back?"

"Dee." He dropped a file onto her desk.

The file was for a new case they'd been investigating involving arms trafficking to and from New Vida. At first, it had been a trickle. But in the matter of weeks, it had become a flood. Avrianna was desperate to put an end to the deadly operation before it could prove catastrophic, but where the weapons were being assembled and packaged was a crucial detail that they had yet uncovered. And when those shipments went out, which routes they took, and their final destinations were so closely guarded that Avrianna and her team were at a loss. Not even security footage had helped to uncover those answers. Nor having extra Defenders on the streets, eyes peeled for any sign of the operation. They had yet to catch them in the act, and that frustrated Avrianna to no end.

"Our hackers stumbled upon chatter on the dark web. Someone let a name slip, and they'd called him the Weapons Lord of New Vida."

Her gaze snapped up. "Dee."

Chuck nodded.

"Son of a bitch."

Was this what Dee Underhill had been doing since he'd miraculously escaped prison? In hiding he'd been quietly building his empire? Producing weapons? And not just pistols and revolvers like Underhill & Co had done, but semi-automatic weapons, grenades, bombs, and weapons like Avrianna had never seen that were now on her streets? Had he been weaving a web of traffickers throughout both worlds to do his bidding?

Apparently so.

He'd become the Weapons Lord of New Vida right under Avrianna's nose.

He'd turned himself from a wife killer to a cosmic killer, and he was turning more and more criminals with bloodthirst into potential cosmic killers, too. With the weapons he manufactured and snuck through the Veil, there was no telling how many people on Earth and New Vida would lose their lives to these powerful weapons. She couldn't allow that to happen. Not on her watch. Not to her world.

"It's time you brought Crystal back out."

Chuck was right. This was a job for Crystal, the badass weapons dealer with a ruined leg whose skill was in crafting one-of-a-kind diamond bullets. With Crystal, Avrianna could uncover the secrets Dee had worked so hard to keep hidden from her. With Crystal, she could bring down the most dangerous man on *both* worlds.

"Do you think you can do it?" Chuck asked, as if reading her mind.

She met his eye and smiled. "Watch me."

Chrys Fey

Author's Note

Dear Reader,

I hope you've had fun getting to know Avrianna Heavenborn and some of the key characters in her story. *Cocky Killer*, *Universal Killer*, and *Cosmic Killer* are three stories I wrote as prequels to the *Heaven Born* series so you could learn a little about Avrianna and discover how she created NVRC before diving into the first book of her series, which will be out July 3rd, 2026 in celebration of Avrianna's birthday.

If you've enjoyed these stories, continue on to read "Chapter One" of *Heaven Born*.

Happy Reading!

Chrys Fey

Chrys Fey

Heaven Born

Sneak Peak

Threat

A black sports car cut across two lanes of traffic, heading in the wrong direction. In the passenger's seat of the vehicle giving chase, Avrianna braced a hand on the dash. She snatched up her radio and shouted, "Vaughn is heading north on southbound Highway 1. Create a roadblock. Stop the traffic. We don't need a pileup."

A reply came through. "On it, Captain."

The sports car weaved in and out of oncoming cars. As the right-hand man to the weapons lord Dee Underhill, Vaughn arranged shipments of weapons, from guns to bombs, between Earth and New Vida. He had to evade arrest to keep their operation going, but Avrianna couldn't allow him to keep trafficking his boss's deadly goods.

She zeroed in on the sports car and what lay ahead—

the Veil. At twenty-feet tall and twenty-feet wide, a veil of air shimmered like opal inside a frame of giant quartz crystals. Vehicles waited to pass through it to enter Earth, while a steady stream of vehicles came into New Vida. Every person to come and go essentially got a clean slate. Their record on either side didn't carry over, which made Avrianna's job that much harder. Sometimes, impossible. If they lost Vaughn through the Veil, he'd escape criminal prosecution. On the other side, Vaughn would be protected. That wasn't an option.

"We have to stop him," Avrianna said. "Go faster."

Chuck, chief of NVRC's Violent Crime Division, swore as he swerved around a car. "I'm going as fast as I can."

"You have to get up beside him."

"I'm trying," he ground out between clenched teeth.

Vaughn narrowly missed two cars. When the blockade of defenders' cars appeared, Vaughn shot back over the median.

Chuck yanked the wheel, and Avrianna bounced in her seat as they sped after him.

Idling cars waiting to leave New Vida came into view.

"Shit," Avrianna hissed.

The sport car's lights flashed red, and the tires squealed. The back end swerved before jerking to a stop. A second later, the driver's door flung open, and

Vaughn dove onto the road, taking off on foot toward the Veil.

Chuck punched the brake. Before the car came to a full stop, Avrianna shoved open the passenger's door. She clipped her radio to her belt and sprang out of the car.

"Captain!"

Avrianna ignored Chuck because she couldn't let Vaughn go free. She was faster than anyone else. Stronger. More powerful. She could catch him…*had* to catch him.

"You're going to lose him through the Veil!" Chuck's voice came through her radio.

She clenched her jaw and balled her hands into fists. *No, I won't.* She pushed her legs harder. The impact of her feet pounding into the asphalt vibrated up her legs. Her badge bounced against her chest. Avrianna and Vaughn cut across the main road to the sound of car horns. Idling cars were a blur as she caught up to Vaughn, but with each stride, they came closer to the Veil and Vaughn's freedom.

"Avrianna, he's going to escape!"

If she could get to her radio, she'd snap at Chuck to shut up. She didn't have the time, though, because Chuck was right; if she so much as paused, Vaughn would get away.

She sped past immobile cars, slicing through exhaust.

The Veil's energy hummed in the air, tingling her skin.

Avrianna was two car-lengths from Vaughn. So close. And yet, he was closer to the Veil.

She spotted an unarmed Veil Protection agent patrolling their side. "Stop him!"

The agent went to intercept Vaughn, but Vaughn plowed full tilt into him, knocking the agent to the ground. The impact didn't so much as slow Vaughn.

Now or never.

Determination roared through her veins, setting her ablaze on the inside. She formed her right hand into a claw and summoned her powers. A bright green orb of burning toxins exploded around her hand, and she tossed the orb at Vaughn. It struck the bottom of his boot.

He stumbled but didn't fall.

When his boot hit the concrete, the melted sole stuck to the ground. He faltered and yanked his foot from the boot. Once freed, he kept on running, but that pause gave her what she needed. She sprinted ahead by two long strides and leapt through the air. Gravity carried her forward. She reached out to Vaughn just as his right foot disappeared through the Veil. A moment later, her body collided into him, and they sailed through the portal.

A tickling sensation rolled over her body from head to toe. The scenery changed from city life to rock formations, orange dirt, and a pale blue sky. The desert's heat swarmed around her. The Grand Canyon was stifling compared to the seventy degrees of New Vida.

They slammed into asphalt beside a truck. Avrianna didn't waste a second. She pinned Vaughn in place. Then she peered up at ten assault rifles pointed at her.

She raised her right hand slowly. *If they fire, they'll find out bullets don't work on me.* And she didn't want anyone to know that.

"Take it easy," she said. "I'm Captain Heavenborn of Reliance Corps."

She lifted her badge for the American soldiers to see. Their faces were partially obscured by their helmets and protective eye gear, but their stern expressions were visible; the US Military patrolled their side with weapons and zero tolerance. Two people hurtling through the Veil and landing face-first at their feet did not sit well with them.

They knew exactly who she was, though. Everyone did.

The driver's side window to the truck beside them rolled down, and someone pointed a phone at her, no doubt recording this for the Internet.

Great.

She shifted her back to the camera. "This man is a wanted criminal fleeing arrest. He contributes heavily to the arms trafficking in both worlds." She eyed the soldiers. "Do you want to deal with him, or shall I?"

The soldiers had two options. They could order her to release him, or they could let her take the problem off their hands. One by one, they lowered their weapons and took a step back.

She blew a lock of silvery-blonde hair out of her face. "That's what I thought." She removed the handcuffs from her back pocket and slapped them onto Vaughn's wrists. Gripping him, she hauled him to his feet.

"Thanks for your assistance," she said to the

soldiers, not even bothering to hide her sarcasm. They looked away, dismissing her. Their disrespect was like a slap to the face.

Scowling, she dragged Vaughn back through the Veil to New Vida.

Chuck paced back and forth on the other side. He and a few defenders were physically blocking the lane to stop the traffic. Wind had tousled Chuck's long, brown hair. When he saw her escorting Vaughn, he met her at squad car where she gave Vaughn his rights.

"Vaughn Wagner, do you understand your rights as were given to you?"

"Fuck you," he hissed.

She pushed him into the back of a squad car, slammed the door shut, and dusted off her hands. "I think he understands."

Chuck grinned. "They let you take him?"

"Of course, they did. If they had let him go on American soil, they'd be blamed for whatever he did over there."

"Or they would've blamed you, for not stopping him in the first place."

Avrianna glared at Chuck. The truth behind his words sent her blood boiling. The citizens of Earth would put the blame squarely on her shoulders. They wouldn't bother to ask how one man could get past several armed Marines, in the middle of the Grand Canyon. Hell, they couldn't even keep track of their own nuclear weapons. Rumor had reached NVRC that one of the U.S.'s nuclear arms had gone missing. They denied it, but every country on Earth, and all of New Vida, knew about it. Sometimes there was truth to rumor.

"Yeah, well, they're not going to use me as a scapegoat." She knocked on the hood of the squad car. "Let's lock him up."

They returned to New Vida Reliance Corps, a massive building of gold metal. Sandy-colored windows reached one hundred and sixty-four stories high. At the top, a pyramid of reflective panels made it look like a beacon with spears of peach sunlight bouncing off its walls.

When Avrianna had thought of the concept for NVRC, an agency that blended law enforcement, investigation, and security with local community efforts, that was exactly what she wanted it to be—a beacon of hope. New Vida had badly needed help, and the police departments that existed before NVRC weren't cutting it. She had seen the problem and knew the solution—unity.

She led Vaughn to a holding cell. With a great deal of satisfaction, she banged the bars closed, relishing the clank of metal on metal that signified a job well done. *Man, I'll never get tired of that sound.* She turned her back on Vaughn and walked away.

"Dee will come for you," he shouted. "He'll make you pay!"

She smirked. "He can try."

On the top floor, she headed toward her office. Sassy, wearing a hot pink feather boa that brought out the warm undertones of her skin, occupied the assistant's desk outside her door. As Avrianna neared, the stench of nail polish clogged her nostrils. Sure enough, Sassy was giving herself a manicure. If Sassy were anyone else, Avrianna would fire her, but Sassy was her adoptive aunt and foster mom, and she loved her. Feather boa and all.

Sassy looked up and nearly knocked over her nail polish when she hopped to her feet. On three-inch heels and in a tight leather skirt, she scurried to Avrianna. "Stop. You can't go in your office."

Amused, Avrianna lifted a brow. "Why not?"

"Because you have a visitor."

She looked toward her office. "And you just let them in and closed the door? I have classified information in there."

Sassy leaned closer. "It's Justice Powell."

Avrianna's eyes widened. "Oh shit."

"That's what I said, although not to her face, of course."

"I would hope not."

The seven Justices were appointed to make fair decisions regarding issues that could impact New Vida. Avrianna had to go through them to get permission to start up Reliance Corps. It hadn't been an easy feat. The fact Justice Powell was in her office now couldn't be a good thing. The Justices never went to anyone; you had to get approval to speak to them, which could take weeks to fulfil. Then you had to face them in the Heptagon while they stared down at you from their elevated seats. And Justice Powell was the toughest of them all.

Avrianna fidgeted in place. "Did she say what she wanted?"

Sassy shook her head, sending dark auburn waves dancing. "No. She just said she had to talk to you and went right on in there and sat down."

"Okay." Avrianna let out a breath. "Do I look as though I just tackled a criminal?"

Sassy eyed her up and down. "Yes."

The knees of Avrianna's jeans were stained orange. She brushed them in vain. In her office stood an armoire full of emergency clothes, including blazers. She'd normally change into a pair of slacks and a button-up shirt in a situation like this, but she couldn't very well shoo Justice Powell out in order to change into fresh clothes.

"Damn. Do I have dirt on my face?"

"No, but you could use some blush." Sassy pinched her cheeks.

Avrianna swatted her hands away. "I don't want to look flustered."

"Oh, right. Sorry."

She wiped her sweaty hands on her thighs. "All right. I'm going in."

"Good luck," Sassy whispered.

"Thanks. I'll need it."

She took another breath to calm her nerves before opening the door to her office. In one of the two chairs on the other side of Avrianna's desk sat a woman with umber skin and short braids. She wore a white pant suit, purple blouse, and a matching silk scarf.

"Justice Powell, it's an honor."

Justice Powell got to her feet. "Captain Heavenborn." Her voice was deep and demanding, as strong as her presence, as her role. She held out her hand.

Avrianna accepted Justice Powell's hand and shook it.

"Captain, please have a seat." She indicated at Avrianna's desk chair.

Feeling awkward, Avrianna took her seat. "You wish to speak to me?"

"I do. First, good work on taking down Vaughn. Our world is a little safer with him behind bars."

"Thank you."

"However…"

Inwardly, Avrianna winced at the sharpness of Justice Powell's tone. Outwardly, she maintained the illusion of calm.

"Your takedown this morning was filmed and is all over the Internet. It's been picked up by Earth news outlets as well." She passed Avrianna a tablet.

On the screen, a frozen video waited to be watched, but it wasn't the recording from Earth's side, as she had expected. The feed showed her chasing after Vaughn. A moment later, her hand erupted with searing toxins. She paused the video, not needing to see more.

"You can't use your powers in public, Captain. Not only could it be dangerous for others, but the majority of people already fear you enough. Displays like this will only make your relationship with the public more difficult."

Avrianna nodded. "I know. It won't happen again."

"Good. I trust that it won't, but that's not the only reason why I am here."

Avrianna braced for whatever she had to say next.

"Rip Goliath spoke to us this morning about you and Reliance Corps. He found out about your contract stipulation to have a partner whenever you go into the field. He wants NVRC shut down and you stripped of your badge. Permanently."

Under her desk, Avrianna balled her hands into fists. Six months ago, Rip opened the doors to Goliath Inc, another so-called law enforcement agency. The Justices had given her authority over the most impacted areas of the island of Aurora, and Rip received permission to govern the areas beyond her jurisdiction on the island. As soon as he did, he had set his men loose for his own personal gain. He wasn't after peace or safety. He didn't care about their world or the people in it. If he did, he wouldn't be going after her agency.

"I wasn't alone during that takedown, though. Chuck Davis, chief of my Violent Crime

Division, was there."

"But is he your partner?"

She shook her head. Five years ago, when she was a detective, Chuck had been her partner, but he wasn't now. She hadn't had a partner since then, and she didn't want one.

Justice Powell sighed. "We let this slide because New Vida needs Reliance Corps. New Vida needs *you*. But we can't look the other way anymore, not with Rip's sights set on your agency. If you don't hire a partner, he will sue and you will lose your badge."

Avrianna nodded. "I will start looking for a partner right away."

"You don't understand, Captain. You need a partner tomorrow."

Avrianna forced herself not to gawk. "That's not possible. I wouldn't be able to find a suitable partner in such short notice."

"You don't have to. I already did." She passed Avrianna a file. "His name is Rainer McCoy. This is the information you need to know about him."

Avrianna took the file.

"He's expecting you in an hour at this address." She slipped a piece of paper across the desk.

Avrianna stared it. "Can I interview him first, to make sure he's a good fit for NVRC?"

"I've already vetted him. He's a good fit." Justice Powell leaned forward. "Need I remind you that you have no choice in this, Captain? You are to go there and meet him, but you *will* hire him to be your partner. Or else, you will lose all this." She lifted her hands to indicate the building. "And our world can't afford that. From what I understand, our world means a lot to you."

"It does."

"Then you will hire him." Justice Powell got up and left Avrianna's office, leaving the door wide open.

Avrianna gaped at the file in her hands. "What the hell just happened?"

Her mind spun. Justice Powell knew her too well. She would do anything for New Vida, but who the hell was this Rainer McCoy, and what sort of sway did he have to get the most influential Justice to speak on his behalf and force Avrianna to hire him?

Curious, she flipped open the file. The application was mostly empty. According to his job history, he had worked at nearly all the Reliance Advocacy Departments, formally known as police departments before they transitioned to assistant roles. His arrest record of violent criminals and arms traffickers nearly tied with her own. Beyond that, not much information was provided. She studied the blank spaces in his application.

Why am I expected to hire him with so little information?

"What are you trying to hide, Mister McCoy?" Pursing her lips, she struck the keys on her keyboard to use New Vida's Database of Information. She squinted when an error message popped up on her computer screen, claiming no records for Rainer McCoy existed. "How is that possible?"

Although New Vida's Database said he didn't exist, that didn't mean information wasn't out there. And if there was, she'd find it. Hacking was a skill she'd picked up from people she'd crossed paths with when she was living on the streets, which she had used to keep herself off the grid. After a moment, information popped up on her computer screen, but more than half of it had been blacked out, including the names of Rainer's parents and his place of birth.

Avrianna frowned. Only one other file looked like that—her own.

She tried to get around the lock, but her hacking skills fell short. She couldn't even find an identification photo of him. Did he not have a license? An Interplanetary Passport?

She got up to pace.

Back and forth.

Back and forth.

She may not know anything about Rainer, but there

was one thing she knew for sure. The Justices were forcing her to hire Rainer because of Rip. His actions against NVRC made fire scorch through her veins. *How dare the bastard threaten me*! Without NVRC, the people of their world would suffer, but the Goliaths didn't care about other people, only each other. They wanted power and money. They wanted to rule. She'd never met Rip face to face, but if she ever did, she'd be tempted to punch him.

"Avrianna…? Are you okay?"

She stopped pacing to look at Sassy, who stood in the doorway.

"What did Justice Powell say?"

"Rip Goliath is gunning for me and Reliance Corps. The only way I can keep NVRC is if I hire a man named Rainer McCoy to be my partner."

"Sexy name."

Avrianna had to agree. Her gaze lowered to the file on her desk.

"Avrianna, breathe."

"I'm breathing."

Sassy pointed at Avrianna's hands.

Avrianna peered down to see green flames swallowing her fists. She blinked, and the flames extinguished. Then she took a calming breath. "Sorry."

"Nothing I haven't seen before," Sassy said. "So…what happens now?"

"I should be leaving to meet him"—Avrianna checked her watch— "now, actually, if I don't want to be late." She picked up the file and her car keys.

"Maybe you should change first. Look a little more presentable."

Avrianna scowled. "I'm not going on a date with the man." And yet, she glanced at her dirty clothes and groaned. "Fine. I'll change."

From her armoire, she chose black pants, a white button-up shirt, and pulled a blazer on over it. Then she slicked her hair into a high ponytail. Professional. Serious. Neat. Satisfied, she slipped her badge over her head, stashed her phone in her pocket, and picked up the file.

Sassy waited for her on the other side of the door. Her brown eyes took in Avrianna's attire. "Much better. And whatever you do, don't screw this up. NVRC needs him. *You* need him."

Avrianna scowled. *I don't need anyone.*

To read more, check out Heaven Born (Heaven Born Book 1) by Chrys Fey.

A word about the author...

Chrys Fey is a disabled, tattooed author of books featuring heroines of steel. Her *Disaster Crimes* series is a unique blend of romance, disasters, and crimes, influenced by her own experiences with natural disasters. The conclusion of her series inspired her to create TheFightingChance.org, a resource for domestic violence survivors.

Fey got the idea for her first book when she was twelve and discovered a rusted screw with a crooked tip buried in grass. That screw was a key to an unknown world with an extraordinary character born in heaven. That story is *Heaven Born*, coming July 2026.

She is a fur baby mom of four rescued cats. For fun, she photographs antiques, makes playlists, and creates flip cup paintings of Avrianna's nebula. She loves Halloween, autumn, and gargoyles.

Website:
ChrysFey.com